IT'S CHEMICAL

A CHAMBERLAIN ACADEMY ROM-COM

BECCA WILHITE

FOUR PETAL PRESS

Kami, This one's for you.

1

GINGER

Why am I spending all this time brushing out my hair when I'm just going to put on a hat? It's like seventy below out there, at least it feels like it, and if I didn't have to, I'd never leave my apartment again. But there is the small issue of employment, not to mention the desire for food and heat.

Employment, too. I love teaching here at Chamberlain Academy.

The thing is, if I want to keep my job, I have to go to this meeting. And I have to go outside to get there.

Bummer.

I'd so much rather stay inside my apartment reading my new book, *You are Made of Stars*, the runaway bestselling empowerment book of the season.

I don't always read books like this.

Okay, that's not true. I definitely always read books like this, even if I'm usually embarrassed about it. I've never reviewed one for my book blog.

But this one is different.

It's so perfect. So inspirational. When I read it (in a day and a half) last week, I felt like if I followed the principles outlined by the author, Portia Bancroft, I could do anything. Now, I'm re-reading.

Slowly. A chapter at a time. Relishing each sentence. Every time I read a passage, I imagine what I could ask her about it in an interview. I'm constantly making notes in the wide margins about how I'm going to implement each self-enabling strategy.

How I'm going to, for instance, "Make Room for the Starlit Miracle" (chapter 2). I made margin notes about expecting wonders in every aspect of my life. So far, I've considered it a wonder that my apartment had heat for half of yesterday. Sometimes the faculty residences kind of fall off the power grid around here.

And now I'm preparing for a miraculous welcome-back faculty meeting. I repeat a sentence from chapter 2. "Keep your eyes alight and the stars will shine on you."

Successful navigation of this meeting is going to require at least half a dozen miracles.

I run the brush through my hair a few more times and then pull on my favorite beanie (the one that I've been wearing, snuggled up on the couch with my *You are Made of Stars* book and a pile of blankets, every day since I got back to Chamberlain after my winter break; the beanie almost makes the frigid Vermont January temperatures bearable).

I check my phone one more time, but in the last thirty-four seconds, I haven't heard back from Joey. She is probably here, on campus. She is probably busy. Busy in ways I need not dwell on. Busy with Dexter Kaplan. Leave it to someone like Joey Harker to come here for a first-semester teaching gig and dismantle the outdated and unrealistically Puritan dating laws of Chamberlain Academy.

Go, Joey.

Of course, it doesn't really matter to me. I don't date. Not for years. Living at the tops of Vermont mountains is a great excuse for not dating, but it's not the real reason. We don't talk about the real reason.

Head covered, coat zipped, scarf wound around my neck and face, I open the door to meet the icy blast of wind I'm only marginally prepared for.

The shock of the cold hasn't gotten any easier for me to bear in these few years of living here. Coming from Chicago, I was fairly sure I knew what cold winters meant. And yes. I knew. That piercing, brutal lakefront wind can slice directly through not only the clothing layers but also the good intentions. But when it comes down to it, winter cold in Chicago has the benefit of being in Chicago.

At Chamberlain, it's the frozen mountaintops and me.

Not a match made in heaven. Not a match made at all. If we could move the entire campus to someplace tropical, or even temperate, it would be perfect.

I hold my breath and slog through the icy snowpack that the grounds crew hasn't chiseled away yet. My feet crunch and crack the snow with every step, and I recite the periodic table of elements in my head to keep my mind off the probability that this wind is currently freezing the tears forming in my eyes. I try not to remember reading Jack London stories in junior high, where characters decide how close they are to death based on how and when their spit crackles into ice on its way to the ground.

I'm tempted to try it, except there are two things stopping me: I'd have to unwrap my face from this scarf, and I'm a little afraid to discover that London's research was valid. People died in those stories. Come spring, some sweet Chamberlain freshman might find my frozen carcass in a pile of melting gray slush on the north side of the science building.

I could ruin the kid's whole day.

Almost there. Almost there. I hope I'm early enough to land a seat near the fireplace. The Chamberlain faculty meetings might be tedious (especially for those of us who read email and therefore already know most of the announcements), but nobody wants the sound of chattering teeth to overpower the speaker system, so a decent fire is almost always burning.

When I pull the door of the main administration building open, a wave of heat rolls out, and I hurry to shut the door behind me. My eyes seek out the fireplace, and—first miracle of the day—there is a whole section of empty seats. I head over and start unwrapping, dropping pieces of my winter outerwear on each of the nearest four chairs.

I notice, but don't really care, that there's a crowd gathered near the portable stage set at the front of the room. Something's happening there that has kept these seats empty, and I'm very glad. I can't imagine anything worth giving up fireside seats for. The book's magic is working.

Within a few minutes, I hear the loud laughs of Dexter Kaplan and Hank Grantham, which I hope means Joey is here. I turn in my seat to wave them over, and we spend a couple of awkward moments asking unanswerable questions in rapid succession, figuring out who sits beside whom, and remembering how to greet each other. In a place as secluded as Chamberlain Academy, friendships force close-ness, physical and emotional. Once you find your people, they're completely yours. That's new for me. I'm not great at letting people in, and I'm not one hundred percent convinced that Hank and Dexter are my people. But Dex is Joey's, and Hank is Dexter's, and Joey is very much mine. So, a group by accident and association.

Better than being alone.

As Joey sits beside me, squeezes my arm, and rests her head on my shoulder for a second, I realize that friendship is a whole lot better than being alone.

"Sorry I didn't answer your message," she says. "I forgot to take my phone off airplane mode until I was walking in the door." She gestures behind us toward the Hall entrance. "By the time the texts loaded, I could already see you sitting here." She squeezes my arm again. "I missed you. I'm glad to be back, is that weird?"

I laugh. Joey always makes me laugh. "I think it's a good sign. We'll see how you feel in six days when the kids come back."

"We can do it. We're made of stars, right?" Joey's sister bought her the same book for Christmas. It's on every bestseller list in the coun-try, and probably internationally. Probably half the women in this room got a copy over the holidays. I love that Joey is totally into it. At least as much as I am. She is such a good friend. Miracle two.

I love these pre-term work days. Teaching school is way more fun before the students show up. I hear Hank's English-accented voice say, "What's the kerfuffle over here, then?" and I think he only said that word because no one in the world without an English accent should ever be allowed to say it.

Dexter looks over to the knot of people standing at the front of the room. "Maybe they've brought in a guest speaker for professional development." Dexter and I share a raised-eyebrow look. Guest speakers are so hit-and-miss. Like the time they brought in that pop-psychology podcaster who was clearly sampling the beverages before her talk. If her speech had a title, it might have been "all the ways to alienate an audience of high school teachers." Seriously. Bizarre political statements. Casual racism. Unfounded opinions on educational practices. The failure of the American education system, and how it was all teachers' fault. It was awful. And hilarious. We dined out on that one speech for weeks. So either way, great or horrible, it could lead the four of us to a good dinner discussion.

Dr. Moreau, chancellor of Chamberlain Academy, steps up onto the stage. Most of the school year, like today, her expensive-looking wool suits seem totally professional and appropriate. I look down at the utter ridiculousness of my jeans with the ripped knees (with leggings underneath, of course).

I was not made to dress for weather. Or for looking professional. Which is why I use my chemical engineering degree to teach high school instead of researching for a pharmaceutical company or acting as a safety spokesperson in some lab or earning tenure as a university professor.

I prefer being the best chemist in the room and wearing jeans and flowy, bohemian tops. High school it is.

Dr. Moreau opens the meeting by welcoming us back, then directing us to check our email at least twice each day, control the conversations with parents about what goes on in their children's classrooms, and maintain appropriate behaviors on campus here at the most excellent school in the world. It's her traditional beginning of the semester hype-speech.

I'm examining the damage this cold weather has done to my cuticles when I hear something that she could not have just said. It sounded exactly like, "Please join me in welcoming a visiting faculty member in the science department, Doctor Tyson Perry Miller."

The room explodes into as much applause as you can expect from forty-five people. Well, forty-four. I am frozen in place, my mouth is hanging open, and I'm sure I look as shocked as I am.

It can't be him.

It can't. But who else could it be? How many Tyson Perry Millers are there who have science qualifications and can elicit this kind of ovation?

I see him from behind first.

He stands up from where he's been sitting on the front row and, even from looking at his back, I know it's him. I would know him from any and every angle, whether I like that fact or not.

What in the world is he doing here? And how do I get out of this room?

I want the floor to open up and swallow me, immediately.

What's the opposite of a miracle?

This is the most anti-miracle in the history of the world.

He still walks with that easy, loping stride, showcasing his long legs and wide shoulders. I know before he does it that he's going to hop the last step onto the stage, proving with his casual jump that he's so very eager to make it to where Dr. Moreau is standing. Not to mention that he knows just how glorious his mane of blond waves looks when he moves like that. He shakes Dr. Moreau's hand with both of his, a maneuver he's been using for a decade to make people feel like they have all his attention.

When he turns and shines his Hollywood smile onto the Chamberlain faculty, I can almost hear the sigh. They are smitten, one and all.

All but me.

Because that smile doesn't work on me. Not anymore. Not through the television, and not in person.

Joey makes an audible gasp. "He looks like he's been sculpted out of marble," she whispers to me.

I can't reply. I can't even nod.

Tyson Perry Miller stands at the microphone, beaming. "I'm so happy to be here with you all this semester," he says, arcing the ray of his megawatt smile from one side of the room to the other and back, like a searchlight. "I feel so lucky to get the chance to work with you in teaching the best and brightest—"

I see the instant he notices me. His smile freezes, becomes just a touch less sincere, a bit forced. I'm not sure if he meant to stop that sentence in the middle, but he stops. The sentence is over now. He says nothing more. Not a word. And he's not moving. I can't tear my eyes away, no matter how much I tell myself I really need to look at something else. Anything else.

He raises one hand in a casual wave and steps back off the stage.

"Why did he have to move?" Joey says, her eyes following Tyson Perry Miller back to his seat. "He could have just stayed there and let us look at him a little longer."

Dexter nods. "Agreed. If you decide to leave me for him, I just want you to know, I completely understand."

Joey, still watching the back of that flowing blonde hair as he settles in his folding chair, says, "Same for you."

Dexter laughs. I don't.

Hank, who has never been much of a whisperer, leans across both Dexter and Joey so we can all hear him ask, "Visiting celebrity high school teacher? Really? Hasn't he got important television shows to star in? They could just let him remain on his filming set and pay each of us a percentage of whatever he's getting from the school."

Joey sighs. "He can have my salary. It's so okay with me."

Dr. Moreau is back at the microphone, and I hear her talking about new advisement assignments as I finally exhale.

After Moreau wraps up the pre-term announcements and we hear a short, delightful welcome-back message from everyone's favorite Chamberlain Trust representative, Wanda Chamberlain. Even though I adore the woman, I have a hard time paying attention to everything she says. When she finishes, the meeting breaks up.

"Come on," Joey says. "We're going to meet him."

I shake my head.

Dexter jumps up. "Yes. Let's go." I wonder if he has some actor-to-actor chat planned, or if he's just fanboying.

Hank looks skeptical. "D'you think it looks a little eager, us all rushing him like that?" he says. Which, now I think of it, might be the Hank Grantham version of fanboying.

"He's going to need a friend. We're his best options," Joey says.

Dexter nods. "He will love us." Another one of his weird statements that Joey swears aren't arrogant. Sure.

I back toward the fireplace. "I'm just going to stay over here. I'm still thawing out." I take another step backward and bump into someone. Turning around to apologize, I feel a pressure on my arms. "Hey, Ginger."

That voice. Deeper. Quieter. More confident. But still that voice.

Tyson Perry Miller, Emmy-award winning actor and voted one of the top ten Sexiest Men Alive on pretty much every list for the last three years, stands with his hands on me. To keep me from stumbling? To keep me from running?

I have no skills for resisting those hands on me.

How does a girl fight something like this?

"Hey, Ty."

2

TY

I can't believe it. She's here. In this room. On this campus. I want to say something perfect. Something unforgettable. Something right for the mood and the location and the first time I've seen Ginger since college. But my brain is running Bogart on a loop: "Of all the gin joints in all the world..."

That's not right.

She's surrounded by people. Of course she is. Ginger has always been the quiet center of the group, the soul of the party. People have always wanted to be near her. I know that better than anyone. Or at least I used to.

One look at her face showed me how uncomfortable she is. I know it's because of me.

I want to tell her I didn't know she would be here. How could I know? It's been years since we talked. I don't want her to think I came here looking for her. That can only be weird now, after what happened.

But even after these years, I feel a comfort in touching her arm. In seeing her smile, even if she wasn't smiling at me.

She was obviously not smiling at me.

"You look great," I say, and I try to look like I haven't just been punched in the heart. But it's hard to pretend I don't feel this. Standing this near her, the flood of memories nearly overpowers me.

How many times in the past five years have I wished I could go back in time and change things between us?

"You look good, too," she says, but she's not looking at me. She's doing that trick she has of staring just to the left of my eyebrow. I know that trick.

And why does her compliment sound like it's maybe a veiled insult? Like, I look good but she can see through the looks.

I glance around at her friends, and they're staring at us. Her to me, me to her, like we're the best entertainment in Vermont. I guess we might be.

Ginger's not in any hurry to make this easier.

"Hi. I'm Ty," I say, holding out my hand to one of the guys standing nearby. Is he standing here because he's with Ginger? They're not touching, but Ginger was never the kind who always needed to touch. At least not in public.

"Hank," the guy says, shaking my hand, "pleasure to meet you."

"You're Ty," repeats the short blonde woman. It's not a question. She's trying it on. She doesn't shake my hand, but when she clenches her fist, I know she's avoiding touching me. "Hi. Ty." She looks over her shoulder at the tall guy behind her. "It's like calling Millie Bobbie Brown 'Mill.' Or 'Bob,' maybe."

The guy standing with his arm protectively on her shoulder said, "Or Edgar Allen Poe 'Ed.' Hi. I'm Dexter. Dex."

I see Ginger flit her eyes to the guy called Dex and then back to the floor.

They go on. Imagining what it would be like to call Ruth Bader Ginsburg "Ruthie." It's so weird to them that I'm sometimes just Ty. As if I've always been called by my full name. They mention a lot of names, celebrities they can't imagine referring to as normal people. "Can you imagine calling James Earl Jones 'Jim'?" They all laugh. I don't mention that I met him at a Gala and he goes by James. And I definitely heard Helena Bonham Carter call Daniel Day Lewis "Danny."

Pretty soon we all get bored of this game. Ginger hasn't spoken in a few minutes. Finally, the guy named Hank asks, "How do you and Ginger know each other?" He doesn't look possessive or jealous, so I don't think they're together. But he seems more interested in talking with me than she does, so I answer.

"We dated in college."

Every one of her friends stares at me with open mouths. Shocked. Then they all look at Ginger, who is turning an impressive shade of red. I guess she never told them. It's been a long time since I've seen her blush, and I regret nothing. She is radiant when she's blushing.

I think they're going to ask for details. They don't. Dexter says, "So you really do have a chemistry degree? That's not just marketing?"

I know they could look up this story on any number of entertainment websites, but I've told it often enough that if I have to repeat it, it happens quickly and without much thought.

I begin with the easy part. "I really do."

The woman, who hasn't said her name yet, asks if the stories about my job are true.

Apparently she's read the websites. I did a little TV work in college, commercials and series between semesters to make tuition money. When I got cast in Enforced, I argued about the inconsistencies in the script. Specifically, that chemically, drug making just doesn't work like they wrote it. Not that being an officer worked like they wrote it. But I didn't know anything about that. Or about setting up sting operations. I did know about chemistry. I fought the writers until they realized that I knew what I was talking about. Then they started giving me a consulting credit. Then we did those social media promos.

And that's what's going to come up next.

That's what always comes up next.

This is the part where someone does the line. Dexter poses with his hand on his hip and says, "Time to pack it in. Shut this down, boys," in a voice that sounds freakily like mine.

I smile and nod. "Nice," I say. Which is what I always say when someone impersonates me to me.

The line is so dumb, but it's how the televised version of a drug enforcement squad closes every illegal operation. It's the line I say right before I swagger off into the sunset with the gorgeous guest star.

It's on T-shirts. It's a meme. It's humiliating.

The blonde woman looks like she's having a hard time not giggling. "Okay. Circle back, please. Did you say you dated our Ginger? No offense, Ty," she says, with a smile that makes me want to take no offense, "but this is the first we've heard about it."

I just nod, unwilling to tell more than Ginger wants me to say.

Ginger still hasn't spoken since she said hello, and I can see her discomfort. I'm fine talking about what we used to have, but she doesn't seem fine. I don't mind saying the words. We used to date. Till we didn't. Then I married someone else. That didn't take, either. Now I'm here.

But that leaves a lot of blank space.

I'm not interested in filling in all those blanks.

Everyone is still looking from me to Ginger as if we're going to tell the whole story of our years together.

I'm not going to tell if she's not.

I change the subject. "This seems like a great place," I say, looking around the room. The ceiling is easily a couple of stories tall, and windows frame a picturesque view of snow-covered evergreens.

This is about as far from Burbank as I can get and still be in the country.

The short blonde (who never said her name) smiles at the Dexter guy. I was getting definite *together* vibes from them, and it's becoming clearer that they're a couple. "Chamberlain is magical," she says. He wraps his arm tighter around her.

That same magic doesn't seem to be happening for Ginger and Hank. She's still avoiding looking at me, but I can't see any reason to think it's because she's with him. I'm glad when I decide they're not a couple, but it doesn't make her any softer toward me.

I guess she just still holds what happened against me.

I guess that's fair.

"So what brings you to the Chamberlain faculty, Ty?" Dexter asks.

My name still sticks in his mouth. Like he's forcing himself to stop after that first syllable. He'll get used to it. Eventually.

"It's a deal with the network," I say. This is true.

Not the whole story. But it's true.

I tell them what I've agreed to tell. "I get to do a semester of classes about nontraditional jobs in STEM."

The blonde woman nods again. "Right. Like, go get a science degree and become a movie star."

I've never been a movie star. Just a TV star, I guess. If we're labeling.

"Something like that," I say. I can tell I'm forcing my smile. It feels too intense. I pull it back. "Because, you know, I have a nontraditional STEM job. I think it's just one of those outreach things that entertainment companies like to do," I finish. This is a lie.

It's not "just" anything. It's a very specific punishment for a very specific transgression. And if I don't do it well and under the detailed conditions, I'm going to lose my spot on the show, both as an actor and a producer.

"Ever taught before?" Hank asks.

"I was a TA for a couple of semesters when I was an undergrad," I say.

"Before the Haven Lake show?" the woman asks.

Now Ginger speaks. "Joey," she says. That's all. Just "Joey." I guess that's the woman's name. Ginger shoots her a look. I see Ginger's head shake, like she doesn't want to hear me talk about it. I won't say anything about us if she doesn't want me to. But I can answer her question.

Haven Lake, the teen dramedy that gave me my acting break, was four seasons of summer camp tears and laughter. Pretty lame storylines. Terrible dialog. No nuance at all. Hot young cast. Proved that a show doesn't have to have it all to be successful. "Before and after," I said. "We shot during the summers."

"Is that how it usually works?" Dexter asks.

I'm ready to explain that it's not. Series are usually filmed during the show seasons. This one was a low-budget second project for a team of brothers who wanted to try making a show for high school kids. They had a streaming series for little kids, and hoped for more. The gamble paid off. Haven Lake was a huge hit for four years and still streams on demand.

Before I say any of it, Ginger moves between her friends and me. "I'm going to get lunch," she says. She pulls on her coat, which is hanging over a chair, and as I watch her wrap a long scarf around and around her neck, her friends ask me if I want to join them.

"Lunch at Lola's. Come on, Ty," Dexter says, still putting a little too much emphasis on my name, "you'll love it."

I don't know if Ginger wants me to come or if she wants me to go away. She didn't say. But if her stiff posture has anything to do with it, she wishes I'd leave. I can't read her expression, because her back is turned to me.

The other woman—Joey?—puts her hand on my arm. "Best food in town," she says.

Ginger, already in her coat, starts walking toward the door. Joey runs after her and pulls on her sleeve.

I can't hear what they say to each other, but Ginger does a lot of head shaking. She bends her head low to say something and glances toward us.

I smile at her. I hope it makes her relax about having me here.

She doesn't smile back. She looks a little sick. And then she turns and walks out the door.

Joey walks back to us. Her smile looks forced. "Ginger's going to eat at home. Come on. Let's grab lunch. Ty, do you have your coat?"

They talk quietly as I step away to get my coat from my chair, but I know they're talking about me. And Ginger. A few people stop me and ask me friendly questions while I retrieve my coat. I smile at them politely, but I don't remember what I say.

Zipping myself into my coat, the first functional winter coat I've had in years, I get back to the group. I try not to notice them working to change the subject of their conversation.

"Ready?" Dexter asks.

I shake my head. "Actually, I'm not too hungry. I think I'll go get settled into my place. Thanks for the invitation. It's great to meet you all."

I don't want them to stop me, so I give them a big smile before I turn and walk out the door on the opposite side of the building.

The cold wind makes me squint, but I don't feel it like I felt it earlier.

The thought of Ginger Rogers, walking in her graceful way across this same campus, warms me.

I don't want her to know why I'm at Chamberlain. But I want her to want me here.

If I had known she was teaching here, would I have come?

Probably not. But I didn't choose this. I didn't choose any of it.

3

GINGER

My face burns. I don't even feel the wind as I stomp back to my place. Can't hear the crunch of snow under my boots. My heart is thudding in my ears. I'm breathing heavily, but not because I'm walking fast. Because Ty is here, and I'm never in control of my breath when Ty is around.

At least, I never used to be. Never. Back then, I'd find myself holding my breath until I saw him. Until he walked into a room. Until he smiled at me. Then I'd exhale a sigh.

And when he kissed me, forget about it. Definitely no control. Of the breathing, I mean.

Those days my literal respiration was tied to him.

Things are different now.

He's different. Married. And now divorced. At least that's what the online magazines told me. He didn't tell me. Janie certainly didn't. She and I have not spoken since that awful moment I choose not to think about.

I mean, until I'm forced to think about it. Such as when he shows up at my faculty meeting, all golden and famous and handsome, and announces to my friends that we used to date.

I have to keep reminding myself that he is different in almost every way than the guy I knew.

When I read online that Ty and Janie separated, I felt a shameful thrill of vindication. I knew she was wrong for him. That he was wrong for her. I'd known from the beginning. And I was right, and now the whole world knows it. Well, at least the whole world who pays attention to TV celebrities and their ruined marriages.

Even in my feelings of victory, I hated that his heartache was so public. That had to make it even harder.

But he chose public life. And with public life comes public humiliation.

By the time I get back into my apartment, I feel sweaty. I peel off the scarf and drop it on the floor, followed by the coat. I keep the beanie on.

Firing up my laptop, I flop onto the couch and log into my website. When I started blogging in high school, it was definitely the place to publish. Everyone and her pet dog had a blog, and within a year of posting book reviews, the feedback was a steady and positive stream. Daily comments on my posts were in the dozens, then hundreds.

Companies reached out and monetized my blog. I made money telling people about what I was reading. It was fabulous. I could see this being a fulfilling and satisfying creative outlet for years to come, a side business to balance out whatever I would choose to do with my chemistry degree.

Like many things that happened to me in the next few years, the bottom fell out of my plans.

People don't blog that way anymore. People don't read that way anymore.

Lately, I keep the site up mainly as a journal of my reading, but occasionally an online magazine will reach out and ask for content. I'm on advance-reader lists for a couple of publishing houses, so I get to see some new books before they're available to the general public, but my favorite part is when I reread books I love and review them. Childhood favorites. Classics. My own list of the best of the best.

I can't depend on other people's feedback anymore to prove I'm a good writer or that I'm producing good content, mainly because there isn't much feedback. The entire enterprise serves a different purpose. A creative outlet. Something to get Ty out of my mind. I open my website.

Not that teaching isn't a creative exercise. I create course content and delivery. I create assessments. I create learning experiences and collaboration opportunities. Labs. Tests. Experiments. But none of it is for me.

None but this. My reviews.

I pull out *You Are Made of Stars* and flip through the pages. I want to read this a few more times before I attempt to write about it, but honestly, it's not that I feel like I need to get to know the book better. I want to do something more for this book.

I want an interview. With Portia Bancroft.

I've interviewed authors before. Often agents or publicists will pass along an emailed list of questions that the author—usually a debut—will answer and send back to me. Sometimes that works out great. Other times, it falls flat. A list of questions is not a conversation. I want Portia Bancroft to have a real discussion with me. I want to ask questions that lead her to tell me interesting side stories and prompt further questions.

I put the book down and pull out my phone. In my notes, I have ideas about a couple of books I reread over the break. Besides the new ones I'm reading, I had an urge to review a classic. I could write about Steinbeck or Hemingway. I could give a review of Mary Wollstonecraft. But I'm not feeling any of that.

Persuasion.

That's what I'll review. It's the right thing to do. I don't know why, but I know it is.

As soon as I type in the title, I understand. It's silly, of course, but the whole idea of Jane Austen's quietest heroine awaiting the return of her jilted lover explains why my reactions were so ridiculous during today's meeting. Somehow, deep in my psyche, the memory of holing up at my parents' house, rereading Anne Eliot's story, gave me an expectation for how I should feel today, seeing Ty. Of course I held back. Maybe even appeared aloof or shy.

The reason I felt so weird about seeing him is that I was channeling Anne. Her story's still under my skin.

I need to hurry and get it out. As soon as I write this, I'll feel better.

As I write about Anne's particular elegance as a character, with her subtle internal battle between what she wants and what her family wants for her, I feel glad that this, at least, was not what happened between Ty and me.

I didn't spurn him. I didn't send him away, and I didn't let someone who loves me chase him off. I watched him choose Janie over me.

Hands hovering over keys, I let my mind wander to the days that he would spend sitting on the floor of my apartment, his long legs stretched out, back against the couch, laptop on his knees and at least three notebooks spread around him. How he would tilt his head back to rest it on my leg as I sat on the couch behind him.

We had our places staked out. Ty and I on the big green couch, leaving the leather sofa for Janie and her man of the month.

I know college was filled with more than class and homework, but when I think about it, that's what I remember. Learning. Working. Snuggling. Us in our space, and Janie and her guy in theirs.

Who knew that studying could be so sexy?

He'd set an alarm on his phone. We'd work for an hour, then Not Work for thirty minutes.

We'd read paragraphs of our papers to each other, we'd race to solve complicated equations, we'd debate ethical questions.

Warmth now settles over my skin as I remember our touches.

It's a strange sensation. I never let my mind dwell on those sweet days. Those sweet years.

Never, because I know it will lead to what enters my memory next.

The last day.

Walking into my apartment to find him there with Janie.

I give my head a shake to erase the image, as if my brain were an Etch-a-Sketch. It's not. The picture of them together does not disappear. Hands and legs on the big green couch, and faces and mouths on each other.

Had they waited until the end of the semester to get together? Or just waited that long to get caught? Had they been fooling around for ages? I didn't wait around to find out if they'd try to explain it. As I stood in the open doorway, unable to move forward or back, I said the last words I ever spoke to Janie. "You're in my place. My spot. That's my couch."

Ty looked at me then. There was some misery on his face, I'll give him that.

I probably stormed off. I might have cried for hours, but if I did, it happened behind a closed door. Nobody else had to hear or see or know anything about it. Then I turned in my last papers, defended my thesis, and left. I didn't stay on campus to celebrate my degree. I didn't look back at all, and aside from pictures on the internet, I never looked either of them in the eye again.

Until today.

Today when Ty showed up at Chamberlain Academy, of all places. I watched, struck dumb, as he stood at the microphone, smiling out at his adoring fans. The whole room oozed love for him. And those were the teachers. I can only imagine how the students will react.

I sigh and try again to type my *Persuasion* review. I don't get far before my stomach grumbles, and I fully resent Ty for making me miss my lunch at Lola's. Because there was no way I was going if he was going. Being on the same campus with him is hard enough. I know I can't handle the proximity of a restaurant booth.

I can't explain it. I tried, when Joey asked me what in the world was going on. I can't just say, "Oh, yeah, I used to date the sexiest man alive, but it's no big deal, because he broke my heart long before anyone gave him that title."

When she asked me to give her all the details, right there in the Hall, surrounded, even peripherally, by the entire Chamberlain faculty (not to mention Ty himself), I couldn't say much at all. "Not today," I said, and I know she could hear the hurt in my voice. "Please? I can't do this today."

She held my gaze. She read something in my expression. She chose not to push it.

She nodded and gave me a hug and promised she'd take him away. Get him out of the picture for a while. Give me a long lunch break to let it roll over me before we have to get back to pre-term meetings.

Let it roll over me. It's not unthinkable that I could do it. I'm a pro at letting things roll. I'm very flexible. I laugh things off and pick up messes and extinguish lab fires. Nothing really bothers me.

Nothing but this. Nothing but remembering the last and worst heartbreak. Nothing but Ty walking back into my life.

I've never talked to anyone about this.

Who would I talk to? My mother? There was no way. From the first time she met him, she was smitten. She couldn't stop herself from telling me I should marry Ty. Immediately. She was so crazy about him that I had to lie and tell her that we broke up because I was finishing my program and leaving school, and it was the smart thing to do. I knew that the truth would break her heart, if she even believed me. I didn't talk to a therapist, because let's be honest. I'd look pathetic. And I already know I'm pathetic. I don't need to pay someone to help me arrive at that understanding. I didn't talk to my best friend. Considering that Janie was my best friend, no. I wasn't going to talk with her about how my boyfriend stunned me by getting caught with . . . her.

I changed my trajectory. It was so easy to restructure my life, that I knew it had to be the right thing to do. I declined my place in the PhD program and did an online education certification. I applied for teaching jobs. I got hired at Chamberlain. I moved to Vermont.

And I got on with my life. I do my work. I don't date. I have learned to keep my friends at arm's length, at least I did until Joey came along. I would never tell anyone I used to date Tyson Perry Miller, because they wouldn't believe me. They would think I was delusional. As if a man like him would ever be with a woman like me. I never really even tell myself that I used to date Tyson Perry Miller, because I never think of him as Tyson Perry Miller. Just Ty.

Sometimes, in moments of weakness, I think of him as *my* Ty.

But I try not to think about him at all.

4

TY

The boys' dorm building is cold. Since the kids won't be here until next week, the facility crew hasn't fired up the heat to all the rooms. Just the common areas, and just enough to protect pipes from freezing. My room is on the ground floor, behind a door that says "Rowan Resident Assistant."

I'm living in a high school dorm.

Is this really my life?

I guess so. At least for the next five and a half months. As soon as the semester ends, I can get out.

This is the plan, and I'm on board. I unlock the door and let myself into the tiny room. Twin bed. Built-in desk. Tiny closet with a mirror inside the door. Bulletin board. Tiny bathroom, which at least I don't have to share. I have the benefit of two windows, since I'm on the corner, but it's still a high-school dorm. I'm a successful adult living in a child's room.

At least, as far as everyone knows I'm a successful adult. The plan requires this is all everyone needs to know

My phone buzzes, and my instinct is to keep it stowed in my pocket. I don't want to answer any questions. But then I think it might be Ginger. I grab it and check.

It's not Ginger.

Why would it be?

It's Brady. My lifetime hero. My big brother, who helped me get in all the trouble I'm in now.

'Hey, Ty. Are you in your new place? All settled in?'

I look at the room. Two large suitcases are piled on the bed. I am not settled in.

'Yes,' I answer. No need to hand out too much information.

'Surrounded by beautiful women?'

He's asking where I am without asking where I am. I won't tell him yet. Too much about what's happened between us is still in the air. On the advice of my lawyer, I keep details quiet. But I need him to tell me what he knows. I can't cut him off entirely.

He probably pictures me on a resort beach somewhere. *He's* probably on a resort beach somewhere. The Miller boys, stepping away from the mess they made.

But his comment about beautiful women bugs me. Maybe because I'm cold. Maybe because it's Ginger's face that comes into my mind, her gorgeous auburn hair, her smile. She had a beanie on during the meeting, and it made her look so familiar. It reminded me of good days.

Not that I'm going to tell my brother that I've seen Ginger Rogers.

He definitely doesn't need to know she's in the picture.

'Not what I'm here for,' I remind him.

'Can't hurt to entertain yourself while you do your time,' he responds. Do your time? How can he throw comments like that around? Does he know how close we both are to criminal charges?

My brother is being very casual and unconcerned about this mess.

I don't know how to answer his comment, so I ask, *'Where are you?'*

Not that I think he'll answer. I wouldn't—and I won't tell him where I am. But maybe he'll get careless and I can gain some information without giving any of my own away.

He doesn't reply. Not for a long time.

I open a suitcase and unload a few pairs of shoes into the minuscule closet.

The production company lawyers assured me that it would be winter for most of my stay in Vermont. I believed them. I filled two suitcases with warm clothes and shoes. I've been here a few hours, and I already know it's all wrong. Warm clothes in Burbank means long sleeves. Jeans. A hoodie. Life here is going to require wool sweaters and layers.

Many layers.

I hang the clothes in the closet and leave the leather shoes in the suitcase. One step out in the snow and they're trashed. I stow the cases on the high shelf and look around.

The shelf above the desk is empty. The walls are bare. No photographs. No books. Nothing that makes this place look like mine. Maybe I should have brought some things besides clothes. At least the effort of unpacking warms me up enough to take off the coat.

I wonder what Ginger's room looks like. Does she have it filled with plants like she used to? I bet the shelf above her desk is crammed with books. Is the heat off in the dorm where she lives?

I hear my phone buzz again. I realize I'm tensing all my muscles as I check to see if it's Brady again, but it's from a number I don't have programed.

'Dr. Moreau would like to see you tomorrow at 1:00 in her office in the Hall.'

I guess this number isn't Dr. Moreau's. I can't picture her speaking about herself in third person. She didn't strike me as the kind to send text messages, anyway. There's no question in the message, but I feel like I need to answer regardless.

'The Hall is where we met this morning?' I ask.

'Yes. And where we will meet again this afternoon.'

I toss the phone back on the bed and do a slow spin, taking in the room once again in its entirety. Can I really do this for five and a half months? I miss my house. I miss my pool. I miss my furniture. I miss my palm trees.

I sit down on the bed. I don't remember the last time I slept in a twin bed. And I didn't pack a bedspread, so I hope I don't freeze to death tonight. I wonder who I'm supposed to ask about that? Dr. Moreau? Maybe she's too scary and I'll just put on all my clothes.

My phone buzzes again and I glance at the screen. Brady.

'*Guess.*'

Guess? I reread the last message. Oh. Guess where he is.

I don't want to play. I ignore him and set my laptop and charger on the desk. I need to figure out my Wi-Fi connection, preferably today. It will make my required daily check-ins easier.

Glancing at the clock, I see it's almost 1:30. Looks like I've killed enough time. I put the coat back on and turn the light off. Locking the door behind me, I head back to the Hall.

Maybe I should have gone to lunch with Ginger's friends. I'm hungry and cold and starting to get cranky.

As I walk toward the Hall surrounded by stone dormitories, I think about what I can tell the kids. How do I teach about nontraditional STEM careers when the only one I know is to get lucky?

I guess I'll figure it out.

I can see a few more buildings off to the side of the dormitories. People are coming out the doors.

It strikes me all of the sudden that those must be the teacher housing. And that I don't get to live there. My tiny room in the kids' building must be part of my punishment.

Even though I don't know it's true, I'm annoyed. Twin bed. Cinderblocks. Commercial carpet. Come on. I didn't do anything so bad.

But I did. I know it, and I regret it. And I deserve whatever they give me.

I watch a few people move from their doors toward the Hall, leaning into the wind and keeping their heads down.

I can follow that lead. I can keep my head down.

June eleventh. I can make it until June eleventh.

I walk back into the Hall, my chin tucked into the collar of my coat. That wind is brutal. Someone holds the door open for me, and I reach to give it a push for the next person. "Thanks," I say before looking up.

No reply. Ginger has her fingers on the glass, waiting for me to come in. But it's clear that she didn't know it was me when she started to keep the door open. Her recognition doesn't come with any hint of happiness.

She is not glad to see me.

She must still hold all that happened against me. Of course she does. It was all my fault. And she never let me explain.

I suddenly realize that if she finds out why I'm here, it will only be more ammunition for her. More reason to hate me.

She can't know.

I smile at her and thank her again for holding the door. She doesn't answer.

"Ginger," I say.

She turns and walks away.

"Wait."

She doesn't.

"Please," I add, sounding desperate even to myself.

She stops. I catch up with her.

"Knock it off." She's quiet, but she's angry.

"What?"

"Don't schmooze me." She says the words like they taste bitter.

"I don't even know what that means," I say, grinning at her.

She points at my face. "Stop smiling."

I can't help it. I laugh.

She doesn't.

I try to stop smiling and it makes me smile more. Just being near her makes me remember what it is to be happy, and I assume she must feel the same. But I can see her growing more tense by the second. Okay, so she means it. I'm not making her feel happy. Quite the opposite, apparently.

"Ginger," I say, with an effort to stop grinning. "Come on. We are going to be working together. Can't we be friends?"

She takes a step back. "We are not working together. I am

teaching real science to real students for their real education. You're a celebrity sub."

She was always so witty. I hadn't forgotten, exactly, but somehow it surprises me. Maybe I didn't expect her to joke with me. Or for the joke to cut so deep.

"A celebrity sub—is that a thing?" I ask.

"It shouldn't be." She is not joking. Her face is blank and hard.

Ouch.

"And no. We can't be friends."

No one has ever said that to me before. Not after any breakup. Not even Janie after the divorce. I'm surprised at the words. At her anger. And at how much it hurts.

Like she's closed another door on me. It reminds me how awful it felt when Ginger left that last day. Walked away and never looked back. How many times did I call her? How many voice messages did I leave? Did she ever listen? She never answered a single text. And then the messages stopped going through. I couldn't reach her. I was blocked. She never let me explain.

She turns and walks away again now, leaving me standing in the Hall, cold wind blowing around me as more people come in the door.

I go back to the chairs where I sat this morning, where I looked out at an audience that looked back to me with smiles and welcome. Where I met Ginger's friends. Where I thought that she and I could make a reconciliation.

I sit on a chair at the end of the last row, still zipped into my coat.

Maybe this whole thing is a mistake.

I can call the Fleming Brothers production company and try again to explain what happened, to remind them that I was stupid, not complicit. At least, not on purpose.

Maybe I can go home.

A hand lands on my shoulder, and I am surrounded by Hank and Dexter and Joey. "Hey," Hank says. "Did you find your way around?"

I put the smile back on for them. "All great," I say, which is not an answer. "Getting unpacked."

Dexter asks, "Which building do they have you in?"

"Rowan," I say.

He shakes his head. "No, not for your advisement. I mean for your apartment."

"I'm in the Rowan RA suite." I smile again, and I wonder if he can tell I don't feel it.

Dexter looks confused. "You're living in the kids' dorm?"

I shrug. "Someone has to do it, I guess."

"Yeah, but that someone is usually a senior student on scholarship. As a work-study kind of thing."

Hank shakes his head. "You're being punished for something, mate."

He has no idea.

And I'd like to keep it that way.

"Well, don't park yourself way over here. Come sit with us." Dexter points in the direction of Ginger's back.

"I don't think," I start to say. Joey is shaking her head at Dexter. She can tell Ginger doesn't want me there. The guys don't seem to notice.

"Come on," Hank says. "You'll need someone to mutter your commentary to when things start getting weird."

I have just been put on probation, sent to Vermont to teach high school, moved into a dorm room, seen my ex, had my offer of friendship rejected, and skipped lunch. "It's going to start getting weird?" I ask.

"Almost without question," Hank says.

Joey hasn't said a word. She's studying me.

I say, "I'm not going to sit by Ginger. I think she's uncomfortable."

Now Joey laughs. "Uncomfortable? Is that what you're calling it? No. You're not sitting by her. I am. But you shouldn't sit alone. You can sit by Hank."

Hank mumbles something about being sent to the naughty kids' corner. I follow them to the same place they sat earlier and slide into the seat at the other end of the row. It's impossible for me to look over at Ginger without turning. Without leaning over. Without being obvious.

But I don't know why I'd need to look at her, anyway. I've seen her. I know how she looks. Still beautiful. Still tall. Still striking. But what good does that do me? She isn't interested in being friends. I know she hasn't forgiven me. I know she's not impressed. So why do I wish I could see her better from where I sit?

Why do I turn so far in my chair to talk with Hank? Why do I find myself looking just over his shoulder? Why is it hard to pay attention to what he's asking me?

Why does it matter so much what Joey is whispering into Ginger's ear? Why do I hope Ginger will turn her face this way when she answers her?

Dr. Moreau starts the afternoon's meeting. She gives a short presentation about student engagement, offering a few ideas to get kids to participate. I'm a little surprised. This is a prestigious boarding school, and, I assume, expensive. Shouldn't these kids want to be involved? Shouldn't they come here already invested?

She gives a great example of how to group kids together and get them collaborating on small-team discussions, and I pull out my phone to take notes. It seems like an easy enough idea. I don't have any ideas of how to run a classroom. I'll take all the help and strategies I can get.

When she asks us to gather in groups and do one of the activities that she taught, I hear the general mutter of displeasure.

Hank leans over. "There are no worse students in the world than a group of teachers."

I give him a smile, but I'm watching Ginger as she steps away from her friends to link up with a different group.

Joey sees me watching. "She's going to do the workshopping with the other chemistry teacher. Science stuff. Teamwork."

I really don't want to sound whiny, but shouldn't I be doing science stuff? "Aren't I on that team?"

She gives me a sad smile. "Come on. Cross-curricular learning teams. That's us."

As Hank and Dexter and Joey walk me through the workshop activity, I try to keep Ginger in my sight. I'd love to watch her face, but she makes that impossible. She keeps her back to me in a way that can't be accidental.

Dexter pulls a paper notebook from his jacket and writes down our group's setup, exercise, and outcomes. "For Dr. Moreau. She likes the feedback," he says, but I'm not paying much attention. I'm certainly not contributing.

"She hates me." I surprise myself by saying the words aloud.

"Course not," Hank said. "She hired you."

I laugh, but it doesn't sound amused, not even to me. "Not Dr. Moreau. Ginger."

Hank shakes his head. "She just comes across that way. She's reserved. She keeps her distance."

"Nope," Joey says. She watches me for a minute. "I think you're right. I'm pretty sure she hates you."

5

GINGER

The meeting was too long, as most meetings are, but I worked hard not to stare at Ty whenever our group had to do one of Dr. Moreau's collaborative exercises. He just looks so much the same as he used to. Without the TV show's camera filters, I guess I thought he'd look different. Older, maybe. More experienced. His hair is longer now, and I like the way it brushes his shoulders. And his jaw seems a little firmer, but maybe that's because I ignored him whenever he tried to speak to me, and he was grinding his teeth.

His eyes are the same.

His smile is, too. But it's not for me, anymore. Now all the smiles are for the cameras, even here where the cameras aren't.

I run for my apartment as soon as the day's meetings are over. I spend an hour staring at my course outline, but I make only a few changes. Mostly I stare at the syllabus, stare at my reviving house plants, and stare at the wall.

It's after five, and it's getting dark.

Winter in Vermont, man. I flip the light switch and the lamps come on all over the room. I do love this room, with its tiers of tables holding my green babies. I would love to do a botany club, or even a student garden, but my proposals for any agriculture-based class have always gotten a big no. The growing season is wrong for school time. Kids should be focused on forward-looking science and technology projects, not reverting in time to simplistic agrarian practices.

I just want to give them something green for their dorm rooms. Helps them breathe better. Watch a seed grow into a plant. Make a cutting. Take care of a living thing. Get some dirt under the nails.

According to the faculty council, nobody's all that interested.

So, I grow the plants myself and I keep them here in my living room. Joey calls it my jungle.

I know I have to do something else. I'm fidgety, and I can't pretend it's not about Ty.

I make another effort at arranging my first-day lesson plan for both Chemistry and AP Chem, but nothing I have planned feels like a good step back into the classroom.

I swipe to a new web browser and open Portia Bancroft's author website. The photo she has posted is staged to be friendly but impersonal, a shot of her, huge sunglasses obscuring most of her face, chin tilted up and a galaxy reflecting back at us through the glasses.

She has very little personal information on the site. I can't find anyplace that tells where she lives, even. *You are Made of Stars* is her first book, but there's a Coming Soon tab that hints she's working on a sequel. There's a tab that links to a contact page for her publicist, but what I want to ask for isn't an appearance. I just want a phone call. She's certainly not posting her cell number.

There's a Contact Me tab on her site, and I click it, just to see what comes up. It auto opens an email addressed to t.bancroft@madeofs tarsbook.com

Before I can think too hard about it, I fill in the subject line. "Interview Request."

That wasn't so hard.

As I start typing the body of the message, I get the most solid bout of imposter syndrome I've ever had. "I'd like to schedule an interview with you." That's the worst opening line ever. Because duh. I put that in the subject line. I delete it and start over.

"*You are Made of Stars* is the best book I've read this year."

It's January. That's not much of a compliment.

I delete it.

"I've been reviewing books online for years, and I'd like to review yours." Grr. No. It's not like I'm asking permission to write the review. That one has to go. Every sentence I type is nonsense. I delete each word. I'm sweating. My nerves are jangling. It's like asking the cool kids if I can sit at their lunch table. This is way worse than defending my master's thesis.

I stand up and walk around the room. I ask my plants for email writing advice. They are mute, as always. Ty used to make fun of me for talking to my plants. Well, not really. That makes it sound like he was insulting about it. He never was; it just amused him that I asked them questions, as if I expected answers.

"You're a real scientist, right? You know that they're not going to answer?"

I would respond that a true scientist was open to her hypotheses being proven wrong. He'd laugh. Then we'd make out.

This line of thinking is not helpful.

I sit back down at the table and try again. "Before I publish my review of your book, I'd really love to interview you. Would you be open to a thirty-minute phone call one late afternoon this month?"

Could it be that easy?

I sign off the way she'll see my name in the auto-signature, "G. Rogers, Chamberlain Academy." Before I can continue to overthink this to death, I hit send and listen to the fly-away whoosh.

Now in all likelihood, I'll stare at my computer, refreshing my inbox like a maniac, for the foreseeable future.

Not great time management.

I close my email program and determine to read emails only twice a day. Seven in the morning and seven in the evening should do the job until the students get back. I'll have to check it more often after that, of course, but Portia Bancroft will have answered me by the time the semester begins.

It's only polite.

I decide to go over to my classroom to work on my lessons. Maybe if I'm in the room, looking at the lab, staring into the empty chairs that will soon be filled with teenagers with empty eyes . . .

I shake my head and turn on the TV. I can do the classroom in the morning. For now, I can avoid each of the things that are making me nervous. All of them.

WHEN I WAKE up from an excellent sleep (I am gifted at sleeping), I reach for my phone first thing. I'd love to pretend I'm not immediately checking for an email response from Portia Bancroft, but I can't lie to myself, right? I decide not to be discouraged that there's nothing there yet. It's still the holidays for lot of people. I read the news briefs and glance at a request for a review from an online magazine, marking the message as unread so I can come back to it tonight.

Once I'm wearing all the clothes, I add all the other clothes.

I've been back on campus for a few days, but the January chill has kept me from walking to the science building That, plus the fact that I don't have to leave my apartment to do my planning, but I do need to walk across campus to organize the classroom. And possibly the fear of running into Ty. But mostly the cold. Right? Right.

Even with my coat and gloves and hat and scarf, I find myself tightening all my muscles to protect myself from the wind. I can't remember how to get used to being outside in winter. Every day my muscles have forgotten anything I learned about staying warm the day before There is no preparing for this cold. Unlocking the outer door and then the classroom door, I bump the light switch with my elbow, throwing my room and lab into fluorescent shine. I've asked for updated lighting, but honestly, if they have to decide between LED panel lights for our classes and fixing the heat to the faculty residences? I'd take the promise that we won't wake up with frozen pipes and frozen noses.

Priorities. Even in a place as well-funded as Chamberlain, people still have to make money choices.

I pull the chairs down from where they're stacked, placing them in pods of four around each table. My phone is working its way through my classic 80s hair-band playlist. I'm only wearing one earbud, because I don't want to get surprised if anyone else walks through the building and stops at my door. But since I haven't seen anyone else in here yet, I won't hold myself back completely. I hum along with Jon and Axl and Sebastian and Vince. I do all the harmonies.

Joey laughs at me for this habit, but she's not here, and nobody else is going to care if I'm belting out the background vocals in my chem lab.

I straighten each of the nerdy science pun T-shirts I have hanging on the walls and dust off my periodic table of elements. The succulents need a little water, and I tend to the pots in the back where I am growing a variety of Vermont conifers: pine, spruce, and fir. They're doing great. It's not part of my curriculum, but I sneak in all kinds of ecology lessons whenever I feel like it. Science throws a wide net, and the privileged kids I teach need to be reminded now and then about the earth they inhabit.

I've just nailed the key change in "Living on a Prayer" when I catch movement in the corner of the room where the door is. I get that startled shiver of goosebumps up my arms, but when I realize it's human and upright and nonthreatening, I breathe easier. I start to wave to whichever science teacher is also wandering the classroom building.

Then I notice it's Ty.

"Hey," he says, leaning in the doorway in that very specifically casual way he always had of leaning into a room. It's like a trademark lean. He did it everywhere when we were together. Still does, I guess. As if standing upright is just a tiny bit too much to handle, but his confidence in the solidity of walls and counters can increase everyone else's confidence that the earth is here to support us and life is good and fair and bright.

His character does the lean in his TV show, Enforced. You can see it in all kinds of shots of him. Leaning at the crime scenes. Leaning in the lab. Leaning in the office. Leaning in doorways of love interests.

Not that I watch the show.

But it's impossible to not see images of it online.

I mean, I can't avoid every picture of Ty that shows up in the entire internet.

Okay, fine, so I watch the show. Everyone watches the show. It would be weirder to be the person who says, "I don't watch Enforced," because then people would ask me why, and I'd have to tell them. So, yes. I've seen it. I watch it. Sometimes. (Every episode. Many times.)

So I see that Ty still does the lean not only on TV, but also in person.

I hate that lean. Because I feel pulled to lean toward him. He's irresistible.

No. Ne's not. I can resist. It's only a man, leaning.

Leaning. I've dreamed of that lean a million times.

And here he is, leaning into my classroom. I shove my hands onto my hips just to have something to do with them. Otherwise they will act without my permission and tug at the ends of my hair, or twist a ring, or, heaven forbid, touch my mouth. Nope. "Help you?" I ask.

The words are polite, but I know I'm being rude. Why is he here? What does he want?

"What do you want?" I ask, before he has a chance to answer the first, obviously grudging, question that might seem like an offer.

He straightens up fractionally from the lean. "I'm looking for my classroom," he says.

"This isn't it."

He looks at the floor as his slow, warming smile spreads across his face. If not the smile that got him the job, at least the smile that made him the series' playboy love interest.

I am so glad he's looking at the floor. He does not need to know what that smile still does to me.

I compose myself before he looks back up toward my face.

"Can you help me figure out which classroom *is* mine?" He asks it in such a polite voice, I am sure he must be making an effort not to sound like I sound. "They don't seem to be numbered."

I shake my head. "They have names, not numbers. It's supposed to humanize the experience for the students."

"Hm," he says. Noncommittal. Which, obviously. It's a ridiculous reason not to number classrooms.

"What's your classroom called?" I ask. I'm in Bunsen, because I didn't fight hard enough for Faraday or Curie. The bio wing has Darwin and Mendel and Carver. Physics is Einstein and Pascal. Newton and Tesla are in the intersections, for obvious reasons to people who care.

"Copernicus," he tells me.

I look blank. "I don't know where that is," I tell him. "Are you sure it's not Galilei?"

"I'm mostly sure, but I haven't met with Dr. Moreau yet, so maybe I've got the wrong guy. But, just so we're clear, I know the difference. I haven't forgotten my training." He's trying to be serious, but the smile is spreading again.

He was the best student in our masters program. The smartest. The most intuitive. And the best looking? Let's not even go there.

I want him out of my classroom. He is much too close to me, and I do not approve what is happening in my lungs and my nervous system while he's here.

"Go look around," I say, keeping my voice as emotionless as I can. "I'm sure you'll find it."

I don't want to be cruel, but I also don't want to be alone with him. Can I trust either one of us to act in our own best interest?

He nods and walks out the door.

I keep working on my classroom prep. I write down some more plans, just in case. I look up a few new sites for ordering lab supplies. I try not to watch the door.

When I look at the clock and see it's been an hour, I decide to pack it in. I'll head back to my apartment and not worry that Ty will show up at the door. As I turn off the lights and close up the room, I see him in the hall.

"Any luck?" I ask. I'm only being polite. Any good coworker would ask.

He shakes his head. "No luck."

I'm surprised. "Really?" I wonder why nobody else jumped at the chance to help him.

"Did you ask any of the other teachers?" I say, waving down the hall.

"Nobody else was singing, so I didn't feel comfortable interrupting them."

He didn't ask anyone else for help. Only me.

I'm not sure how I feel about that. I nod and walk toward him, and he doesn't move. I can't risk brushing my arm against his, so take another step into the hallway, and then I point. "Go left," I say.

We walk down the halls, me pointing out rooms and labs, him making sounds of attention and approval without actually saying anything. I don't find Copernicus.

"Maybe upstairs?" he asks.

I shake my head. "Offices up there."

"Do they have names?" he asks, a hint of that smile appearing. Is he making fun of me? Or only making fun of the Chamberlain science building's naming convention?

And I don't know the answer. Are the science offices named? I work in my classroom or in my apartment, so I was never assigned one. We head to the staircase, and as we walk down the upstairs hall, I point out who has offices where. "One of these will probably be yours," I say, pointing at two empty rooms at the end of the hall.

"What's up there?" he asks, pointing to a staircase that I have never, in all the years I've taught here, walked up. This surprises me a little, even though I don't come this way much. And, ask anyone, there are plenty of surprises on the Chamberlain campus.

"No idea," I say.

"You up for an exploration?" he asks.

"Sure."

I regret it the second it comes out of my mouth. It sounds flirty, and I don't mean it. I am absolutely not flirting with Tyson Perry Miller as we walk around the science building. The very thought sends waves of memories. Definitely strong memories of flirting with Ty in various science settings. But that was before.

We walk up the staircase and come out into a wide, square room. Windows on all sides. But windows onto what? From outside, this looks like a normal third floor in the building. Now that I'm in here, I realize that the outer walls, all smoked glass from outside, are yards away from the walls of the only room on the top story.

Here, in the center of the building, is a single room set up with a few high-powered telescopes, ten or twelve comfortable-looking leather chairs, and no obstructing walls. Literally empty space between this room's windows and the outer windows of the building.

Ty points to a name etched into the glass door. Copernicus.

"It's like an observatory," I say, feeling the breath whoosh out of me. How could I not know this was here?

"Kind of a weird waste of space," he says.

He's right. It's bizarre. Bizarre and beautiful.

"This is your classroom," I say, and I'm full of wonder, even though it's not a question. "What did you do to deserve a space like this?"

He shrugs and looks around. "It's a lot smaller than yours," he says.

I mean, yes, obviously, but he doesn't have a lab. Or desks. Or walls. It's just a window to the whole campus. I do a slow spin. Snow is falling, and from here, in this magical space between walls of glass, it's glorious. Intimate. Romantic.

Time to go.

I clear my throat, and, I hope, my head.

"Looks like you'll have a small student load," I say, gesturing to the chairs. Fewer than a dozen. "That will make things easier."

"Heliocentrism," he says.

I blink.

"Copernicus," he goes on. "You know. He said the sun was the center of the solar system."

Every hackle I own is on high alert. "I know what Copernicus said," I say, my teeth grinding at the back of my jaw.

"And here we are at the center of campus," he says, gesturing around and out the windows. "Makes it easy to keep an eye on me, I guess."

I cannot even. As if he doesn't even question that everyone on campus will have their eyes on him. I turn back to the door, grateful for the metal handle that will open it. With my blood boiling like it is after that "I'm the center of the universe" comment, I'd probably walk directly into the glass wall and knock myself out. Is he actually for real? I used to love this guy? As I walk out the door, I answer him over my shoulder. "For anyone who cares to go looking," I say. My neck feels hot.

"Ginger," he says, and I can't help it. I stop.

I don't say anything.

"Thanks for helping me out." He says it in a calm, quiet voice. There is no hint of flirting. He sounds sincere. "I know this is awkward for you," he goes on. "I didn't know you'd be here. I mean, I didn't know you live here. Work here."

It feels like he spoke only the highlights. Like he read the first sentences of his scripted soliloquies, leaving out all the rest of whatever he meant to say.

It's plenty. I give him a wave, which I hope looks casual and not like a major involuntary twitch. "See you later."

"I like your friends," he says to my back as I'm walking away.

Of course he does. My friends are excellent people. But as I walk down the stairway to the floor of offices and then down to my classroom, I sink into the understanding that, for as long as he's here, my friends will also be his friends. He likes them. And they like him, too. I'm not going to change that. I'm not in seventh grade. I'm not going to say, "Let's hate him; ready? Go."

Once again, what's mine is now ours. It feels stranger than before. More difficult. More dangerous.

6

TY

Walking into Dr. Moreau's office gives me the opposite feeling of being in the Copernicus classroom with Ginger. That was beautiful and magical. Hopeful and warm and open. This is pretty much dread.

A guy looks up at me from the desk in her outer office. He's got a pair of thick-framed black glasses balanced on a very thin nose.

"Hi," I say. "I have an appointment with the chancellor."

He says nothing, just looks at me, his expression unreadable.

I hate this part of meeting someone I'm probably going to see again. Total strangers for a random, momentary encounter? No big deal. But someone I'm going to work with? Is he nervous because he's only seen me on TV? Is he feeling shy? I give him the general-purpose friendly smile, warm but not too warm, and wait for him to tell me to sit, or direct me into the office, or something. Anything.

"And you are—?" Anything but that. He doesn't know who I am. On a campus with a thousand students and forty-something teachers, the chancellor's assistant doesn't know that I'm coming. Or that the new science teacher is coming.

"I'm Ty Miller. One o'clock."

His eyes shoot to the clock on the wall, which reads 1:04.

Oh, I am really not impressing this guy.

He nods to a chair and says, "I'll let her know you've arrived." His eyes travel back to his computer screen, and he is very clearly not sending the chancellor a message. I guess he's sending me a message instead.

My watch, by the way, says 1:02. I know. I check.

After another minute, he picks up his telephone handpiece and pushes a button. I work hard not to look.

"Dr. Moreau, your one o'clock appointment has arrived," he says. He waited until the clock on the wall said I was five minutes late.

I guess we all take our chances to make power plays as they come.

The guy hangs up the receiver and tells me I can go in. I give the door a knock with my knuckles as I open it.

"Hello," I say.

Dr. Moreau gestures to a chair opposite her desk. I heard her speak yesterday, and her accented English adds a level of gravity to her air of intelligence. "I suppose you know why you are here," she says.

How do I answer that?

I aim for light and friendly. "I hope it's to get a handle on my class schedule."

"Not here at this meeting. Here at Chamberlain." There is not a glimmer of warmth in her eyes. Nor in her voice. It's deep and rich and serious. But not at all warm.

I clear my throat, which has tightened drastically in the last three seconds.

I nod. Both of the Flemings, the brothers who own the production company, attended Chamberlain years ago. They worked out my stay here as the best way for me to be an asset to both Chamberlain and the Fleming Brothers Productions. Although I'm still not sure how I'm supposed to help anyone further any shows from here, and there's a limit to what I can reasonably contribute to a high-end boarding school. I came with plenty of questions and no complaints. It could be so much worse.

"This is not an ideal situation for me," she says. "I have a long list of highly qualified educators who would love to work here. And you, because you have friends with influence, have been placed on my staff in order to work out a legal probation."

"It's not exactly—" I start to say, but when I see her face, I close my mouth.

"Your unsavory business dealings have thus far been kept out of the media. Your team obviously wishes this to remain true. I have agreed to take you on for the semester because there is reason to believe you will be a significant asset in accessing new donation avenues for our school."

Well, at least I don't have to wonder how she feels.

She goes on. "You must understand that the very nature of your transgression puts my students and my school in danger."

I shake my head. "I promise you I pose no danger," I begin, but her look shuts me up again.

"We hold our faculty, students, and staff to the highest standards," she said. "Embezzlement is an ugly stain on a reputation, even if only the suggestion."

Embezzlement? What does she think I did, exactly?

"I believe you may misunderstand the nature of my misconduct," I say, wishing my lawyer was here to prevent me saying too much. Or the wrong thing. I'm not supposed to talk about how the company's money disappeared, or how I got my hands on it in the first place, but calling it *embezzlement* is a little harsh.

"Did you or did you not pay an emerging business venture a large sum of money from the production company by which you are employed?"

"Well, yes, I did, but—"

"And did you have permission to make such a payment?" she asks, her eyebrows a solid line of menace.

I just shake my head.

"Which means you misappropriated corporate money, to which you were not entitled, to further your own ends." If she would look away, even for a second, I'd be able to swallow. And breathe. She doesn't.

"Which," she goes on, "is rather the definition of embezzlement, if I am not mistaken."

She is not mistaken.

Not that she has the whole story. But I'm not about to tell it to her. Not with that terrifying glare burning into my soul.

"For reasons of protecting Chamberlain and its students, you will have very limited faculty privileges. Your curriculum will be supervised by members of faculty and administration. Access to student records will be unavailable to you outside the requirements of your coursework. Your classroom key will open only your classroom door."

Ginger had let me into the room this morning, and I'd gotten into the science building because I'd asked the guy outside pushing snow if he could open the door for me. Looks like I'll be counting on the kindness of the rest of the teachers around here to even get inside the building to teach my classes.

"Your position as a resident assistant will fill ten non-class hours each week. You will have four classes of what we are calling 'Nontraditional Opportunities for Careers in STEM,' or NOCS as it will appear on student schedules. Your other two courses will be advisement classes, which I expect you to run as study halls."

I'm feeling a little overwhelmed, but I can do this.

She presses her fingertips together at her desk, her sharp chin resting just above her perfectly manicured nails. "I believe you understand that this is an unpaid position."

The last of my ability to pretend this is anything other than a tradeoff for jail time leaves me with my exhale. "I understand." I can feel my spine softening.

Maybe she can see me deflating, because when she speaks again, her voice is marginally softer. "Mr. Miller, I have no interest in your past situation other than how it can help me reach my fundraising goals."

I wonder if that means she doesn't mind that I made a mistake, or just that she doesn't care what it was as long as it doesn't put the school in a bad situation.

"A celebrity visiting staff member—especially one facing criminal misconduct charges—was not my suggestion, but the Flemings seem to think we can help each other. I do not intend to speak of your unethical activities or add to your humiliation in any way. But neither do I plan to allow you to contaminate our school or endanger a single student. You will be watched closely. And make no mistake, should you injure this school or anyone attached to it, your secrets will no longer be safe. I have complete deniability for your actions. I will expose your crimes to protect my people."

She stops speaking and I nod. Got it.

I know it's fair. More than fair.

Fairness doesn't make it less humiliating.

"I will be an asset to your school community," I say, hoping it might somehow be the right message to send.

She nods and holds out her hand. Not to me—toward the door. She doesn't want to seal our conversation with a handshake. She wants me to leave.

I stand and feel my legs shake beneath me.

She must notice. It's not like I'm hiding it. Her face softens. "Perhaps this can be a useful collaboration."

I nod, unsure if she wants me to say anything else. She seems to be a person who appreciates the last word.

"Your curriculum advisor will be in touch within the next twenty-four hours. In the meantime, familiarize yourself with campus and try not to break any laws."

Is that a smile?

I don't dare to hope.

As I walk out of her office and through the outer room, I feel the assistant's eyes on my back.

I turn and give him a patented Tyson Perry Miller smile. The one that's been on magazine covers. The one that's apparently turned heads for years. "Thanks so much for making this happen," I say in the voice that conveys charm. "Couldn't be happier to be here. It's so great to meet you."

The assistant's eyebrows come together. He glances behind him at Dr. Moreau's closed door.

Let him wonder what just happened behind that closed door.

7

GINGER

There is something empowering about stepping into the frigid air protected against the cold. I have enough of my face exposed (eyes, cheeks, mouth, chin) to know exactly how freezing it is out here, but my hat and scarf and coat and gloves warm the rest of me to a bearable level.

Being out here like this, covered enough to face it all, I like to think I'm stronger than the elements. Portia Bancroft would love that. I'm uniting with the stars to overcome all my adversity.

As if the elements hear me thinking, a gust of wind pushes into my face, stinging the un-scarfed parts. Stupid wind.

"Fine," I splutter into the blast. "You win."

I think about shaking my fist at the sky, but keeping my arms at my side definitely conserves body heat. Besides, I can be a drama queen all I want in the dark and private corners of my mind. I should keep it there. Major acts of body language aren't necessary for public consumption.

Not that I'm in public. Campus is still and quiet without kids. Icy and silent. Beautiful. If you can ignore the wind.

An instant later, I'm glad I held in the fist-shaking. Ty steps out of the Hall and onto the mostly-cleared path. The heat that floods me is welcome in a few different ways, but I'm glad he can't see it. I have to figure out how to mask my body's reaction to his presence here, or the whole campus is going to know how he makes me feel. How he used to make me feel. How out of control I feel.

Whatever. I have to get it together, is what I'm saying.

"Hi, again," he says, pulling his hat lower onto his forehead.

I decide to give a small wave. Not sure I want to try to speak to him, anyway. When I do say something, I want to sound calm and polite. And distant.

But I'm not distant. I'm right here. And he's right there.

I point to the Hall, where office and lobby lights are shining against the cloudy afternoon. The building is always lovely, but it looks warm and inviting with all the windows lit. "Did you meet with Dr. Moreau?"

He nodded, brought his head closer to mine, and mock-whispered, "She's scary."

He's not wrong.

"She's fair," I say back. I don't even know why I said that. It's true, I guess. And I have no idea what they talked about in there. Maybe she asked for his autograph. Would he think that's scary? Hard to tell.

"And she's smarter than all of us," I say, mostly just to make more words come out that are not about us. About our past.

"Nobody's smarter than us," he says, bumping my arm with his elbow.

I'm quite sure the air temperature did not just increase, but I feel even warmer. My body is reacting to his closeness in ways that I'm not at all comfortable with. I can feel heat in my cheeks, and as cold as it is out here, I shouldn't be able to feel my cheeks at all.

Why is he leaning so close? Why is he walking with me at all?

"Is it time?" he asks. His voice is soft, low. He's still standing very close to me.

"Time for what?" There are no more meetings scheduled for this afternoon.

"Time for us to talk."

My breath leaves me in what might sound like a laugh. It's not a laugh. "No."

"You've never given me a chance to explain." His voice is quiet, and the wind is doing its best to carry it away from me.

"I don't need an explanation from you," I say, hoping he can't hear my voice shake. "Never asked for one."

He puts a hand to my arm and stops walking. "But I want to tell you. I want you to understand. I've wanted that for years."

I shake my head. I saw what happened. It would be very difficult to misinterpret that data. "I'm pretty sure I understand," I say, taking a step away. His hand is still on my arm. He closes his fingers gently around my wrist.

"Ginger," he says, and dammit if those two familiar syllables in his voice don't melt my resolve again. "You never answered my calls or replied to any of the texts I sent. You moved out of your apartment. You left."

I nod.

"I did that."

I don't mention what he did. I don't lay his crimes out on the table in front of us. "I got a new phone," I add, which is true. And a new number. And conveniently deleted all contacts who weren't in my immediate family.

"Can we go somewhere and talk?" he asks, still holding my wrist. "Please?"

I turn so I'm standing directly in front of him, facing those mesmerizing blue eyes I spent so much time gazing into back in the before-time. I fold my arms across my stomach, take a breath, and say, "You don't need to tell me anything. It's been years. And we were both very different people then."

"Not so different," he says, but he's not arguing. He's just trained to be romantic and say things designed to take women's breath away.

I don't want him to take my breath away. I don't want him to do anything. I don't want him here, poking at wounds I thought had closed over. I don't want to remember. "I hope some of the things are different. Because I can't live with everything that happened back then."

I see it hit him.

I see him cringe away from the memory of what he did. His mistake. Can I even call it that? I sigh. We all make stupid mistakes. And I really didn't give him any chance to explain.

Because, I remind myself, I didn't want an explanation. I still don't.

I can't risk reopening my heart. But I also can't avoid him here on this campus. And I can't run from him every minute, making it horrible for us and awkward for everyone else.

I can do this. I can see him here.

"Can we just maybe start over?" I say, wondering if he can hear the plea in my voice.

He shakes his head, but I don't think he's saying no. "Is that what you want?"

This time, my laugh is more like a laugh. "To forget about the past few years and just meet you as a new colleague? To ignore the baggage? Yes. That's what I want."

He squints at me, but maybe that's the weird light in the cloudy sky. "Meet now as if we didn't know each other before?"

"Exactly." And I'm just a random teacher at the school he just happens to be visiting for a semester. Just someone on the faculty. Someone who wouldn't make him look twice.

"I can't pretend it didn't happen, that *we* didn't happen," he says.

"Sure you can. Forgetting is easy," I say, knowing with every word exactly how impossible forgetting can be. "What were we even talking about?" I ask, trying to grin at him.

"I can't remember," he says, playing along. But then his expression gets more serious. His voice deepens. "Look," he says, shoving his hands in coat pockets. "We're going to be together, I mean, working together here for the next five months. That's a long time for things to be awkward between us. I'll do whatever you need me to do to make it not weird. To make it okay. and I can't stand being at odds with you. What I want is to explain what happened—I have wanted to do that for years—but I get that I don't get to push. I don't get to hurry that. So yes. We should work together here. There are worse settings for friendships to grow."

We stand there, on the sidewalk, surrounded by mostly empty buildings in the fading afternoon light, and snow begins to fall.

Of course it does.

He watches me, his face unreadable, as flurries grow to flakes. Within a moment, it's snowing in earnest.

We don't move away. Snow happens fast here, and we stand on the sidewalk, snow covering our shoes within minutes. I try not to stare at him, but a girl can't work a miracle. I force myself to gaze up at the snow, getting that blinding feeling that the entire sky is lowering. Then I look at him again. He's still smiling.

I can't stand here much longer, watching him look at me, so I try to think about what friends would do, what we did when we were friends. "Are you interested in making a snowman?"

"What?" he asks. I know he's surprised. I guess I'm a little surprised myself. Should it be this easy to start again?

"Colleagues make snowmen here at Chamberlain. It's probably in the handbook." My lies are always pretty transparent. I just nod at myself as if confirming this complete fabrication.

I tilt my head up again, and huge, thick flakes cascade over my face. "It's going to come down pretty fast. And then, soon as it gets dark it's going to be very cold. It won't pack well later." I hold up my gloved hand to let some snow land on it. "It's kind of a now or never thing," I say, watching the flakes pile up in my glove.

He reaches over and takes my hand. He actually puts out his hand and holds mine. I pull away.

I shake my head. "I wasn't trying to make a metaphor. This isn't about us. When I said now or never, I meant about the snow." I must sound as flustered as I feel.

"I know," he says. His voice is light and cheery, as if he hasn't just nudged loose a bolt locking down my heart. He reaches for my hand again. "But I don't know my way around. I need you to guide me to the best place for our project." He tugs on my hand and swings our arms between us. "Show me the ways of Chamberlain snowmen, friend."

It's impossible for me to feel the heat of him between two pairs of gloves. I know it is. But my fingers tingle with warmth anyway.

Friend. Snowmen. Sure. We can talk as friends about snowmen. I started this. Trying to keep my smile from growing too obvious, I say, "The benefit of the Chamberlain snowman is permanence."

He doesn't let my hand go. "Permanence?" he asks.

"Relative permanence," I clarify. "Winter lasts forever here."

He looks at me from the side of his eye. "Permanent. Forever. Your scientific precision has slipped a bit lately," he says.

I shake my head. "Fine, not forever. But it feels like forever. Perception kind of changes reality around here. Hard to explain, because it's definitely only explainable in some nonspecific realm of physics. Not my specialty."

He doesn't answer, and he doesn't let go of my hand. I'm pretending that it's nothing. That I don't even notice. After we take a few steps, he says, "I guess I understand the principle that things can feel heavier than they are. And that time can speed up or drag, depending on what a person is experiencing."

He is not talking about science. Or snowmen. Are we really going to do this right now? Already? I thought I'd have time to prepare before we started the postmortem relationship dissection. It's not a conversation I intended to have with him—for sure not tonight.

I stop at the edge of the main quad and drop his hand, which is easier to manage in gloves than I thought it would be. What I can't explain is how I can definitely feel the heat of him recede. And I certainly can't explain how much I miss it the second we let go. Okay. Moving on. "If we put a snowman here, the majority of students will see it from their dorms."

"That's our goal? Maximum visibility?" He clears his throat. "I don't remember that being your mode of operation." Oh, he is not. Even he would not dare to flirt with me right now. But, really, does he even know how to talk to a woman and not flirt?

"I'm not the person you used to know."

"Because this is new, right? We're starting at the beginning. But I can't pretend I don't know you, Ginger." The way he looks at me, I just can't deal with it.

Why is it so hard to breathe? Maybe I'm not acclimated to the altitude yet.

Nope. I've been back for too many days for that to be my excuse.

Maybe it's some dumb case of chemical attraction. I hate chemistry.

I mean, I don't really hate chemistry. Just the effect of Ty's presence on me in all the ways I'm feeling it. To be fair, most of that is definitely biology. So much biology.

"You can't have changed that much," he says, giving me that look. You know the one. The look he uses on all the female guest stars, playing DEA agents in immaculate navy pant suits and flawless hair. The look where he tilts his chin a little to the side, looking at you/her/me through his fringe of eyelashes that have always been just a little too good to be real. No human being has eyelashes that amazing. (Spoiler. They're real. They are that amazing.)

I turn away from him and start gathering up snow for a base.

Keeping myself busy is not difficult. Keeping my eyes off him? That's a different story.

I can't believe he's standing here, jeans damp almost to the knees, rolling snowmen in Vermont. This close to me. I can reach out and touch him. I don't. I won't. But I could.

Straining with the effort of keeping my eyes on the pile of snow in front of me, I almost don't hear his next comment.

"I haven't built a snowman in years," he says, and there's sadness in his voice.

"We used to do this together every winter," I say, not sure why I feel the need to remind him. If I didn't forget, he probably didn't either. It was a great tradition. Lots of freezing cold snowman building then some very enjoyable warming up. I'm definitely failing at this starting-over business.

"There are a lot of things I haven't done since the last time I did them with you," he says.

Mercy. I can't.

This could be a very sexy line if I weren't thinking about many, many things he probably did with Janie in the last several years. Mood killer.

I turn my back on him. The line was probably from his show anyway.

I mean, no, it wasn't, because I've casually watched every episode five or six times. But it *could have been* a line from his show. Maybe he'll be writing for them soon.

I'm impressed against my will.

And I'm impressed again as he lifts his nearly perfect sphere from where he's rolled it and places it on top of the mound of snow I've haphazardly gathered.

His shoulders strain against the seams of his parka. That can't possibly be as attractive as I am finding it. Wow. This guy can be as sexy in a winter coat as he can be when . . .

Stop that train, I tell myself.

It's not a good ride for any of us.

Maybe this was a bad idea.

I keep the rolling going, trying to keep my focus where it belongs. On the white, frozen ground around us and the snow falling in completely romantic drifts.

No.

Not romantic.

Is this real? Am I standing in the Chamberlain quad in a snowstorm with Ty Miller?

Okay, that helps. Because, no. He's not Ty Miller anymore. He's Tyson Perry Miller, star and heartthrob and celebrity chemistry teacher. The thought of that last bit makes me smile, and I guess Ty sees it. He asks me what's got me smiling.

I had forgotten that phrase. "What's got you smiling?" he always asked. Or, "What's got you thinking?" Or, when the circumstances fit, "What's got you sad?"

I used to be honest when I answered him. Now I say, "I like snow."

Hm. That is not the answer to his question. Nor is it empirically true. But somehow it feels true right now. I like this snow. Today.

"So, how do we make this the most epic Chamberlain snowman in history?" He asks it with the casual expectation that we can pick up snowman making and whatever else we once did together where we left them.

We can't.

My heart can't take this. I can't figure out how I feel. And when I think about it, even that's not entirely true. I can't pretend I'm not attracted to Ty, both the past and the present versions. What I can't decide is if I'm okay with it. Mostly not. I have to get out of here.

I lift the small wad of semispherical snow and drop it on top of our snowman. "It looks good enough to me," I say. "We're all kinds of low-maintenance around here."

Again, not at all true. But I need to go. I can't give this project any more time or energy or effort. I can't even go locate a carrot and some rocks to give this guy a face. His perfect midsection (the snowman's, not Ty's) looks funny layered between my halfhearted efforts of base and head, but I give it a nod and brush off my hands.

"Nice work," I tell Ty, nodding my head as though agreeing with myself. "That will be a great welcome-back for the students."

He doesn't answer. He doesn't need to. I know I said something meaningless, and I know that it chopped off the chance to really talk. At least for now. I don't want to talk. I don't want him to try to explain anything to me.

I need to remove myself from Ty's immediate presence. Bad enough that he's here, in my state, on my campus, in my department. And I need to snip the threads of memory that are trying to pull me backward into the world we once inhabited together. The world of the past.

There is nothing for me there.

I don't want to forgive him. Or her. Really not her. Or forget the past. Remembering on my own terms is what keeps me safe. I'm protected by the memory of how I was hurt, and now I don't get hurt like that anymore.

I won't get hurt like that ever again.

8

TY

I stay outside long after Ginger leaves. I finish the snowman. I find some twiggy branches behind a bush outside my dorm building, but honestly, the grounds crew doesn't leave me much to work with. I give him eyes and a smile from a few stones and eyebrows from some evergreen sprigs I find. He gets a hat from my room, one I won't miss if I don't get it back.

I sling a zip-front hoodie over the left shoulder, and tuck in a pair of canvas sneakers under the lowest mound. I finish it off with a green and yellow striped tie, tying it first around my neck then stretching the knot to fit it over the snowman's lumpy head.

I step back to look at the effect.

Not bad.

Not amazing, but not bad.

I wish Ginger had stayed to help me. She was always so great at giving snowmen personality.

She was always so great. Period.

I think about our months and months and almost years together as I walk back to the Rowan dorm. I remember her laugh, how I could barely keep myself from kissing that smiling mouth. How we fit together so perfectly. How our lives were pointed in the same direction.

It doesn't seem like she remembers the same things about me.

Maybe that's fair. I wasn't always great. Not that last day, for sure.

And I know I didn't really deserve the chance to explain what happened. But it wasn't what it looked like.

Until it was.

But even then, it wasn't what other people thought it was. Not what I'm sure Ginger thought. What she must still think. This could be different if she let me explain. It would be completely different if I'd never done such a stupid thing in the first place. I feel terrible about it still. And I hate feeling like my whole relationship with Janie was a mistake, but I can't pretend that it was amazing. I wasn't great for her. She wanted me to further her career, and I did. But I didn't make her happy. And she didn't make me happy. And it does no good at all for me to wonder how my life would have been better if I'd never screwed things up with Ginger.

I seem to have a gift for messing up. Ginger, Janie, and now with Brady and the Fleming brothers. It's hard to trust myself. I've never thought of myself as stupid, because my degrees prove I'm intelligent. But maybe I'm just really not awesome with humans. I should stick to elements. I can't manage to hurt them.

I sit, staring at the wall in my cramped dorm room in the silent building, a single bulb illuminating my desk. Where I'll do all my teacher prep work, I guess. Maybe I can at least get a decent office chair.

Maybe a poster for the wall.

This place looks monastic.

I guess I deserve this.

My phone buzzes, and I grab it up, hoping it's Ginger. That she saw the finished snowman. That she wants to talk. Or even not talk. Just sit together. She doesn't even have to look at me. I just want her to let me be where she is. This whole place is so foreign, and she feels like an anchor to the real and familiar.

One glance is enough to prove it isn't her.

'I'm going to call you in a minute. From a number you won't know.'

Brady, again.

I should not get this feeling of revulsion when I hear from him.

My brother.

My childhood idol. My hero all the time we were growing up. Coolest kid in any group. Star athlete. Mom and dad's favorite. Everyone's favorite. His picture hangs in the basketball gym in our hometown. Voted most likely to make a splash in the world. Only very recently turned criminal.

And, like in all the other things, he brought me along for the ride.

It wasn't my intention to fall into illegal activity, but try telling a judge that.

Brady had a deal. Brady always had a deal.

When he called me and invited me in on the ground floor of his latest land development plan, he was adamant that we needed to get the production company to fund it. This property, a couple thousand acres in Montana, was the most beautiful place he'd ever seen that didn't include palm trees. It would be amazing scenery for shows, for films. He and his partner planned to build a large retreat facility. Luxury among the mountains. People could rent it out for executive getaways. Fishing intensives.

Fleming Brothers Productions could have first rights. Total run of the place on the best weeks for filming. Gorgeous suites for actors and crew. Part ownership in the endeavor. Each of the Fleming brothers would get a chalet, as would I. As, of course, would Brady.

The only problem was, they had to secure funding immediately.

The Flemings were on a remote shoot, one of the Tongan islands, and couldn't be reached.

Brady understood.

Brady always understood.

He didn't try to talk me into anything. He didn't beg. He was never angry.

He just let me know that the offer couldn't stay on the table any longer. There was another buyer interested, and if I couldn't make the decision for the production company, we'd lose the chance.

The chance of a lifetime.

I okayed the wire transfer. Since the Flemings had given me exec-utive producer credits, I also had bank privileges.

And I knew what the team wanted. I knew the Flemings were looking for some investment properties. They wanted to secure some locations for filming, places they could return to as their filming schedules dictated. Brady was right. It was perfect.

Until the moment it all disappeared. Money. Contract. Investment partner. And Brady.

Montana was probably still where it belonged, but Montana was all that remained.

Brady's disappearance (and that of his partner) coincided neatly with the Fleming brothers' return to Burbank. And the far lighter corporate bank balance.

The drawbacks and benefits of a small production company worked both in my favor and not. There was no hiding what I'd done from the Flemings. Not that I tried to hide. As soon as they returned to cell service, we talked. I'd left them voice messages and sent emails looping them in on the whole process. But as soon as they returned, we all recognized what Brady had done.

And not done.

He had not purchased thousands of acres in the mountains.

He had watched his partner leave the country with (or maybe without) a great deal of money that was not his.

Fled, I think is the proper word.

And then Brady followed. Gone.

Without, as they say, a trace.

My phone rings. Unknown number. I answer.

"Ty!" Brady's voice rings through the line, strong and clear. "How are you? What's up, brother?" He sounds so charming. So unconcerned.

With those few words, I feel myself shift. My mind turns. I was willing to assume the best, to believe he was as innocent a player as I was. But something about his cheerful voice hits me all wrong.

Combined with the unknown number? And the playful texts? I don't trust him.

I imagine this all from Ginger's viewpoint. The whole story seems so sketchy that only a fool would believe in it. Red flags everywhere. I can see now how it would look to a person on the outside, and somehow, I know that I should not have trusted him.

"You're kidding, right?" I say. I want him to answer that. Is this a joke? Could all of this somehow have been a very unfunny joke?

"Good, good." He isn't listening. He may have never listened. Something twists in my guts, and I know that I can't believe him anymore. My trust in his innocence is gone. My adoration for my big brother is gone. And just like that, my patience is gone.

"What do you want, Brady?" I ask. I'm not being cruel. I just don't want to chat with him.

"We need to catch up. Where are you?" he asks.

Not a chance.

"Why? You going to drop by?" I know my voice sounds strained. Because I'm under a lot of strain. I can't believe him.

He laughs. "Not today. Little busy. Kind of far from LA."

I'm far from LA myself, but I'm not telling him that. Part of this deal is that nobody but the Fleming brothers knows where I'm "working" this winter and spring. My mom doesn't know. I told her I'm on a research project, top secret. She doesn't ask.

"Listen, Ty. We need to talk."

I wait.

"I know how this looks. And I just need to make sure you understand that I didn't cheat you."

Of course he cheated me. I almost laugh out loud. But it's not funny. He doesn't wait for me to answer.

"I was tricked, man. Same as you. Ellison lied to us both." Once I believed that. I wanted to believe. It's that voice. Brady has this tone in his voice. It makes people want to believe him. To trust him. I feel myself nodding, even as I think about Brady's lies.

Ellison. That's the name of his partner. The one who made the deal. Finalized the deposits. Organized the sale. And then emptied the investment account. The one who set all the bad stuff in motion. Brady is still talking. "But it's worse for me. I had to leave the country. At least you're still at home."

I look around my bare, cold dorm. Home. Right.

"And you didn't get into any trouble, did you?"

Does he think he's making a point? Or is he actually asking if I took the heat for this?

"Not much," I admit. This is true, and he doesn't need to hear any of the details. I'm definitely on the outs with the Flemings. They sent me away from California. Hid me here, for all intents and purposes, so I wouldn't show up in tabloids or talk to the wrong people. They're not blaming me entirely for what happened, but they're not pretending I'm innocent. My acting career is in serious jeopardy. In order to prove my intentions were pure, I have to do a semester here in the frozen mountaintops. In a dorm. Because I can somehow benefit both Chamberlain Academy and the Flemings. How, exactly, that will happen is still unclear to me. And, apparently, it's my job to figure that out.

But I'm not in jail. And there is good reason for me to feel grateful about that. And I'm not appearing in online magazines looking shifty or hiding my face, captioned with statements about fraud or theft or embezzlement.

Just a nice, quiet exile while I hustle up a way to repay several million dollars to the production company.

All told, it could be a whole lot worse.

"So, where are you today?" Brady asks again, and I can hear his question becoming more pointed.

"New job," I say, hoping to give him enough of an answer that he stops asking. I don't want him to know where I am. Or anyone else. But definitely not Brady. I don't want him any nearer to me than he is.

"Woah," he says, and his surprise sounds sincere. So, at least he hasn't heard about my probation. "Another show?"

He is going to keep asking. He will not let it go.

"Not a show. Chemistry stuff."

He laughs. "Using that big brain instead of those big biceps for once?"

I sigh. He should know that's not what the show is like. "Have you even watched an episode of Enforced? Do you have any idea what it's about?"

He laughs some more. "Come on. You play a heartthrob cop, and nobody would believe in a heartthrob cop without some kind of serious muscle definition."

He hasn't seen it. Nice. Somehow this makes it worse. Like, he doesn't even know what the show is about, he just lets his partner Ellison decide that I am a good source of funding.

An unfortunate truth at the time.

I was so quick to believe that the problem was Ellison. And me. Obviously, me, too. I recognize it now. Ellison was using Brady. By extension, they were both using me. And I was too quick about saying yes. I'm always too quick to say yes to Brady. Or, I was. Hindsight, man.

I don't answer him. There's nothing I can say that would fix anything.

"So, we're okay?" Brady asks.

Did I hear him correctly? *We're okay?* Really?

I repeat his words to him, toneless. "We're okay. Did you just say that?" Really? Is there any way, any possibility that he thinks we're okay just because he called and asked me to be okay? He didn't apologize. He didn't offer to make any restitution. Okay? Does he actually think that's in the realm of reality?

"Great, man. I'm so glad. I'd hate to think you're angry at me."

Seriously?

"No, that's not what I meant," I start to say. "I am definitely not okay. Where are you? Will you at least tell me that, so I can get in touch if I need you?" He interrupts me before I finish.

"Good. Great. I'm so glad. I'll call you again. Take care, man."

The line goes quiet. I'm not sure what just happened, but I think my brother phoned me to ask if I hold this all against him. If I consider him responsible for getting me kicked out of my life.

Of course I do. If I could call him back, I might just tell him. *Yes, I think it's your fault. I think this whole thing is you being your selfish self and me taking the fall.*

I've never said anything like that to Brady. Should I? I think about it. No. It's a bad idea.

My words will mean nothing to him. He just proved he isn't listening.

And nothing I say matters to him. He hears what he wants. And I feel gross about the whole thing. If I could make him listen, I'd say it all. But I can't make him listen any more than I can go back in time and refuse to give him the money.

It's becoming clear to me, though, that he's not being straight with me. And that's just brother-code. He's lying. He's manipulating.

My head aches. I rub my temples with my thumbs.

Talking to Brady lately always ends in a headache.

Awesome. All I need now is a call from my ex's lawyer, and my day will be made.

Not really.

I don't mean it.

I hate that I even think things like this. It's like I'm tipping the odds toward something I really don't want. *Ignore that thought, universe*, I think. I definitely don't need any lawyer phone calls.

I stare at the phone screen as the sun sets behind the clouds. It doesn't light up again.

I don't realize I'm hungry until my stomach growls loudly.

That's when I remember I was going to get some groceries.

But I didn't find a place to buy anything. I didn't search very hard, but without a car, things look a little distant here on campus.

Once I put on all the winter gear I brought, I let myself out of the dorm again, this time into the dark January night. Six o'clock at night, but dark is dark. I walk through campus and follow a paved road to the west. It takes me down a hill, and I can see lights ahead. I walk about ten minutes and find a strip mall sort of situation. There's a shopfront on the end that might be a restaurant, but has no sign. I could push the door open, since there's light leaking through the covered windows, but I can make do with something premade. There's a small hardware store, something calling itself "Essential Handicrafts," which is a bit of an oxymoron, and a convenience store with a gas pump out front.

I go inside the convenience store and grab a sandwich wrapped in plastic, hoping it was made today. Or at least yesterday. Juice from the cooler for breakfast. A couple of small bags of chips for when I crave something salty. A sleeve of those terrible mini donuts. I love those. I want some pretzel fish, but I can't find them. Too bad. They're my favorite.

If I eat only cellophane-packaged food for a couple of days, I will love whatever warm stuff is on the table in the school cafeteria when it opens. At least, that's my working theory.

It's a pathetic theory, but it's inexpensive. And inexpensive is a good look for me right now. Dr. Moreau's voice rings in my head reminding me I'm not being paid for my time here.

The old man ringing me up glances at my face only once. He doesn't recognize me. I can tell. If they recognize me and try to avoid eye contact, that's obvious. It's work. It's effort to pretend. This guy just doesn't know who I am and doesn't care. For this reason alone, I love this shop. He doesn't offer me a bag. I guess I'll carry things home in my pockets. Fine. Great. Save a corner of the planet.

"I'll be back," I say, picking up my purchases and packing them into various coat pockets.

"Why?" he asks, not looking at me. "Did you forget something?"

"No, I mean," I start, but shake my head instead of finishing my sentence. "Never mind." As I turn to leave, I pass the rack of magazines and see my face on a cover. I'm in my Enforced DEA uniform, but I've never heard of the magazine. I didn't talk with anyone from the publication. It's not an interview. Just a gossip rag. "What is ahead for Tyson Perry Miller?" the headline asks.

"Wouldn't we all like to know?" I mutter as I leave the shop and head back out into the cold and dark.

I walk back up the hill to campus. The walk up is longer than the walk down was. Maybe because it's cold. Maybe because it's uphill. I can see the clock in the main building between the trees. My feet slip a bit on the snowy sidewalk, but I make it back to Rowan without any injury.

At the door to the building, there's a brown paper bag with a twine handle. I look around. Nobody else is out here, so I think this is for me. There's no one else living here yet. I'm all alone.

I pick up the bag and peek inside, looking for a note.

No note.

A paperback book and a bag of pretzel goldfish.

From Ginger.

I feel a flush of heat that is decidedly not embarrassment for the juvenile snack. I'm not embarrassed that I crave kid-food. I'm thrilled that she brought it to me.

The book is a well-worn copy of *Lord of the Flies*, a book we both loved when we were at school. It's the book that brought us together.

In our first year of grad school, we were in a study group. That sounds more accidental than it was. I saw her in class. I heard her asking if anyone who lived south of campus wanted to get together to study. I lied and told her I lived south of campus.

It was worth the drive.

Before we got into studying for organic chemistry, we all talked. Got to know each other. Talked about our undergrad and where we grew up. Someone said something about the worst book ever written, and someone else asked if he meant *Lord of the Flies*. Everyone laughed. Except for Ginger. "I love that book," she said. Her face was all serious. "It's an important question: is humanity basically good or basically evil?"

I had thoughts. I did not say them out loud.

"Evil, on that island." This from a guy who seemed fairly sure he knew all the answers.

I watched the guy prepare to spar with Ginger, and I knew right away he was no match for her.

She nodded. "And there's the most important part of the whole question. The book's not a how-to manual. It's not showing the reality of life or telling people how they should behave. Using kids to highlight the worst in mankind (and it's no accident that they're all boys) is for shock value. You don't have to live that way. People don't, mostly. But we all have a little darkness in us. Under the right conditions, the world brings out our worst. We become beasts. But sometimes, something allows us to become people again."

"Given the chance," the guy argued, "people will follow the loudest example."

Ginger shook her head. "I see how you might feel that way, but I disagree. People will follow their hearts. And most people have good hearts. But they need to know they're not alone."

That was my cue. "The tragedy of the book is that there are several characters who want to behave well, but they can't. They each feel like they're alone in it, or too weak to stand up to the others."

Ginger met my eyes. "We want the kind ones to survive. We need to see it. And we see it in the end of the book. Quietly, but we see it."

She smiled at me. Only for me.

We became a team. Right then.

I knew I wanted to find out how to make her smile like that, just for me, as often as possible. Under better circumstances than defending books about savagery in young boys, preferably.

Turns out I wasn't one of the strong ones who survive. I was too weak to stand up for what I should have.

Maybe, by giving me this book, she's telling me she forgives me. Maybe she's reminding me I could have done better. Tried harder.

Maybe she just knows I didn't have any real work to do, so she brought me a book and a snack.

Whatever the reason, I'm happy she did.

She's thinking about me.

Just like I'm thinking about her.

9

<hr/>

GINGER

He finished the snowman. Not that it's going to win any awards for most clever use of ice molecules, but it's sweet that he stuck it out and didn't give up when I gave up last night.

Swallowing my small dose of remaining pride, I texted Hank and asked him if he knew which apartment Ty was assigned to.

Here's why I love text: If we were in the same room having an out-loud exchange, Hank would have teased more information out of me. He would have laughed at my need to know. He would have asked every question that came to his mind. But over text? Hank is not verbose. At least not with me.

'Rowan RA, poor chap.'

A small, mean, mostly-suppressed part of me laughed at the idea of Ty living in a dorm with a bunch of kids. Even when he was a kid, he didn't live with kids. Certainly not younger ones. He idolized his older brother, and as far as I could tell, the brother let him tag along everywhere, up to and including a college apartment for Ty's first year.

And now, View Magazine's Hottest Actor Under Thirty was living in a cinderblock dorm room. When I dropped off the book and the pretzels, the rooms were all dark. Not that I would have knocked. I'm not going into his room. But we can't have our visiting faculty starving to death, not when there are fish-shaped snacks to sustain them.

Okay. Fine. I was flirting. But flirting from a distance, which is all I can manage right now. And yes, flirting opens doors. Doors I'm not ready to walk through. I can't pretend his presence isn't affecting me, but I can hold off on the deep discussions. I can keep him at arm's length. Sort of.

At least I think I can.

He's ready to talk history. Our history.

I'm not.

But the history is looping itself in my head. Constantly.

I open my laptop and glance through my messages. Maybe email can distract me from Ty-thoughts. As I scroll the inbox, I tell myself to shake him off. Most of these messages I can ignore. But one makes me look twice. I have a reply from Portia Bancroft.

I have a reply from Portia Bancroft!

Telling myself not to make too much of this, because of course it's an auto-reply, I open the message.

There's no opening greeting, which is understandable, since I didn't really give my name in the request, but it only takes a sentence to realize she's really responding to my request. It's only a few lines saying, "I'd love to do a phone interview, but my time is seriously limited right now by my touring schedule. Are you near any of the cities I'm appearing in? We could meet for a few minutes after one of my signings." There's a link to the Appearances tab on her website. I scan the list of cities, sure that no publicist in his or her right mind would schedule a winter appearance in Vermont, and I'm mostly right. Mostly right but delightfully wrong: On the first day of spring, March twenty-first, she's coming to Burlington. I was definitely preparing to go to Boston, if not all the way to New York. But she's coming to Burlington.

Why Burlington? Who arranged that?

And why would she rather meet than have a phone call? Maybe because she's still new at this. Maybe she's worried that her bookstore signing won't draw a crowd in Vermont. But I bet she's going to have a huge showing.

I don't ask why. I send a reply. "Burlington, VT is close to me. I'd love to see you there." I continue typing for several minutes, look over what I wrote, and delete everything that sounds aggressively eager. That leaves those first two sentences. I send it.

Can I really wait two months for this?

I mean, of course I can. Not that it's ideal, but her tour begins in California and moves its way across the country. I can't imagine how grueling a two-month tour must feel, moving from hotel to hotel every night, wondering what city you're waking in, being at the mercy of public appearances every evening. It sounds awful.

I begin imagining what she'll say when we sit down together and immediately hit it off. I put her at her ease, and she gives a relieved sigh and tells me how good it feels to meet someone who is so comfortable to talk with. Someone who feels familiar, like we've known each other for years.

I'll laugh demurely (no fangirl giggling in this fantasy, thank you very much) and tell her what *You Are Made of Stars* means to me. I'll ask interesting, intelligent questions that will definitely occur to me sometime in the next two months, and she'll mention how refreshing it is to discuss such thoughtful points.

When it comes time to leave, I'll insist on paying for her coffee and pastry (we will eat delicious pastry, of course) and she will hold my arm and say how she wishes I could stay a bit longer. She has so many questions for me.

Later, when my review goes viral, she'll insist that we continue our collaboration, demanding (politely) that her publisher gives me first rights on all advance copies of her work, and when she dedicates the next book to me, I'll smile calmly and hold the book to my chest, reminiscing on the surprising path that life takes me.

Yeah, right. Like I wouldn't squeal in a register only dogs can hear. Like I didn't just give such a squeal when I saw her message.

But I have two whole months to get myself together, to prepare to be impressively cool.

I jump up from the couch. What am I going to wear?

Real cool, Rogers.

I sit back down and pull my computer back onto my lap. Okay. Time to prepare some labs.

Two hours later, I'm prepped for the first two weeks of classes. Plans laid. Orders placed. Delivery of chemical supplies scheduled. I know exactly how lucky I am that my courses are repeated throughout the day. Most of the juniors take chemistry, and between Perla Sandoval and me, we teach them all. I don't know how I'd do it if all my classes were different courses. Poor Joey—she handles it well, but her classes are all doing different things all the time. I don't know how she keeps track.

I shoot her a quick text since I'm thinking about her. *'How's planning going?'*

Within a few seconds, she responds with a picture of her snuggled into Dexter's couch, his arm around her, two laptops open.

'I meant planning for CLASSES,' I say.

'Mmmm. So well. Very, very well.'

'Gross.'

She sends me a laughing face.

I keep teasing. *'And who's that guy you're with? He almost looks like the theater teacher, but he's not wearing a bow tie.'*

She responds, *'Well, he acts like he likes me, so I'm keeping him.'*

Joey and Dexter are so great for each other, and I can say that now without visible flinching.

Not that I didn't like him before Joey showed up, but—no, okay, I didn't like him. He's got this wide streak of arrogance that runs through him that has always rubbed me the wrong way. Joey says it's a defense mechanism, and she ought to know. But before Joey came to Chamberlain, I didn't really have a friend here. For all the reasons I don't want to talk about, I kept my distance from colleagues. Somehow Joey slipped into a chink in my armor, and I knew right away that she was going to be one of those friends who makes life so much better. It was true. She does. And when she and Dexter Kaplan started hitting it off, I didn't love sharing her with him.

Now that I see how happy they make each other, I can be a grown-up and at least not actively make it difficult for them. Joey is great at sharing her time with me, too. We get an afternoon together at least once a week, and we all have dinner together every Thursday. At least, we did last semester. I hope that's still the plan.

Besides, what would happen if all those together times now included Dexter? Would that be so bad?

Okay. Yes.

But I don't mind sharing Joey at dinner. And Hank can come. And Ty.

Nope. Not Ty. Where did that come from?

I am not that eager to open the doors of my life and let him walk inside and poke around. I still have too many raw edges.

Not that I'll exclude him. I mean, tradition is tradition, and when the guys invite him to Lola's for the first dinner after classes begin, I'll go. I'll be polite. I'll eat amazing food, because I'm the kind of friend who is willing to make these sacrifices. And we're going to be friends.

But nothing more. Despite what my traitorous body keeps trying to tell me when I'm near him.

There are some pains that don't heal.

You know that thing where you get a bruise, and even before you see it, you can feel it? When you run your fingers along the place you know it's forming, you can feel the tender spot? I guess I'm mature enough to admit that I'm all kinds of tender spot where Tyson Miller is concerned.

It occurs to me now that my visit with Portia Bancroft will be right about at midterm. The halfway mark of enduring this semester with Ty.

Enduring is kind of a negative word. It's not like he and I will be in close proximity. His classroom is far away from mine. His apartment (dorm—ha!) is farther. Maybe he'll be at weekly science department meetings. Maybe, now that I think of it, he's not even required to go to those since his classes aren't core. So I'll see him a couple of times a week. For eighteen weeks. I can do that. I can see him thirty-six times and not revert to a heartbroken grad student.

Maybe no more snowmen, though. And I should not leave snacks and books at his dorm. That probably won't help me stay distant.

I curl up on the couch with a couple of blankets, a cup of tea, and my *You Are Made of Stars* book. The book that Portia Bancroft and I will discuss in March. I laugh out loud just thinking about it. I have an appointment to sit down and chat with Portia Bancroft!

I reread Chapter Nine, "It's Written in the Stars," which challenges the pervasive and crushing fatalistic mindset. Even though the chapter title says "It's Written," Portia suggests that we can interpret situations, historical events, and other people's actions to create our best outcomes. I scribble a few thoughts in the margins, ideas I might want to explore when we talk.

I can't believe we're going to talk.

I also can't believe I have to wait so long before we do.

I'm not going to read anyone else's interviews with Portia. I'm going into our meeting with only the understanding of her philosophy and the connection I feel to her writing. I don't want anyone else's attitudes to color my opinions, and I want to avoid both the implausibly complimentary and the unreasonably unflattering commentaries that interviewers make when they do celebrity interviews.

No baggage. Just two intelligent women discussing self-actualization and empowerment. What could be better than that?

I close the book and stretch, getting up and looking out my window across the dark quad. Most of the winter, I can see more of campus at night than I can during the day, or at least the lights make more windows obvious. This week, without the students, the campus feels large and almost barren. Of course, that could be the dormant trees and the ice covering everything. There's a light on, far away, and I wonder if it's Ty's. I picture him stretched out on his twin bed, leaning on the cold cinderblock wall, hands behind his head. Maybe he's looking out the window in this direction.

He's not. Because that's not his light.

It's not. The light isn't even in the right place to be a dorm window. Because how strange would it be to have a sightline from teacher residences to kids' dorms, anyway? No, thank you. Not going to happen.

But now that I've thought of him, I can't help wondering what he's doing tonight. I love to think of him reading the book I left him, but how likely is that? What are the chances that Tyson Perry Miller reads in bed?

Not that I'm thinking about what Tyson Perry Miller does or does not do when he's in his bed. No. I'm not.

Never. I'm never going to think any version of that thought ever again. Nor am I thinking about how he took my hand as we walked across campus. In the snow. Nope.

I'm definitely not pondering the changes in him, how his jaw seems a bit more angular than it used to—I thought that was camera magic, but it's real.

How his smile still twitches at the edges of his mouth, flashing and then hiding his dimples, but how his mouth is gentler now, like he's been trained to let the smile build slowly instead of the old Ty's knockout grin that came on, full force, out of nowhere.

A swooping feeling lunges through my stomach, that pain-and-pleasure flutter that might mean I'm thinking about how Ty used to smile just for me. Or it might mean I'm hungry.

I'm not hungry.

Grrr.

I'm going to clean the bathroom. A far more useful outlet for my excess energy than staring out the window at a perfectly innocent random campus light.

When my porcelain is glinting in the bathroom, I attack the kitchen sink. It's not exactly rage-cleaning, because I'm not enraged. I'm not even angry, unless it's at myself for allowing my mind to leak down the path of What Might Have Been. But productivity is productivity, and my backsplash grout is getting every attention of this toothbrush. I scrub. I rinse. I scrub some more. I realize I'm humming.

"What About Love" by Heart. You have to be kidding me. Come on. Of all the eighties songs available for my brain to land on—and there are so many great ones—I have to come up with this? But now it's in my head and it's not going anywhere. I just run with it. No more humming. I sing. All the words. Even the ones I might make up, if the actual lyrics don't come quickly enough to my mind.

I feel better. Less frustrated, more powerful. I don't know if it's leftover Portia Bancroft or the cleanest tiles on Chamberlain campus, but I feel more than better. Good.

I don't think it has anything to do with Ty, but I'm willing to concede that I don't actually know. Maybe there is something about having him reappear in my life. Maybe it's time to tie up loose ends. Maybe like Portia says in Chapter Fifteen, "The Stars Align," and forgiveness is on the horizon.

I won't discount the possibility. I won't ignore my chances. I won't decide what is going to happen before it happens.

10

TY

Meeting with my advisement mentor turns out to be the least of my worries. Jackson Powers, science department head and biology teacher, has me come to his classroom to meet him Thursday morning. His room is in the same building as Ginger's and mine, but in a separate hallway.

"Biology and chemistry don't usually mix," he says, shaking my hand. "So you might not see much of me on a daily basis. But I guess you're not really doing chemistry, are you?"

He doesn't wait for an answer. "They've got you up in the observation tower. Guess they want to keep an eye on you."

I can't tell if he's kidding. I don't know how to read that eyebrow lift.

"Or they want to give the kids in my classes the best views," I say. "Maybe it will help fill my classes up."

Jackson shakes his head. "I don't think you're going to have an issue with that."

"Because there are a lot of kids interested in nontraditional careers?" I ask, hoping he doesn't say anything about my celebrity status.

"No. Because your class will be an easy A." He has said a lot in the minute we've been talking, and most of it could be interpreted as rude. But I don't feel like he's being rude. Just honest. And maybe a little abrupt.

I take a minute to decide if I'm offended by his "easy A" comment. Eventually, I figure I'm not. "I take it this isn't a school where good grades come easy."

"Not in the serious classes," he says in a voice that leaves no doubt that he teaches serious classes. Possibly all of them. But still, not unkind.

"In keeping with the department norms," he says, "you'll hold class every day, you'll give a weekly reading assessment, a biweekly test, and maintain a list of essential targets for the kids."

He might see me flinch, because he finally smiles like he means it. "But nobody says what your assessments and tests need to look like. Since your classes aren't core, nobody's counting on you to teach certain concepts that will become essential to following years' courses. So. Let's bust out your essentials and work from there."

He pulls a chair out from a black-topped science table, the heavy kind that look the same in every school I've attended. Flopping a yellow legal pad down in between us, he straddles his chair and says, "So what are you hoping the kids get out of your course?"

I splutter about broad understandings and valuable experience and employability for a few minutes before he stops me. I notice he didn't write down any of my ramblings.

"These kids are between fourteen and eighteen years old," he says, a smile on his face that proves he's not testing me. At least not anymore. "Most of them will be doing jobs after university that haven't been invented yet. What do you want them to care about?"

Am I supposed to have an educational viewpoint? That was not part of the agreement. Did I ever have to state such a thing when I was getting my doctorate? I decide to wing it. "Learning is always good."

He nods, writing on the paper in front of him. "And?"

He wants more? "Nothing you study is wasted."

He smiles at me. "Great start. Let's refine."

We spend an hour working my cobbled-together philosophy into manageable, testable targets. We talk about weekly quizzes, about different assessment methods, about alternate ways to have kids report on their learning. He's patient, and reminds me a few times that these people we're serving are children. "We have to hold them to high standards, but they're going to act like kids. Which they should. Because they're kids."

When I leave his classroom after an hour, I feel so much more confident and prepared. Not that I know any more about teaching than I did this morning when I woke up. But I know a little more about expectations. I have a few ideas on making tests (not the multiple-choice kind, but more like the measures-of-understanding kind). There are ways I can make this easier on myself, and there are ways to give myself a whole lot of work. I am leaning in the direction of the former, especially since I'm not being paid.

I know how to survive the first days of teaching. At least I think I do.

And I know Jackson is tasked with keeping an eye on me. His watch is more metaphorical than someone who is literally sitting and watching my classes happen, either from inside the room, or from pretty much anywhere on campus above a third-story level. But he's responsible for me. I like the guy, so I want to make it easy for him to trust me.

I decide to get to know the campus, wander around and see which buildings are the most likely watchtowers. It's a weird feeling, walking around to see where I might be watched from. Everywhere. I mean, people could be looking from behind any of the windows. I guess that's always true, but I don't usually feel so . . . targeted by the idea. Now I feel like people are waiting for me to mess up. Because I've messed up pretty seriously, and it makes sense that it will happen again.

The kids' dorms are only two stories tall, so at least I don't think

Dr. Moreau will have student spies watching the Copernicus windows. The Hall, the main administration building where we had our first faculty meeting, has third-floor rooms, as does the library. A few of the classroom buildings are on higher ground, so technically someone could watch me from the math building and from the foreign languages building. History is also set high, but there are literal forests between the history building and the science one. Well, one literal forest, I guess. Actually, I don't really know what constitutes a forest.

I look it up on my phone as I walk across campus. Turns out that what separates the science building from the history classrooms is technically a wood, not a forest. Square footage. Density. Height. All factors in determining the difference. Okay. I amend my statement. There are *woods* between us. It would still be hard to spy on my room from a history class.

Why do I keep using the word "spy"? I have nothing to hide. At least nothing I'm going to take to class.

Dr. Moreau made it clear that she's just sitting up there in the Hall waiting for me to place a single toe outside the proper line so she can dismiss me from her campus. In her terrifying French accent. With her sculpted eyebrows.

But if she really thought I was going to mess things up, would she have let me come?

She did mention money.

Somehow she expects me to be a source of funding. I think I'm at my limit of finding that funny. Nobody else better ask me to arrange donations. For anything. Ever again.

I hear someone call my name, but with the empty campus and the snow and the surrounding hills, it's tough to tell where the shout is coming from. I could do a circle and try to see the source of the yell, but I would look dumb, so I stop walking. A minute later I see the British guy, Hank, coming toward me across the snow. He lopes over and slaps an arm across my back. "All right?" he asks.

I tell him I'm giving myself the grand tour of Chamberlain.

"Have you found all the campus secrets?" he asks.

"Buried treasure? Secret society codes scratched into the walls? A system of tunnels?"

Hank laughs. "Don't forget ghosts. I think all of those are requisite for east coast boarding schools."

"I guess there's more for me to discover," I say.

He nods. "And allow me to introduce you to Lola's tonight. Dinner." He points toward what I think is the west. Hard to tell with such heavy clouds. "Best food. Just off campus." He stops, rubbing his fingers along his wispy blond beard. "What have you been eating?" he asks, as if it only just occurred to him that I don't have a kitchen in my room.

"I went down to the convenience store and stocked up," I tell him. I think about eating fish-shaped pretzels and smile, but I keep that part to myself. If Ginger never told her friends about us, she might not be eager to have me say anything about gifts of simple carbs.

I can live without saying anything about it. I can keep it to myself.

At least as long as the bag of pretzels lasts. Then I might have to ask her where she found them.

"You can use my kitchen if ever you need," he says. The words of his invitation sound so formal, but his tone embodies chill.

"Thanks," I say.

"But for tonight, we all eat whatever Lola offers. And we all like it." He nods sagely, like he's just imparted some great wisdom.

I don't know what this means, but I'm happy to be included. "Glad to come along," I say. He puts my number in his phone and, as we stand there in the wind and the snow, he sends me his.

"Now you're connected."

"Thanks," I say. I mean it. It already feels better knowing that if my phone buzzes, it's not automatically Brady.

I want to ask Hank about Ginger. About him and Ginger. I don't think there's anything between the two of them. I'm almost sure not. But I don't know how to ask without looking like I'm a possessive ex. Or I wish I possessed something (someone) that's no longer mine. I can't figure out a cool way to ask. So I stand there, saying nothing.

He's watching me, and before too long, he says, "Look. I'm just going to ask it. What are you doing here?"

Somehow, it's a surprise, even though I should know it's coming. It's not like I don't expect people to ask. Of course, they'll be curious. But nobody has asked directly yet. This is the first time I've needed to use the line that the lawyers approved. The Fleming Brothers production company's keeping very quiet. They don't want anyone to know where I am, let alone why. Nobody seemed to hide anything from Dr. Moreau, but she's not exactly chatty. I doubt she'll be talking.

If someone is saying something about why I'm here, it's me.

I get to make this what I want it to be. Or at least what the lawyers and I agreed on. "I want to give back. I'm so lucky with my education and my career, and now I have a chance to help other people." It sounds chivalrous. Gentlemanly. Generous.

Hank looks at me with raised eyebrows. "Giving back." He says it without inflection, but in his accent, he sounds doubtful. He's not buying it. "That phrase generally presupposes that you're giving to people in need. You know, like the disadvantaged. The marginalized. Those in, say, inner cities." He gestures to the campus in general. "Chamberlain Academy isn't a hotbed of underprivilege."

I laugh. "Yeah, okay. Maybe I need to tweak my statement." I'm not willing to tell him any details, but maybe he can help me offer a more convincing explanation.

I keep going with the honest-but-not-full story. "I'm trying out something new."

He shakes his head. "That sounds like something you'd say if you outgrew your show. Or your character is getting killed off. You're not getting killed off, are you? You're still doing the show, right?"

If they'll have me. "That's the plan," I say.

"Try something else." He doesn't offer any help. Thanks for nothing.

"Spreading my wings?" I ask, wondering if I just need to use a tired cliché to explain myself.

He doesn't even comment. Just shakes his head. We walk across the campus, and we're the only people outside as far as I can see.

I tuck my chin inside my coat collar. It's so cold. "Maybe I'll tell anyone who asks I'm secretly recruiting actors."

Hank laughs. "Moreau would hate every bit of that."

I nod. "Luring kids away from her campus? Yeah, I guess that's not ideal. And I bet she'd especially hate the 'secret' part. She strikes me as a pretty straightforward person."

He agrees. "The chancellor is forthright. Sometimes painfully so."

"I'm learning that," I say.

He nods in sympathy. "Happens to all of us, mate."

"How about this? I'm reigniting my interest in academia."

His eyes open wide against the wind. "Oh, yes. I like that one very much." He claps his hands together once, his gloves making a muffled thwack. "Say that when people ask you. And you should say it when no one has asked. Say it in front of cameras as often as possible. That's your bit."

He might keep going on like this. I nod and say, "Thanks."

He clears his throat. "Anything else you're particularly interested in reigniting while you're here?" he asks.

I stop walking and turn to face him. Without meaning to, I find myself standing up straighter. My arm muscles clench.

He laughs again and shakes his head, gesturing to me. "Stand down, mate. It's not a challenge. Just wondering. As a spectator. Will there be some interesting chemical reactions on campus this semester?" He gestures toward the science building.

I don't say anything.

He shakes his head. "Ignore me. Since there is nobody else here to warn you, I guess I must tell you myself. I often say the wrong thing. I regularly put my foot in it. And I always want to know things that aren't my business." He puts a finger to the side of his head. "Occupational hazard," he adds. "Intellectual curiosity."

"That's one way to say it."

He nods his head in agreement. "*Nosy* works just as well."

"But sounds so much less formal." I feel all my tension release. He's not a threat. He's a bystander, hoping for a show. He's not preparing to fight for Ginger. He wants to know if we'll get back together. Maybe he wants to see her happy.

Or maybe he wants to see me fail. Always a possibility, but Hank seems like a sincerely nice guy..

I bet I can arrange something entertaining for the benefit of the observers.

11

GINGER

There are a lot of things to love about teaching at Chamberlain. It's a good job, and I have decent compensation. More than decent. I like kids, and it's fun to watch them figure out tough things. I love to give them cool labs, and I don't even mind too much when I have to fix what they break. I like Vermont, even though winter is stupid cold.

I work with good people, even if I haven't gotten close with anyone before Joey. I can see what being her friend does for me, and I am willing to put myself out there a little more within the faculty. I've written it down in my goals notebook. "Be friendly."

I know how dumb that looks. But I have to remind myself, because it's not in my nature to be friendly anymore. Not since Janie. Not since friendship turned on me.

Nope. No. No, thank you.

I don't want to think about Janie today. Because I'm thinking about all the good things about my life, not the terrors of the past.

Healthy body. Strong mind. Good job. Living room full of plants. Friends. Books. An interview with Portia (!) Bancroft (!) to look forward to.

And there's Lola's.

Going to Lola's is a bit like going home for dinner a couple of times a week, if your mom lives in the kitchen and could win a cooking show with one of her hands tied behind her back.

My mom is not that mom. In fact, my mom doesn't cook. My dad is a great baker and griller. Lots of meat and pie and cake.

But Lola is a wonder. Her restaurant hides in an unassuming strip mall west of campus. No sign, no bright lights. Nothing welcoming about the storefront. This is on purpose—she is not interested in being the high school hangout. She doesn't run like a regular restaurant. Maybe because she has a small clientele in a small town. If she had pizza and burgers, sandwiches and fries on her menu, kids would fill her booths and tables every day. But none of that. Not even menus.

You go in, you sit down, she brings you food, and you love it.

It has occurred to me that there are people who have to eat carefully, avoiding certain foods or ingredients. Maybe that crosses Lola's mind, but honestly, I'm not sure. "Take it or leave it" seems to be her business philosophy, and it looks like she's doing just fine.

I psych myself up for Thursday night dinner. I know Ty's going to be there. Hank texted me a warning, which was really nice of him. And I better get used to it. Ty's going to be everywhere this semester. I am a grown up. I can deal with Ty. I have dealt with Ty before. But not as an ex.

We meet outside Joey's place to walk down to dinner together. Joey and Dexter, Hank, Ty, and me. I'm relieved that we're an odd number. I don't need any external, couple-y reasons for this to feel more awkward. Thank goodness Hank isn't dating anyone.

Dex and Joey lead us down the hill toward Lola's and happiness. Hank and Ty are talking about basketball and how the late summer trades were so wild and I don't care. I'm just happy not to need to find a way to talk to Ty in front of all these people without blushing. If I let Hank do all the talking, I can smile and nod and eat dinner and nobody needs to know what is happening inside me. How my heart is thudding every time I look at Ty's face. How seeing him look at me from the side of his eye reminds me of so many shared glances, so many unspoken understandings. If I don't have to talk, nobody needs to hear how my breathing gets erratic. Thank heaven they can't see my heartbeat when Ty's around.

And it's not that I'm not still angry. I'm angry. And sad. And heartbroken in a way that maybe I'll never get over. I mean, I haven't gotten over it yet, and it's been five years of distance. Now there's no more distance. I mean, there's distance. It's eight hundred and seventeen steps from my doorstep to the front door of Rowan dorm. But that's not the same kind of distance I'm used to.

And I can't convince my neurons that they're not delighted we're in proximity.

So I'm fine to walk quietly and watch.

Dexter has his arm over Joey's shoulders, and they are so snuggled up that it's hard to believe that only a few months ago it was her first week at Chamberlain. Life moves quickly. When we get to Lola's, Ty says, "This is it?"

It's what everyone says.

As Dexter opens the door and ushers us in, Ty says, "I came here. I mean, not inside here. I walked right past it and bought cellophane sandwiches from the convenience store."

"Shh," Hank says. "Don't let Lola hear you say that."

Dexter laughs. "She can't be annoyed by it. People walk right by here all the time. If she wanted to advertise, she would."

We sit in chairs around a circular table. There's going to be one empty seat, and I can't decide if I want that open chair next to me or not. I hang my coat on the back of a chair and sit. Ty sits beside me on one side, Joey on the other. She gives me a look, a raise of the eyebrows that I interpret as "are you okay?"

I nod and smile. I glance at Ty and he's watching me. His smile gets bigger.

"Smells good," he says, and he's right. There's practically a garlic haze in the room. Lola's been making Italian food.

"We have chosen well," Hank says, tilting his head as if he's praying.

Dexter explains to Ty how things work here. "She's going to come say hi, then she'll bring us plates of whatever she's making. It's always amazing."

Ty asks, "If it's so amazing, why are there only two other tables filled?"

"You've seen this town, right?" Joey asks. "There aren't that many people who live here."

"Sometimes we're the only ones eating when we come," Dexter says.

"But we usually come early," Joey adds. "Normal people don't eat dinner at 4:30. Only starving teachers and my grandparents."

Everyone laughs.

So far, my plan is working. I haven't said a word since we left Joey's place.

Hank says, "I always try to get Lola to eat with us. She's never done it. She's so busy. I think she's the only one who works back there. I've never seen a cook or a server or a busser or a dishwasher. She's a one-woman operation."

"Maybe her employees are back there working so hard they don't have time to leave the kitchen. Ever."

I get a picture in my mind of oompa-loompas from Willy Wonka's chocolate factory. A funny thought, but secret labor force isn't exactly Lola's style.

Ty hums the oompa-loompa song from the Gene Wilder movie. Do I love that we're thinking the same thing? Maybe I love it. I think I'm the only one who hears him. I smile down at the scuffed table.

The empty chair is between Hank and Dexter. It's as good a place as any for my eyes to rest. Just opposite mine, across the table.

Dexter is still explaining. "She loves us, but she doesn't like kids. So she has to act all cold and tough and heartless, but we know it's an act. Nobody heartless could cook with this much passion."

The kitchen door swings open and Lola emerges in a cloud of steam. She points at our table to let us know she sees us, and I can see her doing a head count. Without speaking to us, she turns back around.

When she re-emerges from the kitchen, she's carrying five

gorgeous plates of salad, and those tomatoes look amazing. Who gets gorgeous tomatoes in January?

Lola. That's who.

She places the salads in front of us and welcomes us to dinner. I see the double-take moment when she recognizes Ty. Her mouth drops open. She picks up Hank's salad and moves it in front of the empty seat. Pointing for him to shove over, she sits down between Hank and Ty, turning her back to Hank. "You're Tyson Perry Miller," she says, her voice soft and low and velvety.

I'm used to hearing her laughing or chattering or explaining how to eat something I've never seen before, but this is a different Lola. She seems even taller than she is, which is weird, since we've never seen her sitting. She's just got that majestic, statuesque vibe about her.

"I've seen everything you've ever done," she says. She's breathless. I know the symptoms.

I can't believe what I'm seeing. Her arms are both on the table. She's leaning into Ty's space. This has never happened before. She's sitting at our table, giving her full attention to one person. She's got her arms on the table. Lola is a completely different person. Dex and Hank are trying not to laugh. Joey's not even trying. Lola doesn't seem to notice. Her eyes have not left Ty's face.

Ty squirms in the seat next to me. Under the table, his hand fumbles for mine. He's not making a pass. He's looking for help. I knock his hand away, but I can't let him suffer. Not too much.

"Lola, this is Ty. He's going to teach science at Chamberlain this semester."

Lola touches Ty's shoulder. "You're so pretty for a science teacher," she says, still in that deep, breathy voice.

Ty laughs. "Thanks, I think. I'm not the only one. Ginger's a beautiful science teacher." He looks at me and his smile is a little desperate.

Lola shakes her head and leans closer to Ty. "We're not talking about Ginger right now. We're talking about you."

That doesn't deserve an answer, and he doesn't give one. She goes on. "All those things you say on TV about being a real scientist? They're true?"

Ty nods, and I see him swallow. Like, gulp. Hank and Dexter pick up their forks and spear some of their salads, but Joey has her elbows on the table and her hands in fists beneath her chin. She's in this for the entertainment. I am invisible to Lola. The rest of the world may be invisible to Lola.

She asks questions, but nothing Ty needs words to answer. "Do you love working with all those famous actors who do cameos on your show? My favorite was in season three, when Calvin Humphries played that undercover double agent. I knew he was one of the dealers as soon as I saw him on the screen. He just had an air about him. Untrustworthiness. Aren't the Fleming brothers having a lot of success right now? I hear they're expanding into longer films along with series. Isn't Yolanda Cuevas amazing for a woman of her age?"

He nods, he shakes his head, he smiles. All the time he's batting at my leg under the table. His SOS is clear, but what does he expect me to do? Okay, in fairness, there are dozens of ways I could probably save him. But I am enjoying this as much as Joey is. More than Hank and Dexter are. For sure a thousand times more than Ty is. Lola inches closer to Ty with every question until she's in such a lean that I'm worried she might end up in his lap.

Okay. Rescue time.

"Lola, this salad is delicious," I say, even though it's clear I haven't taken a bite. "Do you want to bring one out for yourself and join us for dinner?"

Ty glances at me, his eyes wide with what looks like terror. I give him the same smile I'm giving Lola. Welcoming. Inviting. Total fakery.

My question takes a second to sink in past the fangirl haze, but when it does, I see it. Lola's eyes clear. She shakes off the mystifying glamor of the celebrity encounter and stands. She recalls who she is. It's the moment she remembers that she has a job to do.

"Eggplant parm, coming right up," she says, her smile far too bright for eggplant. There's still way too much air in her voice, but our Lola is returning to herself.

Or so I think. She turns to Ty. "Do you like eggplant? I can make you something different. Veal? Would you prefer chicken? Or veal?"

Hank splutters. "I want veal," he says, a look of disbelief on his face.

Lola doesn't even glance his way. "Not for you."

He's indignant. As well he should be; he's always been her favorite. Until now. "Why not? And do you actually have veal back there in the kitchen?"

Now Lola shoots Hank a quick glare. "I know where to find some," she says, returning her gaze—and it's definitely a gaze; she is fully gazing—back to Ty.

"I'm happy to have what everyone else is having," Ty says, giving her his most gracious look, the one that comes with the soft, dimpled smile that whispers, "I'm in your hands." He probably can't help it. He's trained to respond like that.

Lola's mouth is open. Not wide open. Not hanging slack. Her lips are parted. Kind of like she can't help it. Yeah. I know that feeling, too.

She walks away from the table, backing into the kitchen, as if she's worried Ty will disappear from her sight before the door swings closed between them.

Joey claps her hands together in delight. Dexter is laughing, and Hank looks a combination of amused and annoyed. "She offered him veal," he says, shaking his head. "She. Lola. Offered someone a substitution. And not just any substitution. *Veal.*"

Ty is visibly relaxing. I watch his shoulders lower. Putting his elbows on the table he turns to look at me. "You're no help."

I shake my head. "I would never come between you and your adoring fans." I can't help the little laugh that leaks out.

He lets his head drop. His fingers slide into his hair as he clutches his skull. He used to do this when he'd get headaches from reading for too many hours. The gesture really works with his long hair. I wonder if he knows how much tension it carries to the audience.

I touch his shoulder. "You okay?"

He looks at me without letting go of his head. "That was painful," he confesses.

I give his shoulder a little squeeze and move my hand down his arm just a bit. He's very tense under this shirt, all those coiled muscles, each of which I could name but probably shouldn't. I don't need any more reasons to think about human anatomy right now. Sympathy. That's what I'm going for.

"Was it really, though?" I ask. "You barely had to answer her. Just smile and nod and give her a thrill." I realize my hand is still on his arm and I take it off. If I clench and flex my hands under the table, nobody needs to know.

It's Hank who answers. "Not such a big deal here. We're all adults. Probably going to be an issue in class." He forks up a slice of golden beet and starts to chew, gesturing to Ty with his fork. When he swallows, he says, "You'll probably get a version of that from a few of the kids in each of your classes." A knowing nod and another bite of salad.

I didn't think of that. It's probably always weird for a teacher to be close in age (within a decade or so) to the students in class, and we're all careful to be way more than appropriate. Some of us are even cold, at least at first, to our students. No question. No misunderstandings.

But it's different for Ty. Some of these kids are—statistically speaking—already in love with him. It's not only that he's new and handsome and under thirty. He's Tyson Perry Miller. It's like if someone had thrown Harry Styles into my high school in 2012. Or into any current classroom, come to think of it. That guy has staying power. I wonder for a minute if Ty has met Harry Styles. I get a little fangirl shiver and feel nothing but empathy for the kids in our classes who are about to lose their minds.

Poor teenage superfans. Poor Tyson Perry Miller, who has to deal with it.

Lola manages to serve our amazing dinner to us while also making it look like she doesn't care much if any of the rest of us like it.

She fills Ty's water glass so often that it's a wonder he doesn't float away. She returns to the empty seat at the table, the one she moved Hank out of, every few minutes to ask Ty if everything tastes all right. She brings Ty tiramisu and cannoli and panna cotta. The rest of us fork things off his plate when she leaves.

Joey smiles at Ty between bites. "You have definitely made a good impression with Lola. But this might cause the rest of us some trouble."

"Why?" he asks.

"You'll have to be ready to come eat with us at the drop of a hat," Dexter says, licking caramel drizzle of the back of his spoon. "She probably won't serve us ever again without you."

Ty glances at me, but my mouth is full of panna cotta, so I don't say anything. I'm smiling at my dessert, but he's allowed to take it personally.

He grins at the table, and I wonder if he knows what a gift that grin is. "I'll do my best. I'll make it to dinner whenever I can."

"You're in, mate," Hank says.

And it's that easy. As long as it took us last semester to become four, we've now become five over the course of one excessive Italian meal. It's not bad. In fact, it's great. And not just the special attention from Lola. It's easy to be with him when we're all together. I'm actually glad.

Ty is in. With us. All of us.

I allow myself to wonder what might happen if I crack open my heart, just a little bit, and see how it behaves toward Ty. Can there be a way? My instinct says no, but my instinct has been wrong before.

12

TY

Walking back up the hill to campus, I laugh with everyone as they mock me gently for the way Lola treated me at dinner. To be honest, I was surprised she still brought us a bill. When a restaurant owner goes all gooey like that, I usually get my meals comped.

I was more than happy to chip in, though. Obvious appearance aside, I'd love to be normal here. I'd love to belong to this group. I'd love to belong to Ginger again. As soon as the thought hits me, I realize it's been true for a long time.

Maybe forever.

Not that I sat around thinking about Ginger when I was married to Janie. Gross. Of course not. I knew I had to put her out of my mind when I was with Janie. That's what you do. I gave Janie my best effort. But it was always effort. Always work. With Ginger, it's natural. Maybe even easy. And I want this feeling to carry on. To get even stronger.

She's quiet. I bump her arm, and she looks at me. I mouth "Okay?" and she nods. Five years. It's such a long time. She carries it well. She looks amazing. Beautiful, of course, but also calmer. Less anxious about what people are thinking or saying. Maybe that's just growing up. I guess if I had a normal private life, I could grow up that way, too. But I'm public, so I have to consider what people think and say.

I'm lucky they're not saying much right now. I'd love to be radio-silent for a few months until someone can discover where Brady and Ellison (and the money) went and get it all back where it belongs.

Hank is saying something that makes Dexter laugh, and Ginger looks at me out of the corner of her eyes. A smile twitches in the corner of her mouth.

"What?" I whisper.

She tilts her head toward Hank and Dexter. "Them."

"I wasn't listening."

Now she turns to face me. "Are *you* okay?" she asks, looking surprised. Surprised by my distraction? Surprised that I'm thinking? She must think I'm not a person who has genuine human feelings anymore. Only acted ones, rehearsed out of all shades of sincerity and perfected for cameras.

I nod and gesture around us. "Absorbing."

She smiles. "And digesting." She points to the south. "There's a great sledding hill right over there." I can see a hill through a thin stand of leafless trees, lit by a few of the classic iron column and glass-topped lamps that dot Chamberlain campus. I wonder for a minute if they were ever gas lights. The campus has been around long enough that electricity was a definite afterthought.

Is this an invitation? Is she hinting? Saying she wants to be alone with me? "Want to show me?"

She shakes her head. "Not in the dark," she says. With an "of course" tilt to it.

I shove my hands into my coat pockets. I'm getting the impression that it's going to be dark most of the time that we're not in class. Does that mean she doesn't want to be alone with me?

I can't figure her out. It used to be easy. She wore every emotion right on her face. Up to and including that awful last day. I want to fix it. I make sure my voice is quiet enough not to be heard beyond Ginger. "Can I say again that I didn't plan this, but I'm glad you're around?"

She slows down a little. The others move fast in the cold, and they outpace us before long.

"Do you want to tell me what you're really doing here?" she asks, keeping her eyes on the path.

"I'm teaching kids. That's what we're all doing here." Even to my own ears, that's lame.

She gives a single nod, as if that was nothing more or less than she expected. She knew I'd dodge the question.

I don't want to be that guy.

I sigh and try again. "It's complicated. And full of legalities. And it doesn't make me look very good."

She nods again, still staring at the sidewalk. She doesn't even look disappointed. Just unsurprised, like this was what she expected. She tugs at one of her braids. I forgot that she did that, but now the gesture looks so familiar.

"It's important that you look good," she says. I wonder if she means to be unkind or if it only sounds that way.

"Ginger? Can I please explain something to you? About . . . before?"

I watch her back straighten, her hands clench in her gloves. It's like she's bracing for a punch. "Okay," she says. Her voice is quiet.

"Can we go somewhere?"

She shakes her head. "Keep moving. Let's walk. I don't want to look at you if I can help it."

What does that mean?

Okay. "Janie." I breathe in and out after I say it. It feels like I've conjured her, and it's not a comfortable feeling. But I need to say this.

I let her name hang there for a minute, like a probe. Ginger doesn't run away, so I keep going. "Janie wanted to do Haven Lake."

She knows this, I guess. But she doesn't say anything, so I go on.

"She wanted it for her summer job. You know how much she loved the show. She arranged an audition, saying she knew me."

Ginger nods.

"The Flemings were auditioning a few people for new parts. She got a slot. She wanted to run her audition lines with me. Actually, she wanted me to go to her audition with her. She figured it gave her a better shot if I was there."

Ginger's breath is coming out in tiny puffs.

"But I didn't feel like that was super fair. You know, to the other people trying out. But I told her I would help how I could. So, we practiced. I read with her. She needed more practice. Hours more. I kept reading the lines with her. We tried out all the scenes. She asked how we could increase our on-camera chemistry."

I clear my throat. Remind myself that we're both adults. And that we were then, too. But more adult now. This shouldn't be hard.

"Increasing the chemistry was as easy as keeping the scene going. And then it was more. And then you came into the room."

I can feel every nerve in my body replaying that moment. Hearing the door. Realizing what I was doing. Pulling my hands off Janie's back like I was burned. Sitting up so fast I almost knocked Janie over. Calling for Ginger to wait. Hearing her voice, so quiet. Broken. Watching her walk away. Waiting for her to come back so I could explain.

Now I have the chance to explain. But I have no words. You'd think in the last five years, I would have figured out what to say. No such thing. I stumble my way through the next part.

"After, I looked for you."

She turns her face away.

"I called your mom. I showed up at your parents' house."

The humiliation of being asked to leave their property? It still burns.

I don't tell her I stalked all of our favorite places. I don't tell her I sat across the street from the entrance to her favorite coffee shop, watching to see if she'd go inside. Or that I watched the library doors. Or the testing center. I don't tell her I almost missed an exam, waiting for her to show up.

There's a lot I don't say. I don't say that it was only that day. I don't say that it was for Janie to get a part. I don't say that I regretted it instantly, and that the regret has simmered in my brain for years, even when I tried to ignore it. So much that I don't say.

But I have to say more.

"And when I couldn't find you, I kept going with my life. I did another summer of Haven Lake. Janie was a hit. I guess you know that."

She mumbles something.

"What?" I ask.

Now she turns to face me. "I never watched Haven Lake again. I don't know how the series ended. I never saw you on TV until Enforced started." Her voice is soft. Not cruel. Not angry. But I feel gut-punched. I can see the hurt in her eyes.

She didn't see it. She didn't watch Janie and me fall in love. She didn't see how great our screen chemistry was. She didn't see what Haven Lake's nine million viewers saw. She didn't take the love-story journey of the decade with us. (Thanks, Hey-You magazine. That one's in my head forever now.)

How do I summarize that? "We were together all the time. It was fun. The two of us were good for the ratings. I guess you don't need to know more than that." If she needs to know, all the interviews are still online. Unfortunately.

"And it was good until it wasn't. She didn't like it when I told the Flemings I wanted to bring Haven Lake to an end. She resented my role on Enforced." I sneak another look at her out of the corner of my eye. "If I tell you she didn't like that there wasn't a part for her, will that make me look better or worse?"

Ginger shakes her head. Not better, not worse? Or she doesn't want to hear it?

"We tried to make it work." That was mostly true. *I* tried to make it work. Janie tried to convince me to use my leverage to get her another part. She didn't care if it was on Enforced or on another of the Fleming brothers' shows. I was her ticket to roles, and she liked that part of me. When it got ugly, she made it clear that was all I was useful for.

"There's a lot of story in there," I tell her, "but you don't need it all. It didn't last. She needed something different. We tried," I say, knowing that at least I had tried. "Then we fell out of love, whatever measure of love we had."

I can't keep talking about this.

I want her to say something, but she doesn't owe me anything. I'm not going to press her. But I want her to know for sure that I wasn't cheating on her. "I hope you can believe me. It wasn't intentional. I was helping her out and I lost myself in the moment."

I lost myself. Never a truer statement.

I lost myself in mid-list celebrity couplehood. Not that I'd say that out loud. It sounds ugly. But if I look into my heart (as at least two therapists have told me), it's clear to me that I liked "us" more than I loved her.

And, while we're measuring, I loved her more than she ever loved me.

Ginger turns to me when I stop talking. "And the moment lasted five years?"

Ouch. "Something like that."

She nods. "Your warped sense of timing can only be a blessing here in Vermont, where nights are like eighteen hours long, and February lasts seven years."

Her smile tells me to move on. But I can't, quite. "Ginger, I'm so sorry for how I behaved. I'm sorry I hurt you."

Is that a laugh? "Sorry?" she says, a snort in her voice. "*Sorry* you hurt me? Dude. My little heart has never been so broken."

Oh, no. I asked for it, I know. I really hoped we could skip this part. I was hoping my apology would be enough, and we could move on. Now that I think about it, that's totally selfish and unreasonable. So, sometimes a guy is selfish. And unreasonable. I wait for her to unload five years of anger and hurt on me.

She doesn't. She bumps my arm and smiles. "No worries, though. I'm a real grownup now, with a decent job, a healthy self-image, and a brand-new, stone-cold, unbreakable heart."

"Unbreakable?" I ask, hating that word. It implies way too much rigidity and way too little passion for a woman like Ginger.

"Definitely unbreakable," she says, thumping her chest with her gloved fist.

From the top of the hill, Hank turns around and shouts down to us. "Do either of you two need rescuing?"

Ginger waves at Hank, and I shout that we're all right.

"Are we?" I ask Ginger.

"Are we all right?" she repeats, clarifiying.

I nod.

"Sure, we are," she says, bumping my arm again.

"We can start over?" I ask.

She turns her head to look at me. The wind whips a few loose strands of hair across her face. "I thought we could, but I'm really not sure how to do that," she says. "We've both changed, but there's a lot here." She gestures at the space between us. "Maybe it's impossible to start over."

"Okay. I get that. But can we start now? Make it new?"

When Ginger speaks again, her voice is quiet and careful. "Our friendship?"

"If that's what you want," I say. I stop walking. She does, too. Her arms cross over her stomach in a protective gesture. She's not looking at me, but she's not looking away. And she's not walking away.

"What do *you* want?" she asks, a whisper.

I start to shrug and pretend it doesn't matter what I want, but now she turns her eyes and meets mine. She's asking. So I should be honest when I answer. "I want another chance."

I hear her inhale, a stuttering sort of surprise. After a few seconds, she asks, "Another chance at what?"

I don't think she's testing me. Or teasing. Or playing dumb. I think she knows how easy it is for us to misunderstand each other.

So I'm clear as I can be. "Another chance to be with you."

I'm surprised how natural it feels, and the words almost take my breath away. I want to be with her. I've wanted it since the moment I saw her again in that first meeting.

She shakes her head and makes a frustrated noise. "You don't even know me anymore."

I take a step closer. "I know everything about you except this unbreakable heart I've heard about."

"That's a pretty important part of the new me." The cold breeze has grown into wind, and she's speaking so quietly that the sound almost blows away.

We are standing close together, but the space between us feels huge. I take another step to close the distance. "Then I want to know that part, too."

"You might not like it," she says, and I can see a tear forming in her eye. She blinks, and the tear falls. I wipe it off her cheek with my thumb.

"Will you give me a chance to decide that?" I slide my hand down her arm and to her hand. Unfolding her arms takes her a long time. Like she's making a difficult choice.

When she takes my hand, heat flows all through me.

"I guess that's fair," she says. "And you know, I might not like you anymore. You're different, too."

I laugh and squeeze her hand. "I'm a little smarter now," I say. "I know how much more I don't know."

"Oh, philosophy," she says, and her smile warms the words. "The kids will love that. You're going to do fine here."

I tug at her hand again. "It feels pretty fine now."

She doesn't pull away, but I feel her stiffen as we walk side by side.

"Ty." That's it. Just my name. I can hear a warning there.

"Yeah?" Do I sound as nervous as I feel?

"We're going to have to take this slow," she says. "Like, really slow."

All I can think about it getting somewhere warm and getting these gloves off and putting my hands on her face and feeling her skin. Kissing her mouth. Holding her close.

I wonder if she can see that want in me.

I nod. "Of course," I say. "As slow as you want. Whatever you say."

"Whatever I say?" That playful tone in her voice is so familiar, so perfect.

"Within reason," I tell her. I look into her face again. "But you're in charge of acceleration speed."

I remember how fast she drives and smile again.

I can't believe how good it feels that something that matters this much is going my way.

13

GINGER

I sit with Joey on the frozen concrete steps of her place and watch the kids arrive back on campus. Even though I might not sleep well tonight (I always get that pre-first-day insomnia), I love the chaos of arrival day, the family dynamics, the dozens of little dramas. Kids who show up on campus, for whatever reason, unaccompanied. Some of them look like they're trying to be brave, while others appear not to care at all. And then there are the moms and dads and various guardians in every version of readiness to end the winter break, from the clingy to the temperamental. Not to mention the roommate reunions, the secret (they think) reconnecting with boyfriends and girlfriends, and the shouts across campus.

Joey is wrapped in a fuzzy blanket, and I have my coat zipped up to my nose, but kids are calling to us and waving across the quad. Dexter and Hank took Ty to the gym, or that's what it sounded like to Ty. He told me Hank asked him if he wanted to play ball, so he dug up a pair of basketball shorts and some shoes. If I know Hank at all, they're playing Madden in his living room. But I didn't feel like I needed to tell Ty that. He would figure it out soon enough.

Joey, sitting a step lower than me, leans against my knee. "All right. I gave you days. Days, Ginger. You're going to tell me all of it now, right? All the gossip that's fit to repeat?"

I know what will make her crazy. "There's nothing to tell."

She makes a sound of frustration. "I knew you were going to say that. Come on. Spill it."

I laugh, and as soon as she realizes that I'm playing with her, she laughs too.

I shift, hoping to prevent my bum from falling asleep on the frozen steps. "Okay. So once I went to grad school in Chicago."

"I already know this part," she says.

"Hey," I say, flicking at her shoulder through all her layers of clothes and coat and blanket. "Do you want this story or not?"

She snaps her fingers, or would if there weren't gloves on her hands. "Give me the good-parts version."

I shake my head at her and sigh. "You have no appreciation for nuanced storytelling."

"You can use all the nuance you want when you get to the steamy stuff," she says, snuggling against my leg again and watching the cars and shuttles and Ubers unloading students. "Go."

I don't mind telling her. I might have told her before, not using his name, of course, but she never asked. I mean, not directly. We talked a little about a terrible ex she had, but I was not interested in opening up my heart and spilling it across a table. My standard answer was, "I dated a bit in college, but nothing that lasted."

The truth was, it had lasted. Three semesters. Almost a year and a half. He'd been to my parents' home for two Thanksgivings. And I thought he'd come home with me forever.

"I liked him so much," I tell Joey, hoping my voice didn't give too much away. The wound felt pretty fresh after our walk home last night. And all that honesty.

"No kidding. How could you not?"

"It wasn't because of Haven Lake," I said, feeling defensive.

Joey turns to me. "Of course not. I didn't mean—" she says. I shake my head. I know what she means.

She goes on. "I mean, sure, he's gorgeous. And even back then, I guess pretty famous. But he's more than that. He's great, right? He's funny and generous and he seriously doesn't seem all that impressed with himself." She laughs. "I'm impressed enough for both of us. For all of us. And I think Dexter's a little in love."

I know she's kidding, but it feels so good to know that, even through the jokes, my friends approve.

"I thought he was the one," I say.

Joey is very quiet for a few minutes.

"And then he wasn't?" she finally asks.

"He was the one for Janie instead."

Now she turns fully around, facing me. "You knew her? I mean, before they got married? You knew Janie Banks?"

I look past Joey's shoulder. "My roommate."

"Shut. Right. Up." Each word is accompanied by a slap on my shoulder. "That's awful. And awesome. What a great story. I'm so sorry you were in the middle of it. Oh my goodness. Janie Banks was your roommate. And she stole Ty from you? How has this never been a story, like, publicly?"

I wonder if Joey remembers that she's talking about real people. Me, specifically. "I think the falling-in-love-on-set angle was preferable to the truth," I say. But really? I think they both wanted to write me out of it as soon as they could. For which I was very grateful. Limiting their complications in the story protected me from being the spurned other. The left-behind. The woman scorned.

Even the words felt sticky and gross.

It may be great content, but we all look better if I'm left out of the story.

"I ran away." I'm talking to the air above Joey's shoulder again. "I never saw her again. And I never spoke to him until he showed up here."

I look at her to see if that's enough. Her hands are clutched to her chest, and she's practically a heart-eyes emoji.

"And he's been in love with you this whole time. I mean, obviously." She reaches out with one hand to give my face a little pat. "Who wouldn't be? But the way he looks at you, and when he wouldn't come to lunch without you that day, and how you two lagged behind last night for a romantic walk in the dark. . . It's like you've had his heart in your hands all these years. It took him until now to come back to reclaim it."

She's winding herself up into such a state of excitement, she might not stop.

"Joey. Joey. You are getting carried away. He was happily married." I don't say for how long, or that he was only happy until he wasn't. That part's not my story to tell. "And he's here for who knows what reason. I'm secondary. Not even secondary. Tertiary. Quaternary? Is that a word?"

She gasps. "He came looking for you." Her hands cover her mouth as if the story she's making up is overwhelming her and she wants to keep any more truth from escaping. "He hired someone to find you and he arrived just in time to win your love."

"You watch way too many Hallmark Christmas movies," I say. I don't know what Ty's really doing at Chamberlain, but I believe he didn't know I was here. I saw him see me from that stage the first day. He was surprised. Shocked. Even Tyson Perry Miller isn't a good enough actor to fake that look.

I don't need to tell Joey any more of the story. She's doing a great job of making one up. And enjoying herself. I lean back on my elbows as I watch a shuttle pull up to a curb. A guy jumps down from the shuttle steps and his feet go right out from under him on an icy patch of sidewalk. Winter hazards at Chamberlain. He gets back to his feet quickly and brushes himself off, grabs a couple of suitcases, and hollers for someone to wait up. As more kids get out and gather their bags, I think about where Ty and I stand now.

He wants to try again. Us. The thought of it makes my insides swoop around like they're in a wind tunnel. Some of that swooping is excitement. So much swooping excitement. Some is fear. I know perfectly well what might go wrong. And some of the possibilities for disaster, spinning around in my head, are silly—but some are very, painfully possible. I know what could happen because I know what did happen.

But I didn't say no to him. I can't imagine starting back from where we left off, but I'm willing to begin again from somewhere. I don't know what that means, exactly, but I can't pretend I don't feel the attraction I feel. Honestly, I can't imagine anyone not feeling attracted to Ty. He is all kinds of fabulous. He's glorious to look at, obviously, even when he's not posed and lighted and airbrushed. He's always been a little too good-looking to be real. He's more than that, though. He's brilliant, and I've always had a thing for smart men. And he's funny. And thoughtful and kind and sympathetic and generous and why am I even letting my mind go like this?

The point is, he wants to try again, and last time it ended, it shattered me. I became a completely different person. I lost all my confidence. I turned away from myself; stopped being the woman I was becoming. Shut down my open, welcoming, warm personality. Receded into solitude, like a character in a book just a little too dramatic to be believed. I decided it was better to go forward alone. I closed myself off. Moved on, just me. I knew I could be successful and useful wherever I landed. And I could do it on my own. I zipped my heart into a fireproof box, and now Ty's knocking on the door and asking me to open it up. And I don't want to say no, even when saying yes opens me up to getting my heart smashed again. How can I even consider letting this happen?

I lean closer to Joey, who still sits on the stair in front of me.

"Are you ever afraid that Dexter is going to hurt you?" I ask. I make sure to keep my voice very quiet, because even though the quad is noisy with unloading and reuniting, sounds carry across the snow. And this is not a conversation for public consumption.

Joey moves up to sit on the same step as mine. She wraps both her arms around my arm. With her head on my shoulder, she sighs. "Of course I worry about that sometimes, but I can't let it stop me from falling for him."

I shake my head. "See, I don't think that's an 'of course' situation. For some of us, the possibility, or, worse, the probability of getting hurt is exactly what stops us from falling. I mean, *falling*. It's so dangerous. So unstable. Why do we have to *fall* in love, anyway? Why can't we walk into love? Or slide into love? Or step in? Or even slip in? Why do we have to fall?"

Joey doesn't laugh at me. She doesn't make fun of my question, and I'm grateful. I'm not being funny. It may have never occurred to me in words before, but the falling is terrifying.

We sit quietly on the freezing step a little longer, and then I stand up, pulling Joey up with me. "It's too cold out here. Let's make tea at your place. Or cocoa. Or something."

Joey looks at me, guilty.

"You have no food or drink in your kitchen at all?" I ask.

She shakes her head. "I haven't been to the store."

"Come on," I say. We head over to my place. If nothing else in my world is fully functional (and I'm not saying *nothing* is), at very least I can feed us from my kitchen.

When we walk inside, Joey takes a dramatic inhale, like she always does. She's only sort of laughing at me and my belief that the air in my apartment is healthier than anyone else's because the living room is full of plants.

When I was a kid and learned about the carbon dioxide / oxygen exchange, I started carrying a potted fern around the house with me. I couldn't sleep if it wasn't on my bedside table. I think I really believed that I might stop breathing in the night. I fully recognize that this was a strange stance to take, but there it is. I have always loved plants, even when I was a weird little kid. Now that I'm grown, it's not about fear. I just really love the feeling of being surrounded by green and growing things; besides, it makes my apartment look like a forest glade, and I'm all over that.

I pour water into the kettle and pull down some mugs. "Tea or cocoa?" I ask, even though I know what she's going to choose. Joey loves sweet things.

"Cocoa please," she says. She fingers the edge of a snake plant on the kitchen table. "I like this plant. I should put one of these in my kitchen," she says. I pour water over the packet of hot chocolate mix in her mug and hand it to her.

"Don't bring a plant into your home if it's going to die of loneliness," I say.

"Do you mean, like, buy it a friend?" she asks, slurping a sip off the top of her drink. It's too hot, but she can't wait.

"Or go into your own kitchen once in a while," I say with a smile.

She nods. "Both good options." She blows across the top of her mug to cool it a bit. Then she blows on the plant. "Have some carbon dioxide, little guy," she says.

I shake my head. "You're so weird," I say. But she knows I don't mean it. I'm the one who couldn't sleep without a fern, after all.

Joey leans back in her chair, cupping her mug in both hands. "So how many plants would I need in my place to provide enough oxygen for me to live?" she asks. I know she's joking, but I have actually done the math, so I tell her.

"If you have a mature plant, say with twenty-five leaves, you'd need something like 675. Round up to seven hundred for good measure. Of course, you're small, so maybe you can round down. But if you add Dexter to the equation, you need to double the number of plants."

She pretends to consider this. "Hmm. Fifteen hundred plants will not fit in my apartment. Even if I never get around to decorating it or furnishing it. Besides, Dex has a very nice place. I'll just start giving him plants as gifts, and we can keep hanging out over there."

"I think that's a great plan. But you should still get some food into your kitchen."

Joey nods. "I will. Want to grocery shop with me tomorrow?"

I take a sip. "You just love me for my car," I say.

"Not true. I love you for your car and for your taste in self-help books and for your connections to hot TV stars." She wiggles her eyebrows as she takes another sip of her chocolate.

"He really is gorgeous, isn't he?" I say, unable to hide my smile.

"And he's so into you."

I don't deny it, but I take another sip of my cocoa to give myself a minute to process. I mean, yes. And I'm not all the way sure how to feel about that.

There is a lot of history. With *us*, sure—years of good history. But in the space between us? The apart time? It's full of Janie and his rising fame and Janie and my retreat to the mountains and Janie.

How do I navigate that?

How does he? Is it even a question for him? He moved fast from me to Janie. Is he moving almost as fast from Janie back to me?

I wonder if he's hiding his own version of heartbreak.

If that's possible, if he is, he's dealing with it differently. I hid. I locked up my heart. He seems to be time traveling to before, going back to when it was good with us. Him and me.

Maybe I can go back, too. Maybe I can unbolt the lockbox around my heart.

Maybe Portia Bancroft can help me.

I get up from the table and go to my room to grab my copy of *You Are Made of Stars*. Back at the table, I scoot my chair right next to Joey and show her the chapter I'm thinking about.

"Right here," I say. "Chapter eleven. 'Stars Arise.' This is where I'm going to find my courage."

Joey claps her hands. "Yes! I love this chapter. You know the part where she talks about aligning your spine with your mind and pointing toward your goal?"

I nod, so happy that Joey feels the same about Portia Bancroft as I feel. Portia must have experienced so much of life to be able to encapsulate all the meaning in each metaphor. And every chapter feels relevant to what I'm experiencing right now. I wonder if it will continue to mean so much to me as my realities change. In each new phase of our lives, as she tells us in the introduction, there is room to reflect the light of the stars within us.

Before long, Joey and I have our heads together, reading out sentences and paragraphs and talking over each other about how well Portia captures exactly what we're figuring out in our lives.

Joey sits back in her seat and sighs. "She's amazing. I want to be her. Okay, maybe I just want to meet her."

I haven't told her. I haven't told anyone. But who better to share my excitement about the upcoming interview with?

"Can I tell you a secret?" I ask. Just in case, I speak in a whisper. It's premeditated secret-mode.

"Always."

Joey's phone buzzes. She pushes it away and leans in. I love this about her. She's so good at being present. Like Portia says in Chapter 12, 'Seeing Stars,' "One of the most generous blessings of the universe is our ability to see the starlight in one another. Seek to connect the light in you with the light in others. Resist the distractions that would try to outshine the brightness of human association. Link your lights, and burn brighter and brighter."

Joey is great at this. She's showing me, right now, that our connection is more important to her than whatever's on her phone.

"I emailed Portia Bancroft."

She gasps. "You did? To tell her you love her?"

I laugh. "That might have come up. But then I deleted most of the fangirl stuff. And I asked her for an interview."

Joey bangs her fist on the table, a huge smile on her face. "You're going to have a call?"

"Even better," I say, lowering my voice for dramatic effect. "I'm meeting her in Burlington."

Joey leaps out of her seat and screams. She's jumping up and down in my kitchen and laughing. Everyone needs a friend like this, someone who gets way too excited for your happiness.

"When? Where? I'm coming. How did this happen? What are you going to ask her? What if she's totally awkward in person? What are you wearing? Are we taking anyone else with us? How much time will you spend with her? Tell me. Tell me. Tell me."

I pretend to be calm; I gesture to her chair. Joey sits back down, but her hands won't still, and she keeps clapping and squealing as I attempt to answer a few of the questions I can remember her asking. And a few she didn't get around to.

14

TY

This could be worse. When I saw that I'd be in charge of a hundred boys, I got flashbacks of summer camp when I was eleven, and I was a monster. Self-aware enough to know I should behave myself better, I still ran wild in a place without parents. And I wasn't even the worst of the kids. Not by a long shot.

This isn't that, but it's still a little terrifying. The three-story stone building, surrounded by Rowan trees (I read that on the website—there's no way I'd be able to tell from the skeletal, leafless trees outside), has fifty dorm rooms in it, twenty on the second and third floors, and ten on the main floor, along with the big living room and my tiny office next to my tiny cell—I mean bedroom. A hundred teenage boys. All of them in my care. It makes me sweaty just thinking about all the bad ideas that must float around the atmosphere in this building. At least Rowan Hall isn't a freshman dorm. Even if I barely know what's going on, the junior and senior guys in my building have been around the block a few times.

An email detailing my Resident Assistant duties is in my inbox, and I check in the students as they come through. It takes all after-noon. I point out the RA office hours and remind them that our dorm meeting will happen tonight at eight.

I don't think it matters too much what I say to these guys. They're not listening to me.

I get approximately sixty kids asking where Chad is. I can only imagine Chad is the name of the previous RA whose room I'm now living in. Probably, according to what Hank told me, a senior scholarship student. But really, I have no idea who Chad is, much less where. I consider, after about twenty kids ask, making up answers to their questions. Chad had an excellent winter break in Tahiti and has decided to stay. Chad's now in witness protection—it's best if you don't ask. Chad quit school to become a circus performer. Chad has been drafted into the Navy. Chad is undergoing intensive psychotherapy to combat the strain on his psyche of living in a cinderblock dorm room. Chad had a terrifying but nonfatal car accident and is currently having his face rebuilt in a Swedish hospital. Chad had just about enough of the way you people snicker at each other when you ask "Where's Chad?"

I keep all of these answers to myself.

Some of the kids recognize me. Some ask for selfies with me. They tell me who I am. (Thanks for that reminder.) Some shake my hand and introduce themselves as though I should know who they are. A few look unsurprised to find me checking them into their rooms and reminding them about linen laundry service options. Three different boys ask me if I'm here researching for a part. I don't tell them how unlikely it is that anyone would watch, let alone create, a show about an adult who gets demoted to babysitting high school students in their prep school dorm.

Most of the kids don't seem to know who I am, which feels strange. Unexpected, I guess. I can't decide which option I prefer. Sometimes I forget that Enforced, though pretty central to my life, is not even on the radar of a whole lot of people. I decide I like the fact that more than half the kids in the dorm don't see me as anything different than an older Chad.

Until the meeting that evening.

I shouldn't be surprised. Somehow I manage to be surprised,

anyway. By the time the Rowan residents gather for our eight o'clock meeting, every one of them is dressed in a suit jacket over a button-up shirt. I wonder if they expected a dress code for this meeting. I look down at my long-sleeved Henley and faded jeans and feel under-dressed. If there was a clothing expectation, I missed it.

Someone makes a throat-clearing noise, and every one of them— each of the hundred boys who lives in this building—stands, pulls on sunglasses, and says, "Time to pack it in. Shut this down, boys." As the line ends, they each pull out a phone and take a picture. Of me, looking shocked and standing there with my mouth hanging open, no doubt.

What is happening? How do they even know the line when so few of them even recognized me? Are they mocking me? Is this some kind of a roast? How am I supposed to react to this? When, exactly, did I lose control of this meeting? It's only 8:03.

Panic rises along the back of my neck, and I look out past the boys crammed onto the leather couches and chairs and floor of the Rowan Hall common room. Standing at the door, leaning against the frame with a smile of absolute victory on her face, is Ginger. Holding her phone and definitely filming this.

I point at her, all my questions in my face, I'm sure.

If this ends up on TikTok or YouTube, will I be busted? For what, I'm not sure, but this doesn't seem like a great beginning.

She points back. That's all, just a point.

Wait.

Did she just wink? Is that for me? A kid who sits near the door reaches over from his perch on the arm of a couch and gives her a knuckle-bump. She waves and turns around, her long auburn braids whipping over her shoulders, and walks out the door. I think my mouth is still open. I want her to come back. And not only because I don't want to be left alone with these people.

The boys are looking from me to the door and back, waiting to see what I'll do.

What will I do? What an excellent question. How do I move on from this? I can't pretend to be in control. There is no way for me to take back the room after that, so I just run with it. I start slow-clapping. Watching the guys, spread around the room, tucking sunglasses and phones back into pockets as they start laughing, I speed up the clapping. A few of them join me, and before too long, the whole room is applauding.

Do we even know what we're clapping for? Ginger's joke? Their own cleverness? Who cares? They're cheering and laughing now, and I can deal with this. I think.

I motion for them to settle, and they do. I try not to show my surprise that they obeyed.

I look around the room. "Well, that was fun. Thank you for your generous welcome." A few more guys clap and whistle and cheer.

"I'm Ty. I think you're probably supposed to call me something else if you're in any of my classes. But here, in Rowan, I'm Ty."

I wonder, even as the words are coming out of my mouth, if this is against the rules. Which are definitely posted somewhere and which I didn't read. I really need to do that so I don't get on the wrong side of the law, so to speak. Again.

Oh, well. For one semester, they can call one adult here by his first name.

"You know how things work here better than I do," I say, "so let's set some expectations. You know how rules work. Let's follow them. And inside those rules, let's have a little fun."

I don't know what I expected them to do, but they're all paying attention, and they're all nodding.

Okay. Receptive audience.

We walk through the bulleted list of rules from the email, the website, posted on the cork board beside the office, and probably stuck to the back of every dorm room door. They know. I can feel boredom creeping in. So I rush it, finish that part, and introduce myself.

I tell them that I went to public high school, and about my undergrad and graduate studies. My love for science, and for chemistry in particular. I don't say anything about acting, because I don't know where to stop that train before it derails into unmentionable legal territory. I don't mention my failed marriage. I don't say a word about Ginger. But I want to. I want to ask that kid sitting near the door if she contacted him and arranged this little Enforced prank. Because she had to, right? It's not like any of the kids would know to go to her.

I smile thinking about Ginger, finding one of her students who lives in Rowan and asking him if he's up to play a joke on the new RA. Of her organizing the prank. Telling the kids what to wear, what to say, and what to do. Sure, she's teasing. But she's teasing *me*. She's getting the kids to play a joke on *me*. It means she's been thinking about me.

After we finish my intro and revisit where they can find all the posted rules and my office hours, I tell them we should wrap this up so they can get on with having fun on their last night before second semester classes start. I thank them for coming to the meeting and remind them about curfew. A few guys get up, grab coats, and leave. More stay. Most stay. A few of them pull out their phones and within minutes, girls start trickling in and sitting close to them. Which is good, as long as they stay out of the dorm rooms. I read the rules. I know that they know. Common areas only.

Some of the Rowan guys come talk to me, and I sit on the fireplace hearth. Some come over and shake hands or fist bump or high five each other before wandering out of the common room. Before long, a few dozen boys are left on the couches and on the floor around me, and we're talking about video games.

"Don't you have something better to do tonight than this?" I ask, when I realize we've been sitting here for ninety minutes. "You only have two more hours before curfew."

A few of them mutter about this being their last chance to relax, and I realize that, as long ago and far away as high school is in my memory, this is their life. And it must feel like a lot of pressure to succeed in a place like Chamberlain. And for these thirty or forty kids, an evening of sitting around talking about nothing is a gift.

I'm happy to stay. Especially since I'm secondary to most of the conversation. And I seem invisible to the few couples that occupy corners of couches. I imagine a few of these girls got here after their own dorm meetings and will stay until that magic moment of just-before-curfew.

Sometimes kids sitting here in this vague circle ask me a direct question, but mostly, the talk is just happening, about not much. I have a good view of the door, and I try to be subtle about watching for Ginger to return. Nobody says anything about her, and I know I can't bring her up, but I hope that as the kids get more and more comfortable with me, they'll talk about her.

I want to hear conversations where she's mentioned.

I know I can't be where she is all the time, but she's on my mind all the time.

I smile thinking about her, standing in the doorway, filming her excellent prank and smiling behind her phone.

That smile.

I want it to be for me. All the time. Every day.

Checking my watch, I see that it's only forty-five minutes until the kids' curfew. I imagine that, since I live in the dorm, it's mine, too.

I stand up. "I'm going to walk around campus a little before it's too late," I say to the people who didn't ask. Before it gets weird, I go to my room and grab my coat.

As I head out the door, a few kids call out.

"You know where you're headed, Ty?" a kid asks.

Someone laughs. Someone else says, "He's only Ty until he walks out the door. Then he's Dr. Miller."

"The doctor is leaving the building," someone else says. I wave over my shoulder and head across the quad in the general direction of the faculty residences. I guess I could have asked one of the kids if they knew which was Ginger's place, but that feels like a creepy move on every possible level. Besides, she asked me to take it slow. So I will. Very slow. And if I happen to walk, very slowly, past her living room window, and she happens to look, very slowly, outside and see me here? That's not creepy at all.

Okay. Maybe there's a possibility for creepy still. But I'm just stretching my legs. Getting a bit of fresh air. Fresh, subzero air.

Man, Vermont is cold.

No more walking slowly. It's no good. I'll freeze to the sidewalk.

Moving faster, I take a loop around the paved sidewalk that runs around the south quad, the one bordering the faculty's housing. There are lots of lights on inside, and I'm determined not to look into anyone's windows, even though all the windows are appropriately covered up. Just like you'd expect them to be.

When I finish the second loop, I know I can't do one more without possible muscle damage from being so cold at such a high altitude. I can feel all my cells. That's not normal. It's like climbing Everest or something, but without the base-camp training. I was definitely not warned about this.

I turn back toward my dorm, and keep my eyes on the building, watching lights come on in all three floors as I get closer. My eyes are watering in this frozen wind, and the lights are like stars, haloed and spread in shining points.

A few other people are moving across the sidewalks between dorm buildings, probably beating the clock to curfew, someone stops in front of me. Not a kid. Ginger.

"Hey," she says. "Out for a walk?"

She sounds a little breathless. Nervous? Or just freezing?

I nod. "You too, I guess?"

Did I forget how to make conversation? Is the weather and the altitude affecting my neurons?

She smiles. It's warmer now.

I point to the door to Rowan Hall. "Want to come in?"

She shakes her head and laughs. "Definitely not."

I must look surprised, because I'm surprised. "That's a little harsh," I say.

She keeps laughing. "It's curfew for your people. No more visitors."

I hope that's the only reason for her rejection.

She rubs her arms. She probably wants to keep moving, but I don't want her to leave. We are standing in perfect view of the snowman. Our snowman.

"Your prank was pretty good," I say.

"I like how your snowman turned out," she says. Under the light, the snowman sparkles with new layers of frost over the coat and hat.

"I think those shoes are goners," I say.

"If anyone finds out they're yours, they'll be stolen and resold online."

I shake my head, but I know she's right. "Maybe nobody will find out."

"I won't tell if you won't," she says. I know we're not saying anything that matters, but it feels so good just to stand here talking. It would feel better if we were inside, but this is a start.

I see her glance over at the tower of the Hall where the clock inches toward the kids' curfew.

"Good night, Ty," she says. Is there a wish in her voice? "Good luck tomorrow."

She starts to turn away, and I reach for her arm. "Can I come find you if I need anything?" I ask.

She smiles at me over her shoulder. "You know where I am," she says. It's almost a yes. I'll take it. I move faster for the rest of my walk back into the dorm. Probably because it's cold.

As I unlock my door, I grab a note stuck partway inside. When I open the paper, it's a series of numbers.

0112358899

I have no idea what this is.

I turn the note over, and on the back, there's a heart and a G.

Love, Ginger?

I can feel myself grinning. She wasn't out for a random walk. She was putting this here.

This is good.

But what is it?

She wrote me a Fibonacci sequence? And put it in my door?

I look at it again. It's not Fibonacci. I mean, it starts that way. But two eights. And the nines. No. Something else. I hear someone walking behind me.

"Dude. It starts." A kid stands at my shoulder.

"What?" Do I sound guilty? Because I think I sound guilty.

He points to the note in my hand. "Digits." His knowing nod and slow grin don't help me understand him.

"Okay?" I hope he'll tell me what he's talking about.

Still nodding and grinning, he clarifies, sort of. "Someone gave you their digits."

I must still look confused, because he speaks slowly and quietly. "It's a phone number."

I shake my head. "It starts with a zero."

Is he rolling his eyes at me? "They're not in order, man."

Obviously.

Ginger gave me her phone number out of order? This is weird.

Ginger gave me her phone number. This is good.

The order isn't that big a deal. I turn to the kid. "Is this a thing?"

"D'you mean is this a Chamberlain thing? Like do people give each other nearly impossible math problems to solve before you can text them?"

I can tell that's a no. "It's not impossible."

He folds his arms and leans against the wall across the hall from me. "There are like a thousand possible combinations."

"Right. Like a thousand. Not impossible."

A bell chimes. "What is that for?" I ask him.

He points to the speaker in the ceiling. "Five-minute warning."

Doors open and a few people jog past me. A guy waves to the kid I'm talking to and says, "Night, Quincy," then does a double-take when he sees me. "Good night, Tyson Perry Miller," he calls as he heads for the door. I can hear him laughing.

"Quincy? That's you?" I ask the kid. He nods and points down the hall, toward what I assume is his room.

"Thanks for your help."

He shrugs. "Happy to be of service, but I'm not trying out a thousand numbers for you just to find out if any of them go to school here."

"Thanks anyway. I've got this." I tuck the folded paper into my pocket.

I head up to the third floor and do a quick check down each hall, saying good night to the guys. But I'm not thinking about bed checks and curfews. I'm thinking that I can knock off tons of those thousand numbers because none of them start with 0 or 911. I've practically got it figured out already.

15

GINGER

Every semester, teaching at Chamberlain Academy gets better. I know my content. I know the kids. I know the Chamberlain practices and procedures. I know what I'm doing. But I remember the dread and the exhaustion that came with those first few years of teaching. Any minute, I was sure, they'd figure out I was making this all up as I went along.

Not the science. At least that was consistent. Just . . . the rest of it. Being the teacher. Being the adult. In charge. In control.

I almost laugh at the thought. Control is such an illusion.

I wonder how Ty's doing.

It's almost four o'clock, and I haven't heard from him all day. I've heard about him, though. Over and over. Everyone seems to know he's here, upstairs in the Copernicus room, which, somehow, they know all about, even though I spend all day every day in this building and didn't even know the room existed until last week. How many more secret rooms are there on Chamberlain campus?

I set the last few items for tomorrow's lab and lock up my room. It's only polite to go up and check on him. It's what any friendly coworker would do.

Yeah. Right.

If I walk into his classroom and there are fifteen teachers standing around ogling him, I'm going to turn around and walk right back out.

There aren't fifteen teachers. There are two kids, and they're both lying on the floor on their stomachs with piles of index cards in front of them.

I watch Ty, sitting at a kid desk, bent over his own pile of index cards, before I knuckle the door frame. "Hey," I say. "School's over."

He looks up, that amazing star-quality smile on his face. "Hello, Ms. Rogers."

Zing, zing. My entire body is tingling.

He glances at the desk in front of him and then at the kids on the floor. "We have a little homework," he explains. "Grab a seat."

I set my coat and bag on a desk near him. "Need help?"

"In fact, I do." He leans close and whispers, "But I didn't think you'd be eager to get in on this. It's a puzzle you've already solved." He indicates the cards in front of him. "312 area code?"

I laugh. He's got kids staying after school to decode my cell number. Lying on the floor. Surrounded by notecards.

I point at them. "Are they being punished?"

He shakes his head. "They're hackers. I'm reverse engineering coding and decoding. On paper. It will make their online game stronger."

"I hope you at least offered them a sandwich."

At that, both their heads swing around. "Do you have sandwiches?" one of them asks.

"Sorry. No. I could probably find a stick of gum in this bag if you're desperate."

They both go back to their task.

"Are you actually going to call every number in the 312 area code?" I ask.

"Of course not. That would be silly. I can eliminate everyone with a 4, 6, or 7."

I laugh. "Or I could just give you a few hints."

Without even a second's pause, Ty claps his hands together and says, "All right, you two. You're done. Give me your lists and go get a sandwich."

The kids clamber off the floor, and they say goodbye, grab their bags, and walk together out of the room.

As soon as they're gone, Ty hands me his phone. "Put me and my fumbling brain out of our misery, please." He rubs his forehead. "All I can see are numerals."

I type in my name. I'm curious. There's my old phone number, which must belong to someone else now. He's kept it in his phone all these years.

"You're getting close," I tell him. "Here's a hint: you can spell a word with the last four digits." I edit the number to give him the area code and the first digit.

I hand the phone back, but not before I see that he's got a picture of me in the contact. I'm laughing with my mouth open. My hair's in two braids and I'm wearing glasses.

My first thought is that it's kind of a messy picture for him to hold on to for so long.

My second thought is that he's the one who made me laugh like that.

I look happy.

I was happy.

"How did it go today?" I ask him.

He lights up. "It was amazing. They're incredible. And these two?" He points toward the door where the hackers left. "They're brilliant. I can't believe some of the things they've found ways around."

"Excellent. Aiding and abetting cybercriminals. You can put it on your resume."

He shakes his head. "Cybersecurity law. Both their families want them to be doctors or lawyers, and this way, they get the best of an already-honed talent."

"And they'll owe it all to you," I say. "They can thank you for your mentorship when they're both nominated to the supreme court."

"You laugh now," he says, laughing too. "But you never know."

He's right. "That is the truest sentence in the world. I really never, ever know."

Ty leans back in his chair and looks up at me. It's a very good thing that none of my students looks like this when they do this move. "I heard a rumor," he does a quick look around the room, "that we do Lola's after the first day of school." He says the last part in a whisper, keeping his agreement that he'll never tell the students about Lola's.

I nod. "That's the tradition," I say. "Or we could eat at my place."

He leans closer, a wicked twinkle in his eyes. "Lola does takeout?"

I laugh. "Not on your life. She wants to see that you clear your plate." Now I'm nervous. Maybe I shouldn't have asked him. But I can't just leave the invitation hanging. "No, I meant, I could cook for us."

Ty unfolds himself from the desk. I watch him do what, for anyone else, would be an awkward move. He looks like he's dancing. Once he's standing, he steps closer. "Is that what taking it slow looks like?" he asks.

It's not the words. It's the voice. Okay, and the words. I suddenly forget why I thought it was important to move carefully. I want him to take another step. And maybe one more. So there's no space between us at all.

But he doesn't. He respects what I said. That stupid, thoughtless comment about not moving too fast. Sigh.

I realize I'm in a definite lean and I straighten up. "You're right," I say, attempting to keep my breath even. "We should go with everyone to Lola's. Let me see if Joey and Dex have made a plan." I turn aside a little so he can't see my skin turning red. It's not just a blush. My entire body has warmed up, and for what? Because he looks at me through his lashes like he's been trained to? Because he knows how to stand up from a chair? Because he listens to me and respects my wishes? It's very hot in here.

'What's the dinner plan?' I send the message to Joey. While I'm waiting for her reply, I watch Ty clean up the room, stack the index cards, and straighten the couches and beanbags.

After a minute, she responds back with *'We have decided never to go to Lola's again without Ty, so as long as he's willing, we eat at 5.'*

'See you there,' I send back.

I put a hand to my cheek and hope my face doesn't look as flushed as I feel. Something about seeing that he kept my contact in his phone has ratcheted up all my feelings. Turning back to face Ty, I say, "Looks like your presence is requested. Possibly required." I should not keep touching my face. Especially not my mouth. But my hands didn't get the memo, and they simply must touch my mouth. Stupid hands.

It's hard to be in this close proximity to him without my coat and gloves. I need more layers between us if I'm ever going to pull off this moving-slowly thing.

He grins. "I like your friends."

"They seem to like you, too. Or at least they like that Lola likes you." Needing something to do with my hands, I tug on the handle of my canvas messenger bag. "I think Hank's hoping for another offer of off-menu specials." My heart is beating much too fast. Just being in the room with Ty makes all my systems go bonkers.

"Aren't all Lola's dishes off menu?" he asks.

"Good point." Is my brain melting? Can that happen at room temperature?

"What time?" he asks.

"What time what?"

"Dinner?"

I am definitely losing it. "Five," I say, and I can hear my breath. Five is not a sexy word. But it just keeps getting warmer in here.

"What should we do until then?" It's a completely innocent question. Exactly none of the answers in my head are innocent.

"I want to send a few emails out to parents," I say, ready to run out the door. I can't resist this pull forever. And I'm the one who said to take it slow, even though I'm behaving in the opposite way. I wanted slow. I still want slow, right? Something I am going to need to remind myself about. Often, apparently. Constantly.

"Already?" he asks. "Am I supposed to be emailing parents on day one?"

I shrug and try to shake off all the borderline indecent thoughts I'm having in that little movement. "It's never a bad idea to send reminders. Or to tell parents about good things you saw in class. It helps to have a few positive conversations under your belt before you have to bring up plagiarism or serial ditching."

He beams at me. "That's so smart," he says, as if I invented parent-teacher relationship protocols. He points to his beanbag chairs. "Try it out. Send your emails from here."

I am not getting into a beanbag chair. They are made for snuggling. Just no. I head for a couch instead. He pulls his laptop off the corner of his desk and flops down on the floor at my feet.

A rush of memory from the before. Sitting on a couch with him sprawled in front of me. I can't stop it, and it shocks me with its power. My arm wants to reach over and rest on his shoulder. My feet want to tuck in beside him. Even though it's been years, I can physically feel the way he would wrap the crook of one elbow around my ankle, keeping me close to him while he sat on the floor in front of that green couch.

I've spent so many years pushing those memories aside that it's leaving me breathless to allow the feelings in right now.

I pull my legs up onto the couch and sit on them. Totally worth my feet falling asleep to get a bit of control back.

I pull my laptop out of my bag and send a welcome-back message to my classes, giving encouragement for the work ahead, reminding them of rules and expectations, restating my policies on late work and missed class time. I copy their parents, covering all the bases. I read over the email twice, making sure I catch any typos and that I've been clear enough to stand up for myself in any inevitable coming battle. There's always one kid who assumes the rules are there for someone else. Everyone else.

After I fix up the message, I stare past the screen at the back of Ty's head. I really like his hair long like this. I want to touch it. I don't, obviously, but I want to.

Once I send the email, I won't have a great excuse to stay here, sitting this close to Ty. So I don't press send. I pull up my blog and write a review of a funny memoir I read last month. I wrote a few of my favorite quotes in my notes app, and I transfer them over to the post, linking to some online options to buy the book. When that's written, I save it, and then I finally press send on the email. Ty hears the whooshing of the sent message and turns around to look at me.

"That was the longest email in the history of the world. What did you have to say that took you," he checks his watch, "thirty-six minutes to write?"

"Chamberlain parents are very invested in their kids' education," I tell him. "They want to know everything that goes on here. I give them what they want."

"But it's only been one day," he says, like he can't believe it. I mean, of course he can't believe it. Who would describe everything that happened in a classroom? It's unbelievable. But I don't put a stop to it yet. Call it an experiment.

"Right. One day. And if the parents think a single hour of a single day is wasted, they'll start to question the validity of the Chamberlain experience for their kids." I make my voice super serious. "Do you know how much they pay for tuition? If you divide that number between each course and each class period, we have to prove that our subjects are worth their money."

I manage to keep my expression earnest and serious.

He turns around so he's facing me. "Are you kidding me? I need to report what we did, in detail, every day? So parents can feel like their dollars are well spent? Are they all crazy people?"

He looks panicked. Okay, I don't want him to hate me. Or Chamberlain. Or the families. I love joking, but I don't want this to hurt his chances of being successful here. I know when to end it. I nod my head. "Yes. No. No. Maybe."

"What?" His eyes are a little wild.

I nod my head and speak in a soothing voice. "Yes I'm kidding. No, you don't need to do it. Maybe parents are crazy. My email was like five sentences long. I am messing with you."

He leans back on his arms, shaking his head. "What happened to the nice girl I used to know?" The smile on his face proves that he's not really upset that I've been pranking him. And I'm not going to answer that question. Because he doesn't need to hear me blame him for the ways I've changed. He knows. And I know that it's not all about him.

Sometimes people just change.

And sometimes they change again.

"Let's go get dinner," I say. "If you don't show up, Lola might refuse to serve everyone else."

I stand up and slide my computer into my bag. Ty holds his hands up so I'll help him off the floor. As I reach out to him, I'm very conscious that most of our touch lately has happened through layers of gloves and coats. When his warm hands grasp mine, I actually feel my skin spark. I mean, there's a literal static-electricity shock. Probably because it's winter and there's less water in the air. But also, a shock. A shiver. A shudder. Our hands are touching. His long fingers reach up my wrists.

I am losing my grip. On reality and the important things. Not on him. I'm definitely still gripping. I don't want to let go.

Once Ty is standing, I release his arms and shove my hands into my pockets, which lasts as long as it takes me to reach the desk where I left my coat. I need my hands for the next part, but why are my limbs turning on me like this? Why can't my body remember that I asked Ty to take this slow? I'm the one who said to keep the brakes on this.

And I need to take it slow. I need him to keep a little distance. Because I need to figure out if I'm okay on my own before I allow myself to be swept into a Ty and Ginger Volume Two situation.

I thought I was okay on my own. I thought I was doing fine. I thought I knew how I felt about life and work and dating (or not-dating) and history and heartbreak and healing. Until Ty was actually here, I was fine. Then he walked back into my world and everything shook. Now, he's standing behind me helping me into my coat and I can't actually breathe.

My emotional scars aren't scars at all. They're open wounds. Every one of my atoms seems to remember what hurt feels like.

He wants to try again. To be *us* again. And everything about that makes my nerves sing happy songs. Except the one part. The big part. The part about when we were together before, and we were so good, and life was happy until it suddenly, surprisingly, shockingly wasn't.

I don't think I can risk that kind of hurt again. I don't think I can survive it. So. I need to figure out a solution. My options seem to be these:

Take it all back. Tell Ty to forget it. Stay away from him. Let the hurt heal over. Again.

Give it a try. See what happens. Be okay with utter devastation if that's what comes.

Dive in. Full speed. Expect the best. Allow the seedlings of whatever-this-will-be to unfold and grow and be beautiful.

Only one of those options sounds like it will keep me safe. But maybe safety is overrated. I wish I knew how to feel.

16

TY

Laughing over dinner with a group of friends is great. Laughing over dinner with Ginger sitting beside me is close to perfect.

Lola was only a little less bewildered by me than last time, but Dexter let me know she's moving toward normal behavior. Apparently her tendency to check every few minutes to see if we're all doing fine, enjoying our meal, needing anything else? That's still weird. And Hank pointed out, several times, that Lola was only asking *me*. I trust that soon I'll just be one of the regulars, and Lola can heap deliciousness on my plates and ignore me. Sounds perfect.

Even though it's early, when we finish dinner it's completely dark. Hank hurries back up to campus for an English department meeting. Walking back up the hill with Ginger and Dexter and Joey, we talk about nothing, revisiting some of the good parts of the day and of the dinner. Watching Joey and Dex walk so close together that their feet are in step makes me a little jealous. I want to walk that close to Ginger, but she asked me—made me promise—to take it slow.

I don't have a lot of practice taking it slow. My relationships have always kind of taken off at a sprint from the starting blocks. So maybe this will be good for me. I can savor the moments before the moments. Like right now. I want to walk like Joey and Dexter. I want to wrap Ginger in my arms and move together up the hill like one body with four legs. But maybe there's something good in the wanting.

Maybe I'm supposed to be learning something here. Patience. Persistence. Something.

We walk past some darkened classroom buildings, and I can see the light of the clock tower on the Hall glowing like a beacon directing us to the center of campus.

Joey is telling Dexter about the prank Ginger organized in my dorm last night, and I'm only half listening. I mean, I already know the story. I was there. But she has a dramatic style, and Dexter and Ginger are laughing. I love to hear her laugh. Happy Ginger is the real Ginger. The one I know best. The one I loved most. And from what she's told me, I think Happy Ginger has been long gone. I hate to think that she's only now returning. It's been years. Even more, I hate that I'm the one who drove Happy Ginger away.

Not that she's been sad for years. But I can see how she's become tougher. More protected. Less receptive. Slower to take risks.

But things are changing. I can tell, even in these few days. And her friends have noticed and mentioned that she's acting different. Joey said so. Hank said so. Is she happy again because I'm here?

I know I broke her heart, but is it possible I could be helping her heal it, too?

Joey and Dexter say goodbye and head into his apartment to get lessons ready for tomorrow.

I lean over and ask Ginger, "Getting lessons ready, huh? Is that what the kids are calling it these days?"

She smirks. She can try to hide it all she wants, I know she's amused.

"Do you have a lot of work to do?" she asks.

Do I? I spent most of today getting kids to help me figure out Ginger's phone number, so I should definitely plan a more academic lesson for tomorrow. But I have a list of topics, so I'm as ready as I need to be.

"I'm on top of it," I say. "How about you?"

"My lesson plans are a well-oiled machine," she says. She makes a casual nod toward another building. Hers? "Want to come over for a while?"

This is the second time she's invited me to her apartment today. I thought it was a test earlier, but maybe not. Now it just seems like she wants me to come in.

I don't want to play games. I don't want to pretend. "I'd love to," I say.

She exhales loudly enough that I think it's relief. Is she relieved that I said yes?

She can keep asking me things. I'll say yes all day.

She leads me to her front door, one of four residences in a stone building that looks like the other stone buildings the rest of the faculty lives in. There's a wreath of something green on her door and a potted evergreen topiary on the tiny concrete patio, and I remember how she always had tons of plants in her apartments.

"I probably could have guessed that this one is yours," I say, pointing to the greenery as she unlocks the door. "Looks like home."

I'm not sure how to read the look she sends me.

"Have you been trying to figure out which is mine?" she asks, letting herself in and holding the door open for me.

"If there's a non-creepy way to say yes, imagine that I said it that way." I gesture to the blinds covering the windows. "I didn't try any harder than taking a glance and finding that you can't see in any of the windows from outside. But see, even that sounds creepy."

She nods, unwrapping her scarf and taking off her coat. "Yeah. Little bit." She tosses her coat on the couch, so I do the same. "Now that I'm here, inside your apartment, you think you can check my work on the phone number puzzle?"

She laughs. "Talk about creepy."

I shake my head. "No way. You gave me all the digits. And there are so many words we could spell from the last four. Just look and see how close I am. Give me a break. Put me out of my misery."

"Misery?" she asks. "That's a little much."

"Okay," I tell her, nodding. "You're right. I'm not miserable. But I'd like to be able to reach you. To ask you questions and tell you things."

"Like what?" she asks.

"Like when something around here makes me smile, I want you to know about it."

She gives me a long look. "There's a faculty phone list in the handbook."

I grin and pull up the document on my phone. "I'm looking it up right now."

She reaches over and holds out her hand, waiting for me to give her my phone. "Let me see how close you got."

She pulls up her contact and I wonder what she thinks about the picture I still have in there. Can she remember how happy we were when I took that picture? Can we be that happy together again? I watch her key in her number.

"You were not very close," she says, "but it's in there now." As she hands me back the phone, she slides her finger down the back of my hand. If that was an accident, I want to make it happen again. And I have a feeling that pretending I didn't notice will help. Moving slow.

I take a good look around the room and smile. "I love it here," I say.

"Here in Vermont?"

I shake my head. "Here in the garden of your living room."

"Ty," she says with some reproach in her voice, but I don't let her finish.

"You're absolutely right. I know. Sorry. I didn't mean to say that. We need to move slow. I can do it. I'll be so slow you won't believe it." I barely breathe. I keep talking without letting any air into my words, just so she doesn't misunderstand me. Or so she understands what I want her to believe. "Don't think I meant anything but that I'm happy to be back where you are. Because you are a really great person to be around."

She turns away.

Going slow is exhausting.

"Movie?" she says.

"When's the last time you watched *Casablanca*?" I asked.

She looks at me, hands on her hips, and I can't tell if I've just ruined things again. I wait.

"Years," she says.

I wonder if she hasn't watched it since we watched it together. We used to put it on all the time, at least once a month. At first, I did it to convince her that it was good. She hated it the first time she watched. Too sad. He doesn't even get the girl in the end. But after a few times watching through it, she came around to my viewpoint. Well, mine and pretty much every reputable reviewer's. Rick isn't supposed to get the girl. Rick is supposed to come to himself—to recognize that he doesn't have to pretend to be a cynic. That it's best to sacrifice some part of his own happiness, some piece of himself in order for the world to keep turning.

So noble.

And nobody is more beautiful onscreen than Ingrid Bergman.

We spent hours discussing bars of light and shadow over their faces and how it must be a symbol of their entrapment in a world at war. How fast the editing moves, so every time we watched it, we saw something new. The melodrama. The soft focus. All of it.

She grabs a fuzzy blanket from the basket beside the couch and we sit down in front of the TV. I will let her guide every move. If she leans in, I'll put my arm around her. If she keeps space between us, I'll respect that decision.

I'll hate it, but I'll respect it.

From "Round up the usual suspects," I'm completely invested. I haven't watched it in years, either. And this time, I kind of hate Victor Laszlo. Who is he to get between Ilsa and Rick? Who is he to ruin this doomed great love? But then I remember that his face is fully lit in just about every shot, and the filmmakers are literally telling me I have to root for him. He's the best of the good guys.

I lean over to whisper along with one of Renault's lines and see that Ginger's fallen asleep. For about one second, I'm shocked. What kind of person sleeps through *Casablanca*? Then I remember. People who teach school. We are a tired bunch.

I put my arm around her and guide her to rest her head on my shoulder. Her braid slips down over my chest, and before long I realize I'm stroking the little tail part at the end of her braid.

She's breathing deeply enough that I bet she won't wake up, even when I get up off the couch. Among the things Ginger is good at, sleeping is up there on the list. She used to say she was gifted at sleeping.

I don't want to move. I don't want to go. I finish watching the film, and for the first time, I wish it were longer. An hour and forty-three minutes isn't long enough.

I reach for the remote. Ginger shifts and resettles herself against me. This is better. I can see her face, peaceful and beautiful. I hit the button to turn the sound off, leaving the menu glowing. Just enough light that I can watch her. Not that I haven't been watching her every minute we've been together since I arrived on campus. I can't keep my eyes off her. But now I can watch her without worrying that I'm crossing a line, making her self-conscious, giving her stress. It does occur to me that this—watching her as she sleeps—might be a huge line-crossing, but she invited me here. She welcomed me in. She felt relaxed enough to fall asleep.

I'm only looking.

And running my fingers along her arm. Just a little.

Yeah, okay. This is definitely creep behavior. I wiggle my way off the couch, and she settles herself in her sleep. I pull the blanket up around her. Straightening up the coffee table and a few pillows, I kneel on the floor in front of the couch.

It would be rude not to say goodnight.

I put my hand on her arm. She doesn't move. I give a little tap. "Ginger?" I whisper.

Nothing.

I move my hand from her arm to her cheek, letting my fingers just graze her skin. "Ginger," I whisper again.

She doesn't open her eyes, but makes a "mmm" sound that either means something feels good or she's too tired to make words.

"Thank you for inviting me over," I say, taking the excuse to lean close and speak softly. So I can thank her without waking her up? There's logic in there somewhere.

"I'm so happy to be here with you," I say, and without waking, she reaches her hand to her face to cover my fingers. Like she can feel my touch in a dream.

I wrap my fingers in hers and resist the urge to kiss her knuckles. Her cheek. Her forehead. Her mouth. If there was a prize for resisting urges, I'd win it. All of it.

I stand up from beside her. "Good night," I say. Putting on my coat in stealth mode, I keep watching her. Am I hoping she'll wake? Am I staying long enough that she'll wake and say goodbye?

I shake my head and tell myself I'll see her tomorrow. I'll see Ginger again tomorrow. That really makes all of the weirdness of this situation manageable.

I close her door softly and jog across campus to the Rowan dorm. A few couples are on the couches, some studying and some not, and I can hear an old-school Zelda game from down the hall.

This is where I live for the next few months, and I'm smiling about it. Because Ginger Rogers is here.

I feel my phone buzz. Did she wake up? Is she missing me?

But the text is not from Ginger.

It's Brady. I feel a shock, and I'm annoyed. I've allowed myself to forget about him for a while in the sweetness of reunion with Ginger. Of reconnecting, or whatever it is we're doing.

'Have a minute?'

I am not interested in trading my feelings about Ginger and *Casablanca* and the couch for a conversation with my brother. So I lie to him.

'Not alone. What do you need?'

Do my words contain any of my tone? Can he tell from my short responses that I don't want to talk to him?

'Wondering if your new situation has put you in touch with any fundraising opportunities. We have to make up for what we lost.'

We? What *we* lost?

Is he kidding? Is he really putting any of the blame for the loss of the money on me? I am fully ready to accept the blame for using company dollars without permission. That was a terrible decision. One I regretted even before the money disappeared. But to loop me in on the blame for that money's loss?

Only Brady is capable of such bending of the facts.

He's had so much practice.

I don't even answer. There's no way I could say anything approaching honest without losing my chill. And my lawyers are very specific about how important it is that I retain my chill in conversation with Brady. Any or all of it, text or phone, could be used as evidence against his partner Ellison, and nobody wants me looking like a hothead. If they ever prosecute Ellison. If they even find him.

'My new situation is not bringing in any money.' It's all I feel comfortable saying.

'Keep me posted if that changes,' he says.

I don't respond. I hope that's all he has to say. And I also hope, knowing it's not going to happen, that he'll apologize. Take some responsibility for what Ellison did. For how our agreement ruined some pretty important things for me. Maybe all the things.

'You still there?'

I could ignore him. But I don't. *'Yeah.'*

'I'm glad to know you'll stick with me in all this. After all we've gone through together.'

Manipulation. Exertion of control. Undue influence. All of it somehow surprising, even though it's been this way all my life.

And it makes me remember all the times in my life, over and over, that he said things like this.

So many times he said, "I know you'll tell Mom and Dad it wasn't our fault." *Our* fault. Right. And I did tell them, even when I knew it was Brady's fault and his alone.

And then there was this one: "I'm glad I can count on you, man." Whether or not I wanted him to. He always could count on me. I stood with him at his stupidest, wanting so much for him to keep me nearby. I covered for him. I made up excuses for him. I was a dumb kid, but I idolized him and we both knew I'd do anything to protect him.

Anything.

And this, I tell myself as I look at the last text again, looks an awful lot like that.

Maybe Brady is more centrally involved in this whole financial scandal than he says. Maybe he's not as innocent a bystander as he claims to be.

How much more trouble can I get in for this mess? I'm not sure I want to know.

Because I'm afraid the answer might be a lot. A great big whole lot more trouble.

I don't need any part of it.

Before I put away my phone for the night, I type Ginger a quick message. *'Thanks for the movie night. We'll always have Paris.'*

No. Sounds too regretful. I delete the last sentence, change it to *'Sleep well, kid'* and press Send before plugging in the phone and going to bed in my cinderblock room.

17

GINGER

I hate that I fell asleep. I hate that I missed any of the time we had together. But mostly, I hate that, when I woke, he was gone.

Of course he had to go. He has RA responsibilities. He has to check on the kids in his dorm. He has to be in by curfew. Even the thought of that makes me laugh a little. Curfew. Like a kid. He's definitely in some kind of trouble, and I want to know what it is.

Doctor Moreau is certainly not going to tell me, not that I'd ever ask. So I go to the next best source.

Wanda Chamberlain.

Head of the Chamberlain Trust, Wanda sits on the board and attends every important meeting and activity at the school. She has to be pushing eighty-five, if not older. And she will, by all accounts, live forever. She has no intention of slowing down. Or of missing out on anything interesting.

Wednesday afternoon there's a faculty council meeting, and Jackson sticks his head into my classroom on his way out to the Hall. "Need me to bring anything up at the meeting today?" he asks. He always asks. I never have much I want to say. I avoid the faculty council with as much vigor as Joey courted it last semester. She wanted some extra validation and a little sticking power. I just want to keep my head down.

"I'm good, thanks," I tell Jackson. "Keep me posted if there's anything new I should know."

"You know I will," he says. Jackson's a good department chair, bringing all the necessary information to our science department meetings and leaving all the other business, the stuff we don't need to know or care about, for other people to handle.

I figure I have about ninety minutes before I can casually, accidentally run into Wanda, and if I catch her alone, I can walk her to her car. I'd go to the meeting if I could, but I wasn't included, and that'd be weird for me to just show up.

This way, we can have a happy-accident meet up, and I can hope for some casual small talk. She's not a gossip, not at all. But she loves what she calls "making connections," and I know she takes partial credit for Dex and Joey getting together. She's invested (literally) in the faculty here. I bet I can get a few answers out of her.

I work on tomorrow's prep and grade a few lab reports, watching the clock and trying not to look too often at the door. If Ty happens to stop in, that's great. If he doesn't, no big deal.

It was nice of him to send a good night text after the movie. And he's definitely taking things slowly. Just like I asked him to. I'm regretting that now and then. Mostly now.

And last night when I woke up on my couch alone.

But when my rational mind is in control of my senses, I know I was right to ask it. Especially when other parts of my consciousness are delirious with thoughts of him here, with memories of his touch and his kisses, with ideas about how things might go forward between us. Not to mention how quickly this semester will be over and he'll be gone.

I know what it feels like to lose him, and I'm not interested in feeling any of that again.

I glance at the door again. No Ty.

Closing up my computer and locking the room, I make my way toward the Hall, ready to intercept Wanda Chamberlain.

Walking across the darkening campus, I can see into the windows of the room upstairs where the meeting is happening. Perfect timing. Several people stand up, mill around, take their leave. I see Wanda wrapping herself in a fuchsia pink coat and putting on a hat to match. She and Joey stand beside each other, neither of them topping five feet tall.

I make it to the door of the Hall at the same time Wanda arrives there, and I give a her a completely phony look of surprise.

"Oh, hi, Mrs. Chamberlain," I say.

I'm not fooling anyone.

"Is this an ambush?" She asks, reaching for my arm and giving it a squeeze. Then she laughs. "Walk with me."

I'm glad she didn't make me answer the ambush thing.

"How were the holidays?" I ask, just to have something to start the conversation. Appetizers, before we devour the main course. Ty. Ty is the main course.

"Lovely," she sighs. "Such a lot of snow and atmosphere."

I nod.

"And you? Any nice surprises? At home, or maybe when you got back to campus?"

That twinkle in her eyes. She knows. She probably saw me coming with questions about Ty a mile away.

"All right. Tell me what you already know." I might sound demanding, but she knows that she controls this conversation exactly as she controls all of them.

"Dr. Miller," she says. There's not a question there, but I feel compelled to answer her.

"Dr. Miller," I confirm.

"You know," she says, her voice soft and a little dreamy, "from my seat on the stage at that faculty meeting, I could tell just who recognized our newest addition. Admirers. Starry-eyed fans. But your face told a different story. There's a real something between the two of you, isn't there?"

I nod. "There was once."

"Care to share?" she asks, her soft voice taking on a new gentleness.

And I know right away that I will tell her anything. Why is it easy to talk about this with her? It was painful to say the words to Joey. Maybe because Wanda is like everyone's favorite great-aunt.

"It's an old story," I say. "The oldest. Love and loss and one person getting over it." I shrug. She puts her free hand on my arm, so she's got my arm wrapped in both of hers.

"I saw his face, too." She shakes her head. "He's not as over it as you think."

I can't help it. I laugh. "I'm sure he was just surprised to see me," I tell her, but I'm not fooling Wanda. Also, now that I understand Ty's regrets, I know there's more to how he reacted.

"Surprised, maybe, but there's a more precise word. Delighted. Stunned." She nods to herself. Clearing her throat, she says, "Picking it up where you left off?"

How does she get away with asking things like that? Didn't I come here planning to get information out of her?

"I hope not. The end was ugly. But maybe picking it up somewhere before we left off." I glance down at her again. "Unless you know of reasons I shouldn't."

She makes a tutting sound that only an old lady with a great deal of money can make without sounding silly. "I would never dream of getting involved."

I can't help it. I laugh. "No, of course you wouldn't."

She gives me one of her patented twinkly smiles. "I'm not saying he's your happy-ever-after. I mean, it wouldn't work."

Ouch. I didn't expect that. Wanda has a finger on the pulse of everything around here. If she says it's not happening, maybe it's actually not happening. I'm surprised how much her denial stings.

"Why not?" My words come out of my mouth like bullets, fast and loud and entirely regrettable.

She answers slowly. "Because I can't possibly let you go, and he doesn't belong here."

I hate it when people have reasonable arguments against what I want.

This time my voice is lower. More in control. "Why couldn't he belong here?"

She stops walking. "He's not a teacher, dear." When she says it, it's so obvious.

Oh. It's true. He's not. If he were staying, he'd need to have teaching credentials.

"Right. Of course."

She stands here, looking up into my face. I try not to squirm. "But I suppose that could change." She's waiting to see me react. I refuse to do it. I push my tongue against the back of my teeth and pray for no visible flinching.

I can wait her out.

Nope.

I cannot possibly wait her out.

"But we don't really have a need of another chemistry teacher," I say, steadying my voice. I will not give anything away. Not that I even know what I'm feeling right now. And maybe that's why I'm being so careful. I don't want anyone to know more than I know about what's happening in my heart.

"Oh," she says, her voice airy as she tugs on my arm and we walk toward her car. "When the right person comes along, we can make a place for him."

"Are we even talking about teaching jobs now?" I ask.

Wanda smiles. "Don't you just love it when conversations work on multiple levels? It's like poetry." She gives me a satisfied nod of her head. "Now why don't you ask me what you came here hoping to learn?"

She really is unbelievable.

"Why is Ty here? I mean, why now? And, yeah. Why here? Is he being punished? Because RA of the Rowan dorm?"

Wanda chooses the last part to answer first. "That is one of our nicer dormitories. And the young men who live there are lovely."

I nod. "Mmm-hmm." If my voice is sarcastic, at least my words are sincere. "They're delightful. But you don't make the rest of us live with them."

Wanda shakes her head. "I can't comment on the chancellor's housing choices. Nor on Dr. Miller's assignment here. But I can be glad he's come." She gives my arm a squeeze. "And so can you."

Permission to be glad. The way that runs through me is a surprise —I had no idea how much I wanted it. Since when do I need someone's permission? But honestly, what else was I waiting for?

"I understand that our Dr. Miller might be in a position to bring some donations in for the school," Wanda says, a little tilt of her head suggesting that she doesn't want to be vulgar about discussing money. It's cute how some rich people, especially women of a certain age, are careful not to be crude about this thing that sets them apart.

And she must be right. Tyson Perry Miller's got plenty of pull. Donations must follow him like women must.

Oh, no. I don't want to think about that. About them.

Because he's not chasing down a bunch of screaming fans. He's spending evenings eating meals and watching movies with me.

He's choosing me.

At least for now.

For now is pretty awesome.

What were we talking about? Oh. Right. Donations. "I could help with organizing donation opportunities," I say, as if the thought of serving on a committee at Chamberlain is something I entertain regularly.

She knows better. She knows it's not the committee I'm interested in. Or the donations. I can see it in her eyes. They're shining at me, and that's not just the reflection of landscape lamps.

"What a wonderful idea," she says. We reach her car, parked at the curb beneath a sprawling chestnut tree. As she clicks the unlock button on her key, she gives the tree a pat. I love that she loves things that grow like I love things that grow.

"Some things we experience in the past need to stay in the past," she says now. "And sometimes we get lucky. We're able to give things a second try." She takes my hands in hers and looks up at my face.

We're both lit by her car's headlights. I can see the wrinkles around her eyes, the kind that come from years of smiling.

She says, "Be brave when you decide what you're willing to revisit. Life is hard. Hurt happens. And yes, we have to be smart and protect ourselves. But be careful about falling into the trap of shielding your heart at the cost of finding new happiness."

She pulls my hands against her coat, and I swear I can feel the warmth of her heart. It feels good to be comforted, but I still don't know anything. And I have to know.

When she lets go and gets into the driver's seat, I wave goodbye and wait for her to pull away. After she's gone a few yards, she brakes and puts the car in park. I come to the edge of the sidewalk.

Rolling down her window, she says, "I don't want to overstep any bounds of propriety," and I smile as I wait for the *but*. "I can't tell you why he's here, but I can tell you that you don't need to be afraid of it. There are reasons, none of which any of us can share, but I would not have allowed him here if I didn't trust him with what's most precious to me." She gestures at the campus all around us.

"But even without your shared history, and even if he was only a pretty face, this might be worth your time." She smiles meaningfully. "And I think we both know he's much more than a pretty face." She kisses her fingertips and flicks the love my way like a fairy godmother in an Audi.

I watch her taillights disappear into the dark.

18

TY

Something is going on here. Something that's definitely against the rules.

All the guys who live in this dorm (they call themselves Rowan Boys like it's some kind of ancient tree-based secret society) are acting weird.

They're seventeen and eighteen-year-old boys. Weird is to be expected. But still. Weird.

Nobody's breaking curfew. And that's weird. But it's not only that. There's a hum of rebellion running through all three floors of this building, and I can't figure it out.

I don't think it's dangerous, whatever they're hiding. They're giddy, but not stupid. They don't have red, glazed eyes. They don't smell like booze. They don't look furtive, like they're planning something huge.

They giggle. They huddle. They duck into their rooms when I walk down the halls. They smile a lot.

I'm not getting paid enough to solve high school mysteries. I'm not, I remind myself, getting paid at all. So I play dumb.

And I watch.

The first week of classes, interspersed with a couple of dinners at

Lola's and one more movie night (I'm the one who falls asleep this time), goes fast. I'm exhausted. I thought seventeen-hour days on set were grueling. Turns out that teaching is tiring in new and nonscientific ways. I'm teaching in my sleep. Literally worrying and planning and grading and writing discussions through all my dreams.

Almost all my dreams.

Anyway. Tired. More tired than I remember ever being. I'm strangely grateful for the Rowan curfew, because at least I'm in the building where my bed (such as it is) sits.

One of the kids I had helping me try to figure out Ginger's phone number lives in this dorm. His name is Griffin, and he's brilliant. Awkward, but brilliant. Totally either going to run global companies or wind up in prison. Not that those are mutually exclusive. I should know.

But he has taken to sitting outside my door, laptop on his knees, waiting around to see if I have a new technical challenge for him, or if I want to see what he's hacked lately. The scariest one for the week is the camera he placed at the front door to the dorm building. I made him disable it, but we both know that once it's been done, it can always be reinstalled. We had a short talk about privacy and voyeurism. He shrugged and pushed a few buttons. His monitor's camera feeds went dark. My concerns did not turn off so quickly. I'm going to have to keep my eyes on this one.

I think for about three seconds about recruiting him to figure out what the boys are hiding from me, but he's either in on it or he's an outsider, and either way, it won't work.

"So, did you figure it out?" he asks.

I'm shocked he knows I'm trying to uncover the kids' secret. How do I look like an adult when I have to tell him no?

I stall. "What do you mean?"

"Ms. Rogers. The phone number. Because there's a list of cell numbers. It's not public access, but." He lets that hang in the air between us as he gestures to his laptop.

"Don't look up secret lists of teacher cell numbers," I say. "That's gross."

He shakes his head. "I'd only do it for you, man."

I almost believe him.

"I found her number, Griffin. Thank you for the offer."

I'm eager to change the subject. "Okay. Here's what I need. Set up a text service where I can send group messages to all the Rowan guys. But I don't want you to use an existing program. Make a new one."

"Why?" he doesn't seem bothered with my expectation that he'll do a project that is more work for himself. Just curious.

"I have a few privacy concerns. I don't want my number to be public access, even on the back end, on the apps that already exist."

Leave it at that.

He nods, as though he completely understands. "Celebrity problems. But you know you're all over the kids' social, right?"

"I'm hoping for none of that to go much further."

He glances up. "Do you know how social media works?"

I think it's a rhetorical question, because he's already typing on his keyboard. I'm willing to bet we'll have a functional, private, and investor-ready program within a week.

"Make it look cool, too."

He shoots me a sideways glance and gives a hum of assent. "It will look cool."

I go upstairs and walk through the third-floor hall. The boys I see aren't acting suspicious. Just normal-weird.

On the second floor, we get full-bore weird mode. A kid named Kendall runs into a room, holding his stomach and kind of bent over. Like he's sick? But he's laughing.

And something smells strange. Not the kind of strange I'm tasked with noticing. Meaty. Gross.

I put my head into Kendall's room, knocking as I open the door. He's got his head and torso out the window.

"What's up, man?" I ask, hoping it sounds both unconcerned and chill. I feel neither.

"Getting some air," he says, smiling over his shoulder at me.

"It's cold outside," I tell him. Because science is my specialty.

He pulls his head back inside the room and shoves his hands into his pockets. "Which is why I'm staying mostly inside." The smile he gives me takes the bite out of the words. He's just explaining how he can fix his temperature issue. He shuts the window and sits on the sill. "How was your day, Ty?" he asks. Seriously, these people must take classes in overconfidence.

"Very good," I say. "Excellent. Have a great night, Kendall."

I walk out.

There is no way to figure out what they don't want me to know.

At least not tonight.

When I get back to my room, I text Ginger. *'Am I an idiot? You can tell me the truth.'*

'It's not one of the top ten words I'd use to describe you.'

I can see the dots that tell me she's typing again.

'Are the Rowan boys attacking?'

'It's not an attack.'

She responds, *'You sure?'*

'Sure of literally nothing.'

'I'm coming over,' she types, and I stuff my phone in my pocket, put on a coat and hat, and shove my feet into my shoes.

I stand outside the Rowan dorm watching for her.

Eager much?

Living here is taking me back to high school behavior mode. I'm glad she didn't know me in high school. Hard enough for her to over-look the dumb stuff I did in college. I really don't need her to know what a disaster I made of things when I was a teenage boy.

When she comes around the corner and into view, at least a hundred yards away, I know it's her. Would I recognize anyone else at such a distance, at night, with this kind of atmospheric landscape lighting?

Probably. If it was someone really recognizable.

Like Ginger is to me. I can see her with my eyes closed. Her reddish-brown hair, coiled into thick braids hanging over her shoulders, her deep brown eyes, the freckles across her nose, the way one side of her mouth curls into a smile before the other side catches up. I know her walk. I know what her fingers look like, and I can tell when she's nervous, because she chews on her pinky nails. She knows it's an unhygienic habit, but she's convinced the pinkies are the least germy fingers.

I'm letting my mind run away without me, and if I leave it alone, my whole brain will be nothing but images of Ginger. In any case, I know it's her, and I feel lucky that she's walking this way. Toward me.

I lean against the stone wall of the dorm building, regretting that move immediately. My entire back feels like it's frozen in place, the stone pulling all heat out of me.

But I don't want to look like I'm rushing to her.

Even though I definitely want to rush to her. At a sprint.

She looks so confident, walking quickly with that perfect posture, two braids hanging from beneath her beanie. When she gets close enough, I can see her smile.

It's like those scenes in movies where time passing is shown by calendar pages blowing past, but in reverse. Like going back in time, watching her walk toward me with that happy look on her face.

"So you figured it out?" she asks as soon as she's close enough to talk without raising her voice.

Figured what out? "I don't think so. What are we talking about?"

She points to the dorm building at my back, and I am grateful for the excuse to get out of this lean. I turn and stand beside her.

A window slams shut on the second floor, blinds drop down, and the room's light goes out.

We keep watching for a minute, and I see the blinds shift, like someone's pulling two slats apart to peek between them. I can't see the kid, but he doesn't need to know that. I raise my hand in a wave.

The blinds fall back into place.

"What are they hiding?" she asks.

"In there?" I point to the room. "Or in their dark little minds? Either way, I have no idea."

She smiles that smile that makes everything better. "Whatever it is, they're moving their contraband from room to room by passing it out the windows. Those ledges must come in handy. Not all the dorm buildings have ledges."

"How do you know that's what they're doing?" I ask her.

Now it's her turn to point. "I saw them when I was walking over. They must not have seen you down here. They weren't being all that subtle."

"So what was it?"

She shrugs. "I don't know." She holds her hands near each other, showing me a space between her fingers about the size of a football. "Too big for pockets."

"They're pranking me," I say. "I wonder where they got that idea." I give her a smile to show that I'm definitely okay with the joke she helped them play on me.

She shakes her head. "Don't flatter yourself. I bet this has nothing to do with you."

"Boys being boys?" I ask.

She shakes her head again, this time harder. "I hate that phrase."

I know it. We've talked about it many times. The socialization of bad stereotypes, excusing unacceptable behavior on the basis of outdated norms.

"How about human adolescents doing what they do?" I say.

"That's about it, I bet," she says. "Want to walk?"

And this is the moment—the time and the place that our new routine begins. If we're not at Lola's or in Ginger's apartment watching (or rewatching) a film, we walk.

Covered in down parkas and wool hats, we stroll around campus at night, walking and talking and laughing. And occasionally watching the Rowan windows to see if they'll show what they're hiding. But they don't slip up, and I don't know any more than I did weeks ago.

And every night, we're rebuilding and remembering.

At least, I'm remembering.

For weeks, we spend time together doing none of the things I think about after I'm alone, but many of the things that will prove to Ginger that I'm capable of taking this slowly. We talk about work. About students. About the past, in easy and innocent ways, stepping around all the landmine topics that—make no mistake—I'm careful to avoid.

One night a few weeks into the semester, we wander through the sidewalks looking at cool architectural touches on some of the buildings, when out of nowhere, the wind starts whipping.

I thought I knew what cold felt like. After almost a month on campus, I've experienced all kinds of Vermont cold. Almost all the kinds. Nothing I'd felt came close to touching this.

The wind tears through coats and hats and gloves, making our eyes pour tears. It's hard to breathe. Miserable and far from either of our apartments, we duck into the nearest building.

The library.

It doesn't take long for every muscle in my back to prove that it had been on the verge of locking up forever. As I stand in the entrance and thaw, the cramping ache starts at the back of my neck and works its way down. I know how Ginger carries her tension in front of her shoulders, right around her collarbones, and I imagine how painful it is for her, this weird thaw inside the warm library.

A kid sits on a tall stool behind a coffee counter, looking at his phone. He probably has no idea what is happening outside, weatherwise, but he's in for a shock when he has to walk home.

I guess that's too bad for us, too. But for now, I'm happy to be warming inside a building with Ginger.

We walk around to the huge circulation desk that dominates the main floor. A woman with a sleek blonde bob sits behind the desk and looks up as we pass. She and Ginger smile at each other. She doesn't give me a second glance. It's like she doesn't know who I am.

I like her already.

"Ty, have you met Desi Chappell?" Ginger says.

The woman, who is wearing jeans and a brown sweater that somehow makes her blend in with the wood of the desk, sticks her hand out and shakes mine. She's probably about our age, but I don't know if I'd notice her outside this space. She isn't a standout like Ginger. She looks exactly like she belongs here in the library.

"Desi runs this place." Ginger gestures to the library with a wave of her hand.

"Don't let the ghosts hear you say that," Desi says with a small, polite smile. Her voice is appropriately quiet for the scenery.

I try to pass Ginger a subtle glance so she'll say goodbye and we can go sit somewhere cozy. She is having none of it.

"Did you know the library's haunted?" Ginger asks me, leaning her elbows on the desk, looking like she's getting comfortable here. I wonder if she can tell I want to be alone with her and this is her subtle reminder that we're taking it slow. As if I need reminding.

"How would I know that? You're my tour guide, and you've never said." I take a step away from the huge desk, hoping that we can find a quiet corner to sit in and warm up, because of functioning library heaters if nothing else happens between us.

Ginger is not reading my mind tonight. "Tell Ty about the card catalogue," she says to Desi.

Desi grins, and suddenly looks much younger. And more interested. She's excited to tell me. She takes off her tortoiseshell glasses and I notice her bright green eyes. "About twenty years ago, the school made major renovations to the computer network. The board wanted to be on the cutting edge of digital everything, so they decided to remove the card catalog." She points behind me. An enormous cupboard full of small drawers hulks there against the wall. "Two decades later and it still remains."

There's a lot of white space in the story, but I definitely like it this way. Huge, nonfunctional furniture remains in a public space. Only possible explanation? Ghosts.

I'll have to ask the Rowan Boys what they know about it.

"I'll take your word for it, but for my own safety, I feel like I need to ask. Are your local ghosts malevolent or benign?"

Desi glances from me to Ginger, and smiles again in a way that makes me think she'd fit in with our group, even though I'm getting definite shy vibes from her—maybe she works late. I don't think much about it because I'm eager to get Ginger alone. However, the thought that Ginger and I once again have a friend group makes me really happy.

"He's got a decent vocabulary," Desi says.

"Among other interesting qualities," Ginger answers. Do I like that they're discussing me while I stand in front of them?

It's getting warm in here.

"You didn't answer my ghost question," I say.

Desi looks back at me. "You're right. I didn't. But if you're really interested in finding answers, I can point you in the direction of several resources right here in the building."

"About haunted libraries?"

She smiles again. "About whatever you want to learn."

"I have a feeling you're very good at your job."

She looks down at her desk, still smiling. "I bet you're good at yours, too."

So maybe she recognized me after all.

"Learning new things every day," I say and tug at Ginger's arm.

She gives Desi a little wave and we move to sit on a sofa in an alcove behind some shelves.

"This place is cool, even if it's not really haunted," I say as I take off my coat and toss it over the arm of the couch.

Ginger pretends to shush me, looking around. "It makes them mad when you question their existence," she says.

Right. Ghosts and crazy people. "When's the last time you had a doctor's visit?" I ask.

She shrugs. "You're a doctor. After a fashion." She gives me that slow, lazy smile that promises amusements of all kinds.

You have to be kidding me. *This* is taking it slow? She's got to know she's very bad at this.

I clear my throat. "That's not what I meant."

I watch her smile fall. I've hurt her. "Oh, no. I didn't—" I say, but Ginger shakes her head.

She scrabbles back toward the arm of the couch, putting as much distance between us as the small sofa allows. Her head shakes and her eyes are everywhere but on me. I shouldn't' have said that. I made her uncomfortable.

She's stuttering out an excuse. "No. Sorry. I didn't mean, I mean, I didn't want to make it sound like I was, I mean," she's falling over her words and there's no end in sight. "I have no idea what I mean," she finishes. She drops her head into her hands.

"That makes two of us," I say, trying to smile.

"Sorry. I know I'm sending mixed signals. There's a very good explanation for that," she says. "It's because I'm a complete mess, and all my wires are crossed." She points to me and makes her face into a stern expression. "You're doing this to me."

Then she smiles, then sighs, and then speaks again. "I'm all mixed up because I think I know how I feel about you, about us, and then you sit here and smile at me and I can't think straight. When you were gone, out of the picture, it was easy to know you'd be gone forever. That part of my life was in the past. I could use what I learned to move forward. Protect myself from getting hurt. But now you're here. Working in my building. Living so close. Walking across campus with me. Sharing meals and laughing and looking like that." She gestures to me and then throws her hands up in the air in a what-do-I-do gesture.

I wait to see if she's going to land somewhere.

After a few awkward seconds of silence, I say, "I get it."

She looks at me, a question in her eyes. "You do? Because I don't."

I shake my head. "I get the confusion." Hoping we are as alone as it looks like we are, I lower my voice and go on. "I understand the attraction. I can't stop looking at you. I have to sit on my hands to keep from touching your face, and your arm, and your hair. All the time. And I know there's stuff between us. I know I hurt you, and I understand that you have some hurdles to get over if I'm going to be in your life again. When I think about people who have hurt me, it's hard to imagine learning to trust them again."

I don't want to say anything else about that, because I really don't want to talk to Ginger about Janie. Ever. But especially not now, when she's looking at me like that. When she's confessing that she feels a powerful attraction. When she so clearly wants us to be us again.

I put my hand halfway between us, and she grins at the obvious signal. She doesn't immediately reach over to hold it, but she's making no effort to hide her smile.

"I think you know what I want," I say, and the emotion I feel surprises me. I wonder if she can hear it in my voice. I want her to accept me. I want her to believe me. I feel that mix of sure and unsure that makes new relationships so exciting, and at the same time, I remember how good we were together. There's real solidity to our history.

And there's real pain.

I can't pretend I didn't ruin us, even if it was mostly accidental. And she gets to decide what comes next, how soon, and what the rules will be.

She is staring at my hand on the cushion between us. I watch her unwind her hands from her protective posture, both arms crossed over her stomach like she's holding herself together. Her left hand, covered to the knuckles by a long sweater, inches across the space between us. My eyes move between her hand and her face. She stops herself before her fingers reach mine. Just places her hand on the cushion. I think I feel the heat coming off her skin, our hands are that close together, but I won't move. I won't be the first. It's her choice to make. She knows that I want her to choose me.

Her pinky twitches, edging just a fraction of an inch closer to me. It's been a long time since I've felt that anticipation, that beautiful pain of being unsure, but pretty hopeful that something good—very good—is going to happen.

Something. Like she might take my hand on a couch in a corner of a high school library.

That will be enough.

For now.

I stare at her hand, covered with the silver and turquoise rings she's always loved. She's wearing one I gave her. Right there on her pointer finger, an oval of blue stone framed in hammered silver. I wonder if she thought of me when she put it on today.

I'm watching her hand so intently that I feel a shock when her other hand reaches up and touches my face.

"Can I?" she whispers, her fingers as light as a breath against my cheek.

I can't speak. I can't swallow. I can barely breathe. Every effort of all my nerves and muscles is required to hold still. To wait. To let her lead.

I nod. Her left hand stays on the couch cushion as her right fingers trail the lightest touch across my face, stopping at the corner of my mouth. She traces my bottom lip.

"Can I?" she asks again, her eyes roving across my face, taking me in at close range. She leans in.

A whisper of a word escapes me. "Please."

It seems to have been the right thing to say. Before I can even think, her lips touch mine and every neuron explodes into light. I don't know when her hands moved into my hair or when mine wrapped around her shoulders, but somehow past and present and future all combine in a moment of absolute perfection.

When Ginger breaks the kiss, she rests her forehead against mine, eyes closed. I watch her, still unmoving, wanting to be sure she doesn't regret this. As her eyes open, I see a shine of tears. Moving my hand up her neck, I cup her face. My thumb catches the first tear as it falls.

She shakes her head. "I'm not sad," she says, a hitch in her voice.

"Tell your eyes that," I say. I wipe another tear from her face.

She breathes out a laugh. "They know. Every part of me knows."

This time, when she leans in to kiss me, she moves so sweetly, so gently that I understand where her tears came from.

If we broke apart now, she might find a tear in my eye, too.

19

GINGER

I walk into my apartment, kick off my shoes, and text Joey. *'I did it.'*

'Split the atom?' she asks.

'Almost as difficult getting there. But way sweeter results.' When I make my way out of coat and scarf and hat and gloves, I wrap up in my favorite blanket and fall into the corner of my couch.

Her answer comes in all caps. *'YOU KISSED HIM.'*

It's not a question. She already knows. She can tell because she knows me. She knows what will make me happy.

I smile at my phone. Smiling at the memory, and at the happiness of a friend who is almost as excited as I am.

'That is not enough information. Give me more. NOW.'

I type, *'Is kissing in a haunted library a good omen or a bad omen?'*

'Qualify. How haunted?'

'Gently.'

'Totally good omen. Contented spirits are singing happy ghost songs for you.'

A minute goes by and I'm happy to stare dizzily at the wall. I did it. We did it, Ty and I. We're giving this another shot.

'So?' It's Joey again.

I don't answer. I just smile at the screen.

'You just kissed (I'm assuming "just" and it better not have been long ago, because FRIENDS TELL) Tyson Perry Miller. TYSON PERRY MILLER. Tell me everything.'

I fill her in on a few of the details, giddy with the memory. And my confidence is strong. We are going to make this work. Nothing will come between us this time. No secrets. No surprises. Just Ty and me and all the good things.

When I'm done, I think Joey is as content with how this looks as I am. Ty and Ginger. Together. Again. My cheeks hurt from smiling.

I pull out my computer and check my email. I have a message from Portia. Could this day get any better?

Hello, *New Friend,*

I realized today you didn't give me your name. Okay if I call you friend?

My schedule has changed. I will be in Burlington in two weeks. Any chance we can still meet for an interview?

Portia

Any chance? Of course. Every chance. I will go wherever she needs me to. Burlington is easy. I'm so glad she's not cancelling. I get to meet her in two weeks. Two weeks. Two weeks? I have to read the book again. I need to plan my interview questions, and they have to be awesome. I want this to be my best post ever, and I want her to remember it as the most connective interview she's had. I need to arrange a sub, because there's no way I'm going to be able to do chemistry on the day I've got a sit-down meeting with Portia Bancroft. My friend Portia. All the stars have aligned, just like her book promised they would.

I'm light-headed with happiness.

Everything is going my way.

I pull my copy of *You Are Made of Stars* off the side table and open to chapter seven, "Reaching for the Stars." I skim over Portia's suggestions for making goals both specific and all-encompassing. Her suggestions for literal and metaphorical stretching to reach for things just outside my comfort zone. Her wisdom about scope and aim and keeping notes and records of my successes.

I read it over and over and it just feels so good. Like, somehow, I knew all this before, and she's unlocked it so it's available and easy for me.

I send her a quick note back, deciding not to use my name, because I love the idea that she wants to call me "friend." She can call me Ginger when we meet. In two weeks.

I add some notes to my list of interview questions, but I feel so confident. I know that our conversation is going to flow perfectly, and that we'll have so much to say that time will fly.

And speaking of time flying, I have to get prepped to be nonfunctional for a whole school day. Whether or not I miss class, there's no way I'll be thinking about chemistry.

I organize two days' worth of lecture-based lessons, which I almost never do. Kids don't engage much with lectures. But these are going to be fun. I write up the talking points, put together slides, make an assessment, make an alternate assessment, and then send an email to Perla, the other chemistry teacher, showing her the plan and asking if she'd be willing to do one of the days with our combined classes if I did the other.

She answers fast. She's totally up for it. I email the facilities secretary and ask for a small auditorium room for the two days we need it. I should hear from him by tomorrow.

I feel like a character in a film who dusts off her hands after dealing with The List of Things that Must Be Done. I love this feeling of being ready.

So ready, in fact, that I have time to put on sweats and climb into bed with *You Are Made of Stars*. I'm feeling chapter fifteen, "When Stars Align." When I read it the first time, I thought it was pretty specific to situations where outside forces allow us to build strength. But when I re-read it a week or so ago, it felt more like when people align. It felt like advice for making things work in interpersonal ways, if you know what I mean.

Interpersonal ways like today in the library.

I feel myself smiling as I tuck into the blankets and adjust my pillows. My excellent reading lamp shines on the pages of Portia Bancroft's wisdom and I read chapter fifteen. Twice.

When I finish, I'm full of ideas and thoughts and I know I can't fall asleep. But it's late. And it's dark. And, you know, a really small number of degrees with a healthy wind-chill factor. So I'm staying here. Maybe forever.

I pull out my phone and scroll through some news sites. I watch a video about a new AI software that is equal parts exciting and scary to anyone who has ever read a science fiction novel. I listen to the new song that Nonny Throttle dropped. It's good. I listen again. I know that reinstating my social media sites is a bad idea. It's been five years, and I almost never regret not having them. But sometimes, like now, I think it would be nice to just drop in and check out the lives of strangers. Or celebrities. Or celebrities who are not strangers.

Nope. Bad idea.

I don't need to stalk Ty online. I have his phone number.

'Hi. It's late. You still up?' I send the message and snuggle into my huge tower of pillows.

He starts typing an answer almost immediately.

'Nobody sleeps around here.'

'Are the Rowan Boys making trouble?'

'Not yet, but it's only NOT TROUBLE because I haven't caught them.'

'You still don't know what they're hiding?' I know he's been watching for whatever the guys are doing, but if they don't want to get caught, they're not getting caught.

'The trouble is, I'm pretty sure that half of these guys are smarter than me.'

I laugh. *'Impossible.'*

But I know it's very possible. Chamberlain kids are at least two of three things: Wealthy, smart, and lucky. Some of them are the whole package.

He types, '*Why do they like eighties heavy metal bands?*'

'*I don't understand this question. Who doesn't love this?*'

'*I keep hearing Metallica playing. Loudly.*'

'*Well. Obviously. Nobody plays Metallica quietly. What would be the point?*'

The dots show me he's typing. Then nothing. Then dots again.

'*I guess you're right. But now that I think about it, it's really only one song.*'

'*Would it be weirder if they played entire albums?*' I ask.

A minute goes by. Then he responds. '*A quick internet search suggests that there are only a few shows that have sold more tickets than Metallica concerts over the past four decades.*'

'*Longer than any of these people (ourselves included) have been alive. Which concerts have sold more? Do tell.*' He loves to teach me the things he knows. This was one of our favorite games back in the Before Times.

'*Nope.*'

'*I must know.*'

'*Picture me saying this to you while I wear my teacher face: You have access to the entire collected wisdom of the ages. I know your research methods are sound. Look it up.*'

I love picturing his teacher face. '*Sigh. Let's pretend I did and move on. What's the song?*'

'*It's the one about the plagues of Egypt.*'

I laugh out loud. '*Creeping Death?*'

'*You know it? I'm a little worried that it might be literal. And literally happening in Rowan Hall.*'

'*Shh.*' I type. '*Listen carefully. Do you hear frogs? Crickets?*'

'*Very funny. I've seen movies about these east coast boarding schools and the horrible things guys do. It's not impossible. If it starts hailing, or, heaven forbid, the drinking fountain water turns red, I'm coming to your place for shelter.*'

'*Under no circumstances should you go outside in a pestilential hailstorm.*'

I realize my face hurts from smiling, and we haven't even mentioned the kissing that happened tonight.

'I've missed you.' I type the words and leave them sitting there in the text box. Can I send this message? Is it too much? Not enough? Bad timing?

Be fearless, I tell myself. Remember chapter fourteen, "Embrace Each Beam."

I hit send. I hold my breath.

He doesn't reply. There are no dots. He isn't typing. I stare at my phone. Nothing changes.

Nothing. I keep staring.

For too long—way too long.

Oh, no.

I scroll through tonight's entire conversation. Oh. No.

I thought we were sharing some sweet, flirty chat.

I was wrong.

The whole text thread is about kids and school and metal bands and plagues. We could have been any two colleagues from any school anywhere talking about our day. This was not personal. This was not flirting. This was not relational.

Then I had to go and screw it all up by saying something needy.

How could I?

This desperate girl isn't me, not anymore.

How is it possible that I have spent the last five years consciously curating my post-Ty personality, making myself into someone who requires nothing and nobody, only to revert to Ginger the Needy at the first touch of Ty Miller's lips?

I mean, not the first touch. But the first touch in a long, long time. (Really, really long and I could probably count the days if I thought it was a safe idea. It's not.)

I melted instantly into a gooey pile of need.

And let's make no mistake: *I* kissed *him*. I mean, I didn't attack. I asked permission. I'm not an animal. And he granted me permission. Because he's a man. A man who, if memory serves, really likes kissing. So of course he said yes.

And now I've made it something it isn't, something it wasn't meant to be, something it may have never been.

I've scared him off.

I've put myself too far out there, wherever *there* is.

I can't lie here and stare at the phone. I can't just wait until he finds a polite and professional way to tell me that there's no "us."

I slam my phone down onto my duvet and jump out of bed. Slamming the phone onto a down-filled blanket is not terribly good drama, but it's safer than slamming it onto tables and stuff. I stomp around my room for a minute. Then I move to the kitchen and stomp around there.

This is neither helpful nor pleasant.

I pour some water into the electric kettle and turn it on. Within a minute, I've got a cup of tea steeping and I'm sitting at the table leaning my head on my arms.

Why am I the way I am?

Why do I have to make things more difficult than they have to be?

Why do I have to love Tyson Perry Miller?

Oh, no. There it is. I said it. Love.

I let my head drop onto the table.

Love.

Sure. Let's make this just a little more miserable.

But now that I've thought it, I can't un-think it. I love him.

I do.

Dammit.

I love so much about him that it's not even easy to think of things I don't love. I mean, aside from the obvious.

Bright side, Ginger, I tell myself. *Look at the positive.* At least I didn't say "I love you" to him. Because I did that once. One time only. And he never, in all our time together, said it back. I know. I listened for it every day.

And "I've missed you" is bad enough. But not the worst. Not the most vulnerable. Not the most horrifying.

Okay. That's something. I sip my tea, grateful for the warmth seeping through the mug as I cradle it in my hands.

I can live with this. I can work here on this tiny campus with a thousand kids who will talk of nothing but the hot celebrity teacher for the next several months. I can put a smile on my face, or at least avoid actively crying about him.

I'm not crying, anyway. Just moping. Hunched over a cup of cooling tea in my ratty sweatshirt.

It's not my best look.

Swirling my tea around in my mug, I realize that even though it's very late, I'm not even a little bit tired. If I were smart, I'd get into bed and meditate or read a boring book or listen to Zen sounds on my phone so I fall asleep. But I'm not that smart.

I go into the living room and open the leather ottoman where I store extra blankets. I pull them out. Underneath the bottom one, I take out the shirt-box. It's not the original box. That's been smashed and crushed and torn a little from being placed on the bottom of various closet shelves, the backs of drawers, and dark corners of apartments for the past five years.

When I move, I change out the box. But it's always a white shirt box, no labels, no marks. Nobody but me would know there's something inside that's worth noticing.

Lifting the box's lid, I see the little clasp on the book is turning black. Cheap metal-looking materials do that. I press the catch and the strap covering the album opens. It's only a matter of seconds before I have flipped open the photo book and soaked up the nostalgia—both the kind that comes from printing photos and putting them in books and the kind that comes from looking backward in time.

Back to the days of Ty and Ginger.

Back to the happy Chicago times. I thought it was such a fun retro idea, to print out pictures from my phone and put them in a book. It's like going shopping in an actual mall. Time travel. I turn pages. I see his face everywhere.

In my apartment, on the couch. In the kitchen. Lying in the grass under our favorite sycamore tree.

At my parents' house, doing dishes after Thanksgiving dinner.

At his apartment, playing with his roommate's dog, the smelliest indoor animal I ever encountered. In the campus library. In his car. On Segway machines doing that most touristy of Chicago's delights, the Magnificent Mile tour.

There's a picture of him sleeping. One of him leaned over his laptop, concentration all over his face. One where he tried growing his hair long, and he hated it. I stopped at that one, running my finger along the image of his slightly wavy blond hair, wondering if he chose to grow it long again now, or if it was someone else's call.

So many pictures of him laughing. Some of us laughing together. Those pull me in, and I don't know if it's my nostalgic side or my tendency to push at bruises, but I stare at the shots, trying to see if the future was somehow encased within the photos. If I looked hard enough, could I see his coming betrayal? The years without him? Could I see that he'd walk back into my life again? That I'd be unabashed or brave or dumb enough to lean back into this thing between us?

Because I did. I leaned. I kissed him. I confessed my feelings and he walked away.

As I close the book and replace it first in its box and then in the bottom of the ottoman, it occurs to me that it's possible I'm being slightly dramatic.

Did he really choose to walk away?

Or did he actually need to step away? Like, for his job?

I force myself to walk calmly into my room and pick up the phone where I tossed it onto my bed.

Seventeen. There are seventeen texts from Ty.

Starting with *'It's a cat.'*

20

TY

It still feels like summer camp around here, except it's cold and the dorm is nicer than a cabin in the woods and I'm way too old for this.

I figured out what they've been hiding from me. That sounds like I solved something. I didn't. They came and told me.

And their timing is the worst.

In the middle of some very good flirting with Ginger, someone knocks on my door. "Ty? We need you."

The voice sounds a little nervous.

I drop my phone on the bed and walk into the hall, where several guys stand, looking embarrassed. I might say sheepish, if I used words like that.

They all have their hands in pockets or behind their backs.

"We're having an emergency," the one called Nam says.

York interrupts him and holds his fingers an inch apart to show me the emergency is small. "Only sort of. And we can probably handle it. But maybe you know what to do. So come upstairs. Please."

I wonder, all the way up both flights of stairs to the third floor, if I'm being pranked. They're harmless, but I'd rather be talking to

Ginger than following a bunch of kids around the building after curfew. I'd rather be talking to Ginger than most things.

We stop in the middle of the hallway. Nam unlocks his door, pushing it open with a look that broadcasts regret. I don't know if he regrets letting me in, or the smell of the room. It's rank.

I cover my nose with my hand.

"What happened?" I ask.

"Nothing."

"It smells like a dead body in here."

The boys all deny it. Shake their heads. Mutter.

York shushes them all and says, "Not a human one," which pretty much stops the conversation.

"Do I want to know?" I ask.

Three of the guys keep shaking their heads, but Nam steps forward. "Since September, nobody has slept in here. Except Creeping Death."

I stand there in the smelly room waiting for any of these words to make sense.

No good.

"What?"

Joel, I think, repeats a few of the words. "Nam's roommate never came this year, and when my roommate moved back home after three weeks, he moved in with me. And we gave this room to the cat."

Cat.

Gross. Cats are monsters. Forbidden cats can only be the very worst.

That's a piece of the smell. That litterbox odor that makes me gag, along with some lingering scent of what must be cat food. But that's not all of it.

There are a million questions I should ask. I begin with the easiest one. "A dead cat?"

They all shake their heads. Okay. A live cat, then.

I don't ask them if this is against the rules. Because I don't have to. It's definitely against all the rules. And I'm not ready to turn them over to the chancellor, mostly because it's after one in the morning.

And because I'd get in trouble too. I can just imagine the look on Dr. Moreau's face when I tell her there's a horrible funk hanging over the Rowan Hall dorm and it's because I'm no good at forcing teenage boys to obey basic rules.

The boys, as one, point to a vent in the ceiling.

I take a deep breath and deliver my next line with no emotion whatsoever. "Have you got a cat living in the ceiling?" No judgment. No anger. No doubt.

"He doesn't *live* in the ceiling," York says, a bit of condescension in his voice, as if I should know better. "He lives here, in this room. That's not the problem. He's currently stuck in the ceiling. That's the problem."

A pitiful mewling noise floats down from above. I can't help it; I give in to the urge to rub my forehead. I traded a late-night conversation with Ginger for this?

I look around the room. The two beds are pushed together, making one king-sized bed in the center of the room. On the mattresses sits a manky green cat bed that has definitely seen more sanitary days. A bed sheet hangs from the open space in the ceiling where a heater vent grate should be. The sheet fans down and attaches to the mattress in a weird parody of a headboard.

"Keeps him from sitting in the windowsill and getting discovered," one of the boys says, noticing where I'm looking.

Of course.

The desk on the left is lined with bowls. Probably stolen from the cafeteria. In the bowls in the source of much of the smell.

"Is that tuna?" I ask.

Nam points. "That one is. He likes it better than the crab." He gestures to another bowl. The other six bowls also contain what we're going to refer to as food. And there's one with water. On the desk on the right, there's the litter box. Which may have never been emptied.

I swallow down my gag reflex.

"You have a cat."

York nods. "His name is Creeping Death."

I nod. Because much of this now makes a strange kind of sense.

York's not done. "Like the Metallica song? You know? We thought he'd like to hear where his name comes from. But when we played it, he climbed up into the vent and now he won't come down."

Obviously.

I resist the urge to shout, "What do you want me to do about it?" Instead, I try the old standby teacher trick of waiting them out.

They are way more patient than I am.

I finally take my hand away from my nose, realizing that the smell isn't as bad as I thought. Just kind of feral. And, yes, meaty. Okay, it's still so bad. I carefully breathe in tiny sips of air.

"Can we go over the facts, please?"

The boys nod at me.

"You have a dorm cat."

"Creeping Death," York says again. "Like the plagues." He grins at me.

I can't think of a single nonthreatening thing to say to that kid. I ignore him.

Same voice. Calm, bland statements. No cursing. "You have adopted a stray."

"A rescue," Nam says.

Another kid nods his head. "We find the term 'stray' hurtful and offensive."

I am not getting paid enough for this.

"And your cat lives here, in this room, where presumably, administration thinks you sleep." I point at Nam.

They all nod.

Joel shakes his head, then nods again. "I mean, yes. The cat sleeps here. Mostly. He usually kind of roams around outside during the day. And if he falls asleep in someone's room, he just stays there."

York agrees. "Until he asks to go out. He scratches on the windows. Then we pass him to the end of the hall and let him climb down the tree. There are big rowan trees at all the corners of this building. I think they did that on purpose."

It's a struggle not to roll my eyes. I am very proud of my restraint.

"I can't believe I'm asking you this, but how long has the cat been in the ceiling?"

"Three days," Joel says. "I know, because Nam made me promise not to say anything to you until at least three days had passed."

Nam nods again. He looks a little sick.

"So the music you played tonight?" I ask, not sure how I think asking this is going to help. "That's not what scared him up there?"

"Same song. Different day." Nam's voice is quiet.

York nods. "We were hoping to lure him back down. It didn't work."

No kidding.

These are the best and brightest of the American prep school scene. I sigh again.

"How do you know he's not coming down and then going back up when you come in?" I ask. I can't believe I'm having a logical conversation about this.

Joel is the one to answer again. "He's never alone. Someone stays here at all times to monitor the situation."

I stare.

"We're very worried," he adds.

York says, "We have assigned everyone shifts. We all have hours that we stand watch. There's a spreadsheet."

I really cannot with this one. "You're skipping classes to babysit a feral cat in the air ducts?"

One of the guys makes a protesting sound. "You don't have to say it like that." He sounds offended. Sad.

"Maybe we should call maintenance." I don't want to call maintenance. I don't want anyone else to call, either. But if these guys think *I'm* climbing up on furniture and sticking my head into an air duct to rescue their reeking dorm cat, they've really got to think again.

Now I hear from each of them. All of them. In unison. "No."

"Aren't you worried about his safety?"

This is leverage. Somehow I can use this situation to my benefit.

Nam says, "Of course. But we toss food up there now and then.

And he's not constant with his noise. Just enough to let us know he's still there. Don't tell maintenance. Just tell us how to get him down."

I can't believe them. What do they think I know?

"Okay, let's say I don't tell. Here's what I need from you."

They stay huddled close by as I make all my demands. When I'm done, I tell them, "You've got 48 hours. If I don't see legitimate, marketable plans by then, I call maintenance. No kidding."

When they all nod, I suggest they go to bed.

I get back to my little cell and pick up my phone. I immediately text Ginger, because even if it's just the disgusting events of high school boys and their strays, I'm having an adventure. There's no one else I'd rather share it with.

'It's a cat.' Just typing the words almost makes me laugh.

'The thing they've been hiding.'

'And they're not only hiding it from me. The monster's been a secret resident of Rowan Hall since the fall.'

'Would not be surprised to find it has a popular Instagram page.'

'The cat has its own room, bigger than mine.'

'Mine smells better, FYI.'

'My room, I mean. I don't have a cat.'

'Because cats are the worst.'

I'm pacing the few feet from door to window and back, over and over as I type.

'The kids feed it tuna, which reeks.'

'And crab. Etc.'

'They pass the poor thing from room to room out the window.'

'That must have been what you saw the other night. When you came over. Weeks ago.'

'Although I can't be sure it's the size of a football. It's hiding. In the ducts. Where it will probably either live forever or die a horrible, smelly death.'

'Did I mention they named it? Guess what they named it. Go ahead.'

'You'll definitely guess. We talked about it earlier tonight.'

She's not responding. Maybe she went to sleep. I should leave her alone. But then I scroll back and see her last message. 'I've missed you.'

I feel all the warmth of a delicious summer afternoon at the lake wash over me. She's missed me. I grin, wondering if she meant that she missed me in general, for the last few years, or since we were together tonight. In the library.

'Are you still up? Sorry to keep bugging you if you're sleeping.'

I can't just leave it at that.

'I've missed you, too. So much.'

I stare at my words. It's nothing but the truth, but it feels dangerous. Awesome, but like I'm putting myself way out there. Which is only fair. She said it first. She was always braver than me.

The little dots show up in my screen. She's typing.

'It's so late.'

Oops. *'So sorry—I'll leave you alone. Good night.'*

'I'm teasing. I'm not sleeping. I had a cup of tea and a crisis.'

'What kind?'

'Darjeeling.'

'I meant what kind of crisis?'

'Well, there were no cats involved.'

'Then you might be doing it wrong.'

I hope that made her laugh.

She types some more. *'You should teach a class. How To Know Your Crisis is Legitimate.'*

'I'm not qualified.' I drop my phone and change out of my sweater and into the T-shirt I sleep in. She doesn't respond right away, so I switch my jeans for pajama pants. When I pick up the phone, she's texted again.

'Me, either. My current crisis (former crisis? I think it's over) was fueled by over-caffeination and self-doubt.'

I climb into my bed and prop up against the pillows.

'What do you have to doubt?'

'Well, there's this guy.'

Uh oh.

'Yeah?'

It's the only safe response. Welcoming her to say more. Demanding nothing. Being open.

'Yeah. I knew someone a lot like him once. It ended badly. And I'm a little scared that I'll get hurt again.'

It's like a physical pain that runs through me. I want to stop her hurting, but I'm the one who hurt her.

'I guess that is always a possibility in a relationship.'

She says nothing.

I type again. 'Are you in a relationship?'

My heart is beating fast. I realize I'm nervous, wondering what she's going to say.

'I think so. I hope so. And it's probably always going to be a bit frightening to open up.'

I clutch my phone, knowing I have to say something but not knowing how to fix what I broke.

'Ginger. I'm sorry. And I'm willing to keep saying I'm sorry. Forever. Because that's how long I'll regret hurting you. And I can't promise that I won't find new and ever more interesting ways to complicate my life. But I never want to hurt you again.' I shift on the bed. 'Can we talk about this for real, out loud, in the same room?'

I wait long enough for her to read the message at least twice. When she starts typing again, I realize I've been holding my breath. I don't fully relax until her message comes through. 'Yes. Of course. But tomorrow, okay? It's late and I really want to go to sleep while I'm smiling about you. It almost guarantees good dreams.'

'Good night.'

I see the line of dots again.

'The cat's named after the Metallica song?'

I fall asleep with a smile on my face.

21

GINGER

I wake up and roll over, my room still dark in the predawn. I check my phone, and I still have five minutes before the alarm goes off. I love it when that happens. Like a bonus snooze.

Closing my eyes, I realize something is different. What is this feeling?

It's giddiness. I've just woken up silly with happiness.

That doesn't happen every day. At least, it didn't before. Maybe, starting now, it will happen every day. I'm willing to test that hypothesis.

I don't wait for the alarm. I get up and get moving, because the sooner I'm ready for the day, the sooner I'll accidentally-on-purpose run into Ty.

Is this how happy people feel all the time?

Maybe that's not fair. I haven't exactly been an unhappy person. I'm functioning. I contribute to society. I'm friendly, sort of. I do the things I'm contracted to do. But it just feels a little better to be alive today.

I pull out my phone. *'Thank you,'* I send Ty.

He's awake, too, because he responds right away. *'For what?'*

'For nothing. For being excellent. Because I woke up looking forward to the day.'

I can feel my face trying to split open from side to side with the strength of this smile.

'And I get the blame for that?'

'We call it credit.'

'Breakfast?'

'What about it?' I ask.

'Have you grown into a habit of eating it?'

He remembers that I don't like breakfast. *'Not yet.'*

'Does Lola make breakfast?'

I laugh. *'She might for you. But you're special. The rest of us have to fend for ourselves or do without.'*

'If I knock on your door right now, would you come to breakfast with me in the cafeteria?'

There's a knock.

On my door.

Right now.

I definitely do not run to answer it. But I might slide across the floor in my socks.

"Morning," Ty says, that million-dollar smile rolling across his face. I want to pull him into the apartment and pick up where we left off last night. Instead, I open the door wider and keep my hands to myself.

"Good morning," I say. "Come on in."

"You sure?"

I nod. "You're standing in an open doorway in predawn February. Please come in."

He closes the door and leans on it, his hands behind him. I watch him watching me. Finally, I say, "What?"

"Is it too early for me to ask if I can kiss you?"

A flush of heat crawls up my neck. "Too early how?"

"In this conversation? In the day? In our relationship?"

I don't think my smile gets bigger than this. "Not too early in any of those."

He closes the distance between us, his arms around me before I can think about it. He tilts his head to the side and stares at me.

"I can't believe it," he whispers, his hands on my back and his nose almost touching mine. "I'm not dreaming, am I?"

"Want me to pinch you?" I ask, hoping it doesn't sound like a threat.

"I want you to kiss me," he says, almost without making any noise at all.

For several moments I do not move. I do not think. I do nothing but soak in the perfect feeling of how we fit together, breathe together. His lips on mine, spanning the years between then and now.

Eventually I break the kiss to ask him if he still needs breakfast.

"Right now, I'm sure I have everything I need. In an hour, my stomach might disagree."

"I have eggs. And bread."

"Are you offering to cook for me?" he asks, and the absolute delight in his face is magical. In fact, it's almost enough to make me say yes.

I smile at him.

"No, but you can cook in my kitchen while I watch you."

"Lead the way."

He rolls up the sleeves of his button-down and puts on my apron. If the cop-show situation doesn't work out, he can star in a cooking show. I'd watch it.

He tells me about the Rowan Hall cat mascot, and how he promised not to tell on the kids if they'd help him figure out a great fundraising idea. Apparently that's part of Moreau's demands—that Ty brings money in to the school.

"She's making the most of this," I say, spreading hummus on a pita and piling on cucumbers and arugula. "You want one of these for lunch?"

Ty makes a face. "Is there a cheeseburger hiding in there?"

I pretend to dig through the arugula. "Why, yes. And a milkshake. Would you look at that."

"Thanks anyway. I'll pick up lunch that's not a salad sandwich."

He still smiles when he makes fun of my food. I watch him, and for just a sliver of a second, it's not only the past and the present I'm seeing. I can imagine us together, years from now. We stand in a kitchen, side by side, and he adds meat and butter and cheese to all my food. It's kind of a delicious vision.

"So what if the Rowan boys don't come up with a good fundraising idea? You going to toss the cat into the cold, dark world?"

He shrugs and expertly shakes the sauté pan so his eggs turn over without a spatula. "It's not hurting anything. Except my sense of smell. Cat food is disgusting. Not to mention bowls of crab and tuna and a dangerously full litter box."

He shudders.

"Wait. You didn't make them clean it out? You just left it there?"

He gives me a look that shows me he's lost here. "I have no idea how to proceed."

It's terribly cute, but he can't let the cat stay there. Not like that. "Demand they clean up. Immediately. Because, eww. That's disgusting. And probably dangerous."

He agrees to make the demands.

"So, fundraising?" I ask, reminding him we were talking of more than dorm cat safety.

He pops bread into my toaster and pushes the lever before turning around to lean against the counter. Watching me finish making my sandwich, he answers the rest of my question.

He speaks slowly, like he's being careful with his words. "I know someone who recently published a book that's doing pretty well. Maybe she'd come do an event for parents." It's cute that he doesn't want to wave the flag of his celebrity status, including his celebrity friends.

But wait—authors! Books!

I know interrupting is rude. But I'm so excited about meeting Portia Bancroft that I just let the words come rushing out of my mouth. "Oh! That reminds me. I'm going to Burlington in a couple of weeks. I'm crazy about this new author, and I'm sure it's nobody you've heard of because it's kind of girly stuff, and she's on tour, and she agreed to do an interview with me, and I can't stop thinking about what I'm going to say to her and I'm convinced that we're going to become best friends and probably coauthor a new bestselling series."

He stares at me. His mouth opens, probably to ask me to slow down, but I hurry on.

"I know. I'm being silly. I'm a little frantic. But I'm so excited. It's been a long time since I let myself get this eager about something good that's coming. Not the cowriting a series. That's just a joke. But meeting her. Doing an interview. It's so good to have something positive ahead. Life has been so step-after-step, waiting for something happy. Not that I've been depressed." I am talking very fast, because he just keeps staring. Like I've lost my mind. I haven't. And I can prove it. If I just keep talking. Really fast. "I haven't been depressed. Just kind of going through the motions. But lately, just in the last few weeks, things have started really looking up. So I don't want to mess any of it up. Let's never mention any part of what I just said again. Ever."

I smile, and I think he knows I'm joking, but he looks uncomfortable.

"Pretty please," I say. And then I stop talking. Finally. I'm sure we're both relieved. I smile at him.

Walking the few steps from where I'm making a sandwich to where he's cooking his eggs, I don't take my eyes off his eyes. Considering how fast I was speaking, I move very slowly. My smile is convincing him that he shouldn't look away. I don't stop until I'm standing right in front of him. Hardly any space between us. "I know I have you to thank for that," I say, leaning forward and kissing his cheek. He turns his head and meets my lips.

"Ginger," he begins, but I stop him with both my hands on his face.

With one arm around my waist, he moves his pan off the heat. He gives me a long, delicious kiss. He pulls back to look at me, grinning. "Just until the toast pops up," he says.

The toast pops up. He ignores it.

"Your breakfast is going to get cold," I say after another minute. My arms wrap around his waist.

He nods, his hands on either side of my face now. "It is."

"Cold eggs and toast are awful."

"There are things that make up for a disappointing meal," he says, nuzzling my neck.

I kiss him again and laugh. "Eat your breakfast," I say, stepping away. "It's almost time for school."

"Yes, Ms. Rogers," he says, and I swear if he smiles at his students like that, they're all doomed to loving him forever.

I'm sure he doesn't look at his students like that. Pretty sure. But now the thought's in my head and I must know. "You don't give your students that face, do you?" I ask, filling my water bottle.

He blinks a couple of times, swallowing a bite of his breakfast. "I have no idea what you're talking about."

I laugh. "Your innocent act doesn't work on me. I know too much."

He gets serious. "Nobody knows me like you do."

It's a good line, but I'm not sure it's true. Shouldn't Janie know him better? And what about friends from his last few years? The people he works with. I don't answer.

He must notice my silence, because he gets out of his chair and comes over to me. "A lot has happened in the last few years that we've been apart. I have had experiences. Some of them great, some of them pretty awful. But through all that time, I never felt like anyone could see me like you can see me. They notice this," he gestures to his face and hair, "and they like the image and the headlines and the ratings. But you have always seen inside me better than anyone."

Except I still don't know why he's really here. And that seems like a pretty important thing to know.

He runs his hand from my shoulder to my fingertips, interlacing his hand with mine. "If it all went away, I'd be fine as long as you are with me."

I should breathe now. And close my mouth.

Wow.

He's not done. "And it might."

He lost me. "What might? It might what?"

He looks at the table. "It all might go away." His eyes flick to mine and then away again.

The silence of the following pause is excruciating.

"Are you in trouble?" I ask after forever.

"Kind of." His voice is very quiet. "I made a mistake." He squeezes my hand again. "An error of judgment."

I wait for him to say more, but he doesn't.

After another forever, I ask, "Do you want to say anything else about that?" My brain is screaming, "GIVE ME DETAILS," but I know better than to push. I remember that Ty is a man who needs time to say things in his own way. In his own time.

He looks into my eyes. "I do. But not right now. And we'd better get to class."

He picks up his plate and rinses it in the sink.

I will give him space and time to decide what he wants to tell. But I can't help that my brain is filling in these huge blanks with possibilities based on every book I've ever read, every movie I've ever seen, every likely and unlikely scenario that could lead to "errors in judgment."

I tell my brain to forget it.

Not likely.

I can't pretend the mood of the room hasn't changed. The air in my kitchen is stiff and heavy, hard to move through. We put on our coats and grab bags in silence. There is no chance that Ty and I will walk to the science building holding hands and laughing now. Our silence follows us through the lifting dark, as the sky begins to go blue. When my elbow touches his, I draw back and hold my arms in tight to my sides. We walk quickly, staying in step, but I don't say a word. And I won't until he brings it up again.

If he chooses to.

I can trust him to make a decision about how much to share with me.

I know I'm not automatically privileged to know all of his stories.

We made some progress this morning. I feel a lot more confidence in the whole concept of "us" now. He wants to let me know things. But just like there are some things I don't want to hear, there are probably things he doesn't want to say. I have to be okay with that.

Campus is waking up, lights on in many of the buildings. The latest snowfall is cleared from sidewalks but still hangs in gorgeous clumps on the evergreens. The science building's warm interior beckons us as we move across the frozen quad.

He walks with me to my room, and as I unlock the classroom door, he stands behind me, still silent.

I push the door open and flip on the lights, but I don't walk in yet. I want to give him another chance to say something if he wants to.

Turning, I lean on my classroom door frame watching him. I allow a small smile to rest on my mouth, nothing forced or fake. I want to telegraph peace to him—he looks like he needs it. And I have years of practice looking at peace. Sometimes I mean it. Sometimes it's a great disguise.

When he speaks, his voice is barely more than a whisper. "I haven't told anyone who absolutely doesn't need to know," he says, and I brace myself. "And when it's time, you're the next one I tell. Maybe the only one."

My breath leaves me in a whoosh. Okay. I love the phrase "when it's time." It means he's not doing this now. He's not going to drop whatever bombshell he's holding and then leave me here to deal with it in silence as I try to teach chemistry. Okay. This is good. Good.

"Sorry to be all mysterious," he says, a smile creeping onto his face. Now he looks more like himself.

I shake my head. "You know I love a good mystery," I say. I hope he hears what I'm not saying. Take your time. You're safe here.

"I do know that about you," he says, leaning in and kissing my cheek. "Turns out I know a lot about you. Have a great day at school, Ms. Rogers."

"You, too, Dr. Miller."

I watch him walk to the staircase at the end of the hall. When he gets to the doorway, he turns and waves. I'm glad I waited.

All these years, I assumed that I was the injured one. That he stomped on my soul and broke my heart and walked away unscathed.

But Ty has some hurts lingering, too.

Today, I realize everyone's at least a little scathed. Life is tough, and sometimes it wounds us. All of us. Even the happy ones, the pretty ones, the successful ones. Sometimes we make our trouble, and sometimes trouble finds us. But we all get hurt.

I thought I could work through my hurt alone, or at least block off the hurt parts so they wouldn't leak out any more pain. But I know now I was wrong. It started with Joey, the reopening of my heart. I couldn't help it. She moved right in and brought Dexter and Hank with her. And now Ty is back. And there are such great people here, maybe there's room in my heart for more.

Being here for each other is the only way to get through the hurt without turning our hearts into scars.

I bet Portia Bancroft would love that line.

22

TY

The proposal comes in a spreadsheet, of course. And the guys call a meeting using hacker Griffin's (truly excellent) conference-texting app, which he programmed and coded and somehow managed to get us all into. Including me. Where did he get my number? I didn't give it to him yet.

The kid is brilliant. And a little scary.

We meet up together on the main floor of Rowan, which smells like microwave popcorn and instant noodles. High-sodium study-time food.

York pulls up a spreadsheet on his computer. It's a few pages long, but I motion for him to get to the bottom line. He clicks on the tab for "Money-Making Ideas" and hands the laptop over.

"We have more, but the best ones are listed first," York says.

The top three ideas on the "Save the Cat" suggestion list read as follows:

- Get a real celebrity (no offense, Ty) to come do a function and all our parents will pay for tickets. Do you know anyone really cool?

- Have the production company come do a documentary at Chamberlain. Great campus, genius students, a faculty that's pretty hot for old people, cool history. Donate proceeds back to the school.
- Raffle off a date with Tyson Perry Miller. We know a few people who have already pledged $.

I READ IT OVER, and I'm not all that impressed. Okay, I'm a little offended. Do I know anyone really cool? And "pretty hot for old people." Nice. Actually, I kind of want to have that printed on T-shirts for all the faculty. And I don't need help—or money—to get a date. Thankfully.

"I think Dr. Moreau had bigger ideas in mind, guys," I tell them. Specifically, I think, ideas that don't revolve around me.

"Like what?" York asks.

And that's the problem. I have no idea what high-end boarding schools do to raise funds. What's a success even look like?

"I think the documentary idea might be a little self-serving." I don't tell them that their lives aren't that interesting to outsiders. The information might offend them. They wouldn't believe me anyway. "But maybe we can put the school on a list of locations for filming. Production companies pay a lot for locations if they're great ones. Chamberlain is definitely a great one. Is summer pretty quiet around here?"

Joel gives a shrug. "I've heard that some teachers live here all year. But I doubt much goes on."

Of course not. In his mind, teachers all live in their classrooms. I mean, it's fair for him to make assumptions like that, since most of his teachers literally live on campus.

"Okay. I'll make some calls. But don't stop thinking. If something better comes up, let's pursue it."

Joel says, "And Creeping Death?"

I look around and see nobody who's likely to bust me. I lower my voice anyway, just in case. "He can stay. But he probably should get out of the ductwork. Try leaving him alone for a couple of hours and see if he gets bored and comes down."

Nam opens his backpack and pulls out a huge rope with knots tied every foot or so.

"What's this for?" I ask.

"Maybe he's up there because he can't come down," Nam says. "I'm going to attach this to the ceiling vent and see if he'll climb down it like a ladder."

York shakes his head. "More likely he's found a feast of birds and rodents in the ducts and he'll live there forever, getting fatter and happier every day."

"There are birds in our ducts?" Griffin asks, looking like he's now got something new to be afraid of. Poor Griffin.

Time to wrap this up. "Okay, stay focused please. Don't get distracted by nonessentials. If there is wildlife in the ceiling, there's not much we can do about it right now. If the cat wants to live there, he's going to live there. Right? Cats are not famous for conforming to people's wishes for them."

They all nod. Okay. Agreement is good.

One more thing I need from them. "If I were a betting man, I'd bet he's not coming down because nobody's emptied his litter tray. It reeks in there. Put "clean the litterbox" on your spreadsheet guard-rotation schedule starting right now. Just throw the whole thing in a dumpster and start over."

Joel asks, "Where are we supposed to get a new litterbox?"

I just give him the look of an adult annoyed by a kid. "You're all humans of above average intelligence. I'm sure you can figure it out. You did it once."

I hear some muttering about finding the current litterbox in a basement, and I wonder if they mean the basement of this building. Should I be looking in basements? How is it possible that these kids are so good at getting up to trouble I couldn't even imagine? And finding a litterbox is gross, but I really hate to think about the possibility that they found it full. Nope. Not going there.

I head for my room and pick up my phone. I can live every day knowing that Ginger and I are happy together, but there are things I have to fix.

I take a deep breath and text my brother. *'Any progress in finding Ellison? Or the money?'*

I'm starting to worry that Brady's lack of information on Ellison is suggesting that Brady himself is deeper into this than he will admit.

What does that mean for me? It doesn't look good. I give my brother money, money that's not mine, and he flees the country.

Of course it looks like I planned it. Or at least that I was in on it.

Checking the phone again, I see that he's not answering. Maybe it's the middle of the night wherever he is.

I don't want to think about Brady anymore.

I stare at the kids' spreadsheet of ideas for a while. Honestly, as I think about it, the idea of having the production company film a show here over the summer is growing on me. I wouldn't say this aloud to anyone, but if I offered to be in it, it would sell. They could push it through committee by saying I'd be in it and let the whole idea ride on my part.

I know. It sounds gross and arrogant to say so. I don't mean it that way. I just watch the numbers. I'm familiar with how success is measured for things like this. Honestly, I know most actors have a short shelf life, and I'm popular enough right now that this is the time to capitalize on my success.

Pulling up the Chamberlain website, I see photos of what the place looks like in seasons that are, in all honesty, a lot more appealing than winter. Not that it's not beautiful now. It is. But it's stark, not warm, emotionally or temperature-wise.

I type up a few ideas. Playing a character on a popular show gives me a window into the entertainment industry, but acting as a producer for the last few years has opened a few more doors. I understand how and why things work better than I understood them when I was younger, playing roles and being directed, showing up when I was scheduled and staying in my lane. It's been eye-opening and, really, pretty fun to learn so much more about the industry.

The next morning, I wake up to a long string of texts from Brady.
'Are you up? I need to talk.'
'Ty, it's serious.'
'The money's gone.'
I want to bang my head against the wall. No, I want to bang Brady's head against the wall. But that's not helpful, so I keep reading.
'I know the money was already gone from your accounts, but now it's gone from my accounts, too.'
I feel like my stomach is full of lead weights. Oh, no. I'm not surprised, but I'm sad. I was right. Brady lied when he told me Ellison took off with all the money, leaving both of us in the dust. Brady did have access to the missing funds. Until now. I trusted Brady, and I shouldn't have. He, in turn, trusted Ellison, and look where that got him. Wherever he's hiding out—likely somewhere a lot warmer than here—with an empty bank account. And no way to leave, according to the rest of the texts.

I stare at the phone, reading the messages that follow, the wheedling ones that beg for a little help, the angry ones that hurl blame everywhere but at himself, the penitent ones that I don't believe for a second.

I feel simultaneously better and worse. Better because there is no longer any reason to wonder. Brady lied. He cheated. He stole money. He conned me and the Fleming brothers (but mostly me, because I'm the one who stupidly believed him). He lied again and again, and he dragged me through the muck of his mess. I no longer have to wonder if I can believe him, and there's some relief there. I have my answer. He lied. And I never have to give him my trust again.

No more question, at least about blame.

And I feel worse. I can't pretend the blame for this mess falls to some faceless mystery partner. I can't tell the Flemings that it came as a complete shock to me. I can't ever erase my name from this awful chain of events.

I send an email to the Flemings, telling them straight up that I was wrong about Brady, and that I no longer held out any hope that we could recover the production company's money without law enforcement's efforts. I basically told them, "Here's all I know about Brady and Ellison; release the hounds."

It's not a great feeling. I hate that I was duped, and by someone I've always loved and admired. And I hate that it's official. I can't respect Brady. Ever again.

Lying in my bed, staring at the dorm room ceiling, I roll through all these events and the emotions attached to them. And of course, I think of Ginger. It's not long before I realize that the way I feel now, the anger-sadness-humiliation-disbelief-shame must be how Ginger felt when we ended. Before. The way Brady has kicked my trust around must feel exactly the way she felt when she discovered me with Janie.

I send her a quick text. *'Thanks for giving me another chance to prove I'm not the worst. I hope today is a happy day for you.'*

I SEND another email to the Fleming brothers. I want to show them proof that I've been working on new ideas, rebuilding some of the trust that my stupidity cost.

"You both went to school here. You know how beautiful and camera-ready the campus looks. You're both familiar with this place and how fantastic it is. I'd love to get together to pitch a show idea that we could film here, at Chamberlain. In the summer, obviously. Something along the lines of Haven Lake, but about kids during a school year instead of summer camp. Secret societies and pledging and auras of mystery surrounding generations-old traditions. Tunnel systems. Ghosts. People love this stuff. We could give the project to a team of writers, cast in June, film for six weeks in summer and have a season's worth of material in the can before classes start up again in the fall. If you think it would help to sell it through, I'm willing to play a teacher for a season."

I don't mention that I'd do it without pay. I need to keep at least one piece of this on the bargaining table. "Let me know if you'd like to have a conversation about it."

I've written up my ideas for the project for Dr. Moreau, also. I'll wait to request another meeting with her until I hear back from the Flemings. I don't want to waste her time, and also, she's just intense enough that I'm not eager to hurry myself into another meeting in her office.

I don't have anything to grade. I don't have any messages I need to answer.

When Dr. Moreau gave me limited access to student information and accounts, I didn't realize that she may have done it to protect me. Ginger told me that she's inundated with emails from parents and spends a couple hours every week just pacifying all the people who are worried about their kids—academically, physically, emotionally.

Makes me wonder if my parents reached out to my teachers to check on me when I was in school.

They probably did, but they were quiet about it.

But nobody has email access to me here. And it's kind of great. I imagine at least a few of the students in my classes and in my dorm have told their parents that I'm here, and statistically, at least a few of those parents are fans of Enforced. But I'm not getting approached by any of them.

I glance at my inbox one more time before closing up my computer for the night, hoping to get at least a "we'll take a look and talk about it" message from the Flemings. But the message I find isn't from them.

It's from Janie.

"My agent wants us to do a photo op together. Where will you be for the next three weeks? Will you have your people reach out to my people and set something up? Please don't make this a bigger deal than it is. It's good for both of us to appear happy in our new situations, and your success fuels mine and so on.

XX

J"

I sigh. It only takes a second to recognize, thanks to all kinds of therapy, that it's a sigh of tiredness, not longing. I tell myself I don't miss Janie, and now I see that it's true. I don't. And if I compare pretty much any aspect of Janie's personality to Ginger's, there is zero danger that I'll turn back toward Janie.

Now that I think about it, I can't imagine turning away from Ginger for any reason. I feel a tiny seed taking root in my brain, though. A problem. When June arrives, I leave Chamberlain. There will be no more reason for me to stay.

Unless I can get the Flemings to do a school show here.

It won't help if I beg. So I aim for two birds with one stone and send a message to my agent Tanya. It's easy to ask her to get with Janie's guy to set up a friendly photo shoot, but even easier if Janie's traveling. Which she might be. I heard she was doing some promotion.

There's a prickly sensation in my brain, like I'm remembering something I'm supposed to deal with. But I don't know exactly what that is. My brain has just about hit its limit these last few days. Too much excitement. Too much feeling.

I try to shake it off.

I let Tanya know that I can pretty easily get wherever in New England over a weekend if she can set something up.

"And while you're at it," I tell her, "I'd love for you to read over the message I sent the Flemings. I copied you on it. I'm pitching an 'angsty, dangerous mysteries of the rich, hot teen boarding school' show. I already have a perfect location. It's a great idea that will only sound greater when it has your vote."

I know I still have the skills to make things happen. I still have the vocabulary to convince people to do what I want them to do. But I feel like the whole exercise is an excuse. Sure, filming the show at Chamberlain would check lots of boxes: bring in revenue for the school to please Moreau, new project with an expanded viewership to please the Flemings, new acting experience for me. But the most important part in my mind? It keeps me near Ginger for a few more months, and that's all I can manage to care about today.

23

GINGER

The days leading up to my meeting with Portia Bancroft fly by. Maybe it's the anticipation, but I think it's more likely Ty. The time I spend with Ty always moves too fast. I see him everywhere, and I love it. He's in the hallway during breaks. He comes down to my classroom for lunch. We eat at Lola's twice a week, unless he can talk me into going more often. Grading and planning and snuggling and watching movies fill up so many of our non-class hours, and it makes every minute feel immediate. I have not felt so present in my own life in years.

"This is the best school year ever," I tell him one night as he's leaving my apartment.

"Feels like it used to," he murmurs into my hair as he wraps his arms around me.

"Better now," I say.

He pulls back and smiles at me. "Better how?"

"You want an alphabetical list?" I ask, a teasing smile on my lips.

He promptly kisses the smile away. It comes back, the way it always does these days.

"Do you have an alphabetical list?" he asks.

"No, but I could probably come up with one."

He laughs.

I say, "Mostly, I just feel more confident now. It's in part because of you, you know. So, I'm glad about that."

I'm holding back on saying more. I won't say the words that I really want to say. It's been five years since I told Ty Miller I loved him. The words always came easy to me. He never actually said it. He showed me, of course, that he loved me. But for some reason, the words were just never there. And that's fine. But I'm not saying it again, not before he does. So maybe I'm not ever saying it again.

I can live with that, especially since I know this won't last forever. He's gone in a few months. Not that that part is easy. My guts twist when I think about him leaving. I hate the thought of him all the way across the country. But for now, I'm so happy that he's here. In my doorway. Kissing me goodnight.

"Tomorrow is the day I'm doing my Burlington trip," I tell him. He looks surprised. And is that a wince? "Didn't I tell you? I'm heading out right after classes. I thought I'd get a sub, or have Perla take my classes, but then I remembered that it's not too far away, and I can do my job. Even when I'm this excited."

I should breathe, or let him say something, but I'm just so eager to share. "I have an interview with my favorite new author. She wrote this transformative book that I keep reading over and over, kind of obsessively. And she's going to interview with me." I let out a giddy laugh.

He still looks a little stunned. It's fine. He doesn't need to say anything. I have words enough for both of us. "I still keep that book review blog. Remember that I used to do that? Yeah. I still do. This is the most excited I've been for a long time. I secretly think she and I are going to be best friends." I wiggle my fingers together like I'm making adorable nefarious plans.

He smiles, but honestly, he looks a little sick.

"Have a great day tomorrow, and I'll be home on Saturday. Let's get dinner at Lola's. Early. I'm going to have so much to tell you about." I give him a wave.

He just nods and waves as he walks out the door. I guess I talk too much, because sometimes Ty doesn't get in any words at all. Maybe he doesn't always have anything to say. It's possible. A bit of a foreign idea to me, because I never shut up. At least lately, with him. I have been giddy with word-flow. Maybe it's a sign that we make a great pair.

I tidy up the apartment, wash the dishes we used tonight, and go into my room to finish putting together my overnight bag. I'm only taking an extra pair of jeans and another sweater, plus a pair of pajamas. It's all just backup. I can definitely come back to Chamberlain right after we have our interview and she does her reading. We're scheduled for the half hour before it begins, but she might want me to meet up with her again after her signing. I mean, it's possible we'll get what we need in those thirty minutes, but if Portia Bancroft wants me to stick around so we can talk late into the night, I don't want to disappoint her by saying I have to leave. I can grab a room for the night if we stay up for hours, talking over cups of coffee and delicious pastries like new best friends.

I giggle to myself again. This is unusual for me. I'm not a giggler, in general. I laugh, but it's usually too loud. Lately, my laughing has gotten gentle and soft. Like my laugh is in love or something. I grin as I shove an extra pair of socks into the corner of my bag. I wash my face and brush my teeth and I can't stop smiling all through my bedtime routine. Portia Bancroft tomorrow, and Ty Miller every day after that. At least until June. And I'm not thinking about what happens after June. Not tonight. Because, like Portia says, "the stars will guide us to our destiny."

I sleep hard and wake up to the sound of my alarm. It's a relief that I didn't get that first-day anxiety that I used to have when I was starting school. Who am I kidding? I still get it. First day of each new semester, I get this anticipatory giddiness mixed with fear, and it's always a fight to fall asleep the night before. But today, I jump out of bed rested and excited.

I look out the window at the spots of light in the quad. There's an inch of new snow on the ground, so we're going with Protocol A, the snowy roads plan. That means I'll have the car packed before class, and I'll race the kids out the door after last period.

I shower quickly, pull on my luckiest pair of jeans and a sweater that makes me feel both warm and stylish.

I pull out the lecture materials that I put together for me and Perla to deliver to our classes, even though I decided to stay at Chamberlain today. I'll take Perla's classes and she can have a whole day to prepare and grade and sit with her feet up eating something delicious. This way, I have a favor that I can call in when I need it. Maybe for a day off with Ty. That's a nice thought. And today will be an excellent day— just some awesome chemistry and a ride into Burlington stand between me and meeting Portia Bancroft face to face.

I can't believe it.

The day goes perfectly. I should have known. The universe is aligned for me to get what I want. It's like Portia says in chapter ten: "When you keep those stars in your eyes, everything within your view shines in your favor."

In the car, I hook my phone into my ancient sound system and play the audio of the book. I bought it for myself yesterday, a gift for the road trip. The narrator begins the recording, saying, "Read for you by the author."

I feel chills run up my arms.

I'm hearing her voice. And I'm about to sit across the room from her, listening to this same voice. Within a couple of hours, I'll be sitting at a table with her. It's dizzying.

I wonder if she'll look like her book-jacket photo. A laughing face tilted at a drastic angle, mouth open, a straw hat and huge sunglasses obscuring the top half of her face, the picture is just vague enough that as I look at it, I can't tell at all how old she is or what her face looks like.. The picture is mostly of teeth and neck and artful reflections of a starry sky. It's a creative shot made to be that kind of glamourous that doesn't even care if we can recognize her.

Her voice is lovely. Soothing. Familiar.

Very familiar. I can anticipate when she's going to pause. I know how she's going to sound saying certain words. That's weird. I wonder if Portia Bancroft is a pen name. Maybe she's an actor who's done audiobook work before. I try to figure out why her cadence is so familiar, but eventually I give up, letting myself get swept into the lyrical beauty of the words.

I pull into the bookstore about ten minutes before our interview is scheduled. Perfect. Just enough time to hit the bathroom, swish a little mouthwash around, and touch up my lipstick.

The wind is crazy, but I manage not to blow away between my parking spot and the front door. I'm glad I wore my hair in braids so it behaves itself. I can see the corner where the table is set up for Portia's signing, a huge banner with her name on it and a giant blow-up of the book cover, dozens of chairs set up, and a few camera people flashing what must be marketing shots. Perfect. She's not waiting for me. A line of people has formed behind those velvet rope-things I've always thought of as cattle chutes. They must be waiting to be shown to the chairs.

I slip into the bathroom, do what needs doing, and walk back out into the store, anticipation and excitement filling me all the way up. I feel so great. Amazing, even. There's no more room for worry. In fact, I am so calm that I feel my shoulders relax. My breathing is a little fast, but eagerness explains that. I come around the corner of the shelves and I see her.

At least, I think it must be her I'm seeing. She's standing under a blow-up of that jacket photo. But something is wrong. Very wrong. Because I'm not watching some publisher's marketing team take a few snaps of Portia Bancroft posing behind a table at a book signing. I'm looking at Janie Banks, my former roommate, standing in a flowy kimono dress that is adorable, but completely wrong for the weather, staring adoringly up into the face of Tyson Perry Miller.

What?

Ty has his arm around her shoulders. A photographer is saying, "Tyson, just relax. You look very tense. That's it. Breathe. Portia, darling, you can dial back the gazing. You look a bit too eager. You're happy to see him, but you don't want to take a bite out of him."

I hear someone behind me mutter, "I'd take a bite out of him. Where's the line for that?"

What?

I don't know what is going on.

Portia Bancroft is supposed to be signing books tonight. Here. And she's supposed to meet me first, sit down with me and talk about her process, her inspiration, and her rise to success. Instead, Janie Banks is making yummy-faces at Ty.

Our ex.

I think I'm going to throw up.

I get it now. This is so not amusing. Portia Bancroft is, in fact, a pen name. Just like I thought in the car. For an actress who has probably done audio book recordings. But that's not why her voice was familiar.

No. This can't be happening.

Her voice is familiar from weeks and months of talking together in our shared apartment. Only an Olympic-grade emotional block could have kept me from recognizing her voice on that audio recording. An Olympic-grade emotional block I've been constructing for years.

I try to back away, to get out of the space, but people from the line have pressed forward to watch the photo shoot. I'm blocked out of the aisle by a wall of people taking pictures and videos on their phones. I try to escape to the other side, but I knock over a chair and somehow, even in this busy room, it calls everyone's attention. And I mean everyone.

In a split second, I see Ty notice me, freeze, and drop his arm from it's completely unnatural perch on Janie's shoulder.

I see Janie (Portia?) look over at me, gasp, and clap her hands. By the time she squeals, "Ginger? Oh, my stars! I hoped it was you. You're Ms. Rogers at Chamberlain? Oh, my stars!" I have made it only two steps closer to escape.

Janie-Portia has other ideas. She sprints as fast as her completely impractical rattan wedges allow, and nearly knocks me over in a giant hug. "Oh, my stars!" she says again, and I'm sure no human being under the age of eighty has said that phrase since 1978. Certainly not three times in fifteen seconds.

"Look at you!" she says, gripping my sleeves and searching my face. "You look exactly the same. I would have known you anywhere." She tugs on the end of one of my braids. "You're even still doing your hair the same way!" There is not a way to take that in which it's not insulting.

I glance back at Ty, who looks miserable.

Good.

He should.

Janie-Portia grabs my arm and drags me up to where Ty stands. "Y'all, get a shot of the three of us. We were all in college together. Ginger, get out of your coat. Come on. Ty, you on this side. Ginger, you stand right here. Oh, my stars, I can't believe it. What a sweet reunion!"

She's manic, laughing and pointing at photographers and giving directions, and I can't help but remember this is how she behaves when she's nervous. Her voice, almost unrecognizable from the one on the audio book recording, now sounds high-pitched and restless. Still very familiar.

I can't do anything but focus on breathing in and out. What is happening?

A photographer puts down her camera and looks at me. "Um, friend? Can you smile?"

He's asking me. Can I? Great question. I try, and very soon someone ushers me into the front row of seats. "You're the blogger with the interview? Portia will be right with you." The woman barely looks at me before she turns back to the real reason anyone's here.

The photographers get a few more shots of Janie and Ty, and then the woman who seated me waves them away.

"Thank you, thank you. If you'd like to stay for the event, you may join the line." She makes a gesture toward the back wall.

Janie trots back to me and slides into the chair beside me. I can't feel my legs. I must be in shock.

"Why didn't you tell me it was you?" She laughs. "You didn't even sign your full name. You just had to be all secretive, didn't you?" Her giggle is as fake as her nails and far less classy.

I mumble something about it being a surprise to see her here.

"You really didn't know? You couldn't tell I'm Portia? There's a picture of me on the book. On the wall. On buses from Montreal to Mexico City!" She gestures widely, and I see her glance over to see if anyone is still taking pictures. When she sees that there are no more photographers standing by, she says, "Come on. Let's go somewhere quiet."

She stands and pulls me out of my chair by my arm. Portia Bancroft is Janie Banks. Janie Banks is tugging me behind her. Portia-Janie calls to someone named Jean or Janene or maybe Jolene, and the woman who was giving orders snaps to attention.

"Find us somewhere we can be alone for a few minutes, will you?" she says, then turns back to me. "I can't believe it! What a fabulous twist of fate." She hugs my arm. I feel itchy in my sweater and I want to know where Ty went. Before I can do more than glance around, we're being moved through an Employees Only door and steered into what must be a manager's office.

"Oh, my stars," she says again as the door closes and we are left alone together. I finally figure out that this is a new trademark phrase for her, a way to use an antiquated saying to sell books.

I bet it works like a champ.

"Janie," I say, not sure how to continue.

"Portia," she corrects. "Now that I've been to a few big venues, not to mention weird little towns here and there and everywhere, people will make the connection. This photoshoot with Tyson will certainly help with that. Won't everyone be surprised? *You* sure were!" She laughs and I want to turn away. I want to leave.

She's not done. "But now that we're alone, I have to tell you that I knew it was you. I mean, how many people named Rogers teach chemistry?"

Does she think I have a number? Because I don't. I can't respond, but she doesn't seem to need me to say a word.

"And you still have that little book blog. I remember that you did that back in college."

I wonder if it's possible for her words to sound any more belittling. But she doesn't apologize. She doesn't seem to notice that she's said anything offensive. "I think I'm done being Janie Banks. If I do decide to act in another show, I'll call myself Portia. That way, I'll have two entries in IMDB. How cool is that?" She pauses for a breath, but I don't feel the need to tell her how cool that is.

"It's been so fun seeing people recognize me. It's like their two favorite celebrities, Janie and Portia, merge right before their eyes. Me and me!" She laughs like his is just the most delightful story, and she's been waiting for so long just to get a chance to tell it. To me.

Because she knew I was coming.

And she knew Ty was coming.

Did Ty know I was coming? If he knew, and he didn't warn me, well, that's a problem.

She's still talking. "The tour has been amazing. And somehow, the story that Portia and Janie are the same person hasn't broken wide open yet. But it will when these photos come out. Tyson is a champ for showing up here from, well, from wherever he's been hiding."

I nod. She doesn't seem to need more than that from me right now.

"And I'm glad he looks so good. I worried a little that he might have let himself go, after I ended things with him. And taking time off his filming schedule? I thought I might take one look at him and tell the photographers to forget it." She shakes her head.

How generous of her not to kick him out. How lucky for them both that he's still sufficiently handsome. I would like to throw up now.

"It's great to see you," she says now, dropping some of the insincerity from her voice. "You good?"

I can do nothing but nod. Does she really care if I'm good?

I can't sit in this office and make small talk. I decide to ask her my interview questions and pretend all this awkwardness away. "When did you start researching astrology and philosophy and psychology?"

I asked. I hope I'm keeping the judgment out of my voice. Because I know exactly what she studied in college, and none of this was that.

"Actually," she says, leaning over the desk, "and you're going to have to keep this off the record, I took a fortune-telling class." She nods as if I've asked her if she's serious. I didn't ask. I can tell she's perfectly serious.

"All this stuff? It's mostly linguistics and diction, you know? Give your words just enough mystique and shroud all the nouns and verbs in secrecy, and people will make their own connections." She does a little move with her hands that suggests mystery. "Nothing concrete. Everything a little covert."

I blink at her.

She's serious.

"And it really works. People read my words. They feel it however they're feeling it. They're comforted about their life and choices, and I look brilliant. So basically," she whispers as she leans farther across the office desk, "I don't have to say anything at all. Remember that line, *Align your spine and your mind* from chapter seven?"

I do remember that line. I have it highlighted in my paper copy. And my online copy.

She's grinning at me. "I just laughed and laughed when my editor told me I could keep it. It doesn't mean anything. I mean, obviously it doesn't. It's nonsense. But you would be shocked at how many people have sent me pics of their forearms tattooed with that line."

I might be shocked. Or not. I hope I can keep my face passive, but I'm feeling every inch the woman who seriously considered that very tattoo.

There's a knock at the door, and an apologetic face appears. "Ms. Bancroft?" a man says.

Janie-Portia bestows a gentle smile on him. "Yes?"

"It's time to get you all set up for the reading and signing." He gestures behind him.

I worry that she'll tell him we're not done, but she hasn't needed much from me in all the minutes we've been in the room. She doesn't need my consent now to stand up and walk out.

"Thanks for visiting with me, Ginger," she says. "I hope you've got plenty of material for your little article." I'm not sure if she's saying this for my benefit or for that of the store employee who stands holding the door for us. It doesn't matter. I don't answer.

She's not done talking to me—or at least talking *at* me. "I have a seat held at the front. You can sit there and avoid the crazy lines. People have been packing in here for hours."

It's not a question. I don't need to answer. But I give a little hum that might mean yes.

I don't mean yes.

I'm not staying another minute. As the store worker guides Portia-Janie around the bookshelves and into her spotlight, I pull on my coat and walk out the door.

24

TY

I stand close enough to the door that I can't miss her leaving. I've been here since the two of them stepped into that back hallway as soon as the photographers were finished. I'm not surprised Ginger leaves the store before Janie gives her speech. I'm only surprised that she stayed this long. Ginger is a pretty forgiving person —I mean, she's forgiven me, and I broke her heart—but this is a big ask, even for her.

It's hard to imagine how she feels right now. I can't blame her for being angry.

I'm sure she's shuffling thorough every piece of information in her mind, trying to put it all in a logical order and arrangement. Janie. Portia Bancroft. Me. The press.

If I knew earlier, before this morning, that she was planning to be here, maybe I could've come up with a believable, reasonable explanation for everything that happened tonight. But it was too much to process. Too impossible to explain.

Maybe.

Or maybe I was being a coward.

If I knew that she read Janie's ridiculous book, maybe I could have given her a hint that Portia Bancroft wasn't exactly what the hype made her into. But would I? I don't want to hurt Janie's career. I don't want anyone to disrespect what she's created—and she's created a lot. New persona, huge following, bestselling book that actually connects with hundreds of thousands of people, even though it says nothing at all.

But I didn't know that Ginger had read the book. Not until this morning. She may have mentioned it before, talked about being excited, but she never said what the book was. And I didn't stop her from coming because she was so excited. Or that's what I told myself. Now it seems so wrong, and it looks so cruel.

I could have tried to protect her. But how, and from what? From the past? From Janie's insensitivity? From disappointment? And I'm not chauvinist enough to think Ginger needs my protection.

But I knew about Janie, and Ginger didn't. When my agent Tanya set up the Janie photo shoot, she specifically asked me not to mention it to anyone, so I didn't. But I could have. I should have told Ginger.

I've messed up everything. Again. I did something stupid that Janie asked me to do, and it hurt Ginger. Again. How could I be so foolish? Again? Have I learned nothing?

I don't know what Janie said to Ginger during their interview in that back room, but whatever it was, Ginger's had enough. She's not staying around to hear anything else from Janie. I follow her outside and call her name.

She doesn't answer. I holler a little louder, jogging to catch up with her. Is she crying? Did Janie make her cry? Even though I told my agent this was the last interaction I was willing to have with Janie, if she made Ginger cry, she will hear from me.

"Ginger," I say again. "Wait."

Maybe it's the wind, carrying my voice away from her.

Maybe she's avoiding me. Maybe I'm the one who made her cry.

I reach her just as she arrives at her car. There's no more space for her to walk away from me, so she spins to face me.

She isn't crying. Her face is composed, but I can see fire burning in her eyes. She stands in front of me, angry and disappointed, and she has never been more beautiful.

"I can explain," I say.

She closes her eyes and takes a breath before staring at me again. "I believe you probably can." Then she turns back to the door of her car and unlocks it.

She's inside before I realize she doesn't want me to explain this. She doesn't want to hear any excuses from me.

I stop her from pulling the door closed, but she isn't looking at me. She puts her bag on the passenger seat and buckles herself in.

"Can I ride back to Chamberlain with you?" I ask.

She shakes her head, looking straight ahead.

"Are you okay to drive?" I ask.

Now she faces me. The glare she shoots me drops the already arctic temperature out here a few degrees. "I'm fine," she says, reaching for the door and pulling it closed.

I step out of the way because, right now, I doubt that she'll shed a tear if she runs over my feet. She backs out of the parking spot and drives away.

When I was leaving Ginger's place this morning and she told me she was coming to Burlington tonight, I understood. And I felt sick. But I didn't explain, because I promised I wouldn't. I promised Janie through Tanya, and I can't mess anything else up with my agent. She's the only one entirely on my side, professionally.

I would give anything to go back to this morning and break that foolish promise to Janie. Because who cares about Janie? Ginger is everything.

Janie's transformation into a personal-development author has been so far removed from me. I could not possibly care less about how she's "expanding her creative expressions," as she says. But apparently, according to Tanya (and Janie's own agent, who gives Tanya her information), part of Janie's final alteration into Portia is that *we* appear to be okay. Not okay-together. Okay-apart. That our separation is friendly. That we wish each other nothing but success. I'm all for that. Success is exactly what I wish for her. So I agreed to meet her for this photo opportunity. It was seamless, and there's nowhere for the press to go with our story other than that two midlist celebrities can still be polite to each other after their divorce. It's not a story at all. Just the way I like it.

Sure, it was awkward to stand there with her in front of the pipe-and-drape backdrop. Painfully so. Janie seemed to forget the part she was supposed to be playing, and she looked at me like we were having a screentest audition. She stroked my arms. She gazed up at me. She was pushing for chemistry. Too bad for her, there is not a drop of chemistry between us anymore. Not a hint. Not an atom.

And I don't miss it.

As soon as I got to the venue, Janie told me that her interview tonight was with Ginger. She knew. She didn't tell Ginger because she wanted the shock value of us all being in the room together. Something else for her to feel superior about.

When Ginger arrived, Janie went full hostess-mode, inviting her to stand in a picture with us, making sure Janie herself was in the middle, which I can only trust will show up illustrating the chapter of her autobiography where she explains how she came between Ginger and me.

I wonder for a minute how she'll choose to tell that story. Will any of us come out of that looking anything but awful? Not that it matters how I look to Janie's adoring public. But I don't want anyone dragging Ginger into the gossip.

It was awful, and it will continue to be awful, and I could have stopped it. I didn't. And Ginger is absolutely right to walk away from me.

I rub my head where my pulse is throbbing. I'm still standing in the parking lot, and only now do I realize how cold it is.

Calling for a car to drive me back to Chamberlain, I duck back inside the bookstore to wait where it's warm. I keep my head down, standing in a corner with a book in my hands and my back to the crowd. Nobody bothers me. Nobody notices me at all, because everyone in the room is absorbed with Janie. With Portia. With the presentation going on across the store. I hear her using her carefully curated hippie voice, full of breath and meaningful pauses, to convey the deep meaning of her empty words. I feel a little sorry for her audience until I remember that they're actually crazy about her. And her words. They don't seem to care that the entire book says, well, nothing. Somehow it means something to them.

That can't be a bad thing. It's just not for me.

The car arrives and I step outside. When I buckle myself into the back seat, the driver eyes me in his mirror. "Anyone ever told you that you look like that actor? What's his name?"

Not this. Not tonight. I don't reply.

"Um, he was in that show with the guy, in the place? You know the one?"

He's looking at me in the mirror, but he doesn't seem to expect an answer. He pulls out of the parking lot, glancing into the mirror now and then, before he shouts, "Brad Pitt. That's the guy. You look like him. But younger."

This could have gone worse. I'm relieved he doesn't actually recognize me. I'm not thrilled to be Tyson Perry Miller just now. I'd rather be Ty.

"That's flattering. Thanks. He's great. But I'm just a high school teacher, man," I tell him, and pull out my phone. I call Ginger, but her phone sends me right to voicemail. She doesn't answer when she's driving. Which is good. I want her to be safe. I send a text.

'Can we talk tonight when we both get back?'

She doesn't answer that, either, of course. But I send another one, just so she knows I'm thinking about her.

'I want to talk to you, please.'

'I'm sorry about how that all went.'

Maybe she'll answer while she's at a stoplight. Maybe she's looking at the messages right now. Or maybe she'll grab a drink and fill up her car with gas before she drives out of the city. I wait, staring at the dark screen of my phone, until we're climbing up the winding road into the snowy Vermont mountains, and then I close my eyes for the ride back to Chamberlain.

25

GINGER

It's late. It's too late, but I phone Joey anyway.

She answers with a groggy, "Hello?"

"Sorry. Can you let me in?" I ask. "I'm at your front door."

It's only seconds before she pulls the door open, waving me in the apartment and then wrapping me in her arms. She stands there, hugging me around the waist, and says nothing.

Joey is a good friend. I hug her back and don't move until she lets go.

She takes me by the hand, and we walk into her kitchen, where she sets a kettle of water on to boil and puts a tin box full of tea bags and hot chocolate packets in front of me. She may not have food, but she usually has tea. And cocoa. I reach in and pull one out without looking at it, tossing it onto the table next to the mug she sets down.

"So," she says, "I take it that tonight didn't go great?"

I lay my head on the table. I'm so tired. I probably should have driven straight here, but I couldn't do it. I followed twisty back roads and drove through forested hills for hours. Until my tank was almost empty. Until my tears were almost dried up.

Joey lets me lie there for a couple of minutes. When the water boils, she pours it into my mug and starts the tea steeping. With her fingers, she brushes the runaway hairs off my face and tucks them into my braid.

After a minute, she speaks in her soft, gentle voice.

"Remember what Portia says? 'You can't see the stars until the darkness comes.' I think you're there."

From my vantage point, cheek against the surface of her table, I give Joey a look, hopefully one that communicates just how little I care about what Portia says.

But I cared when she was Portia. I cared immensely. Now that she's Janie with a new name and an artsy headshot, it's hard to keep buying into the babble.

"What does that even mean?" I ask, my words muffled by the fact that only half my face is moving. The other half has become part of the furniture, I guess.

She reaches over and gives my arm a gentle caress, halfway between a scratch and a tickle. "You know," she says. "Perspective. Contrast. Openness." She rubs her nose with her other hand. "I guess."

"It kind of means nothing, doesn't it?" I ask.

She smiles. "Probably."

She waits, and I'm glad. I have a big story with a whole lot of dramatic details to tell her, and I love that she can be patient.

When I'm ready to sit upright, I suggest we move to the couch. Joey's couch came with the apartment; while most of us have upgraded our furniture, she's still very much a first-year teacher. We sit down and she pulls my feet onto her lap and holds them there, wrapping a blanket across my legs.

"You are going to wonder if I'm making this up," I warn her. "Trust me. If I were making it up, it would be a lot funnier. And more things would explode."

And I tell her. About the familiarity of the narrator's voice. And the vagueness of the author photograph. And the shoot I walked in on, and the interview that was not much of an interview. I tell her I walked out of the bookstore before the event started, and I see her wince, an acknowledgement that I missed out on something that had seemed so important to me only hours ago.

She nods and runs her hands over the blanket covering my legs. She makes appropriately shocked faces when they're called for. She shakes her head in disbelief. Joey is the perfect audience for something like this, because I know with her artist's eye, she's playing it all visually as I give her details. And in her version, I'm the main character. I'm the hero. I'm blameless. And I win.

What do I win, though?

When I stop talking, she waits for a minute before she starts asking follow-up questions.

"So, you drove away and left Ty there?"

I nod. "He got himself there. I'm sure he managed to get himself back here before his curfew." I have no energy for spite. The words come out soft and matter-of-fact.

I look at Joey. "Why didn't he tell me he was going to meet her?"

"I guess he didn't know you were doing the same thing." Joey pats the blanket over my legs again.

I shake my head. "He knew. But that's not what I mean. Ty and I are dating. We're together. Why would he not tell me he was meeting his ex-wife?"

"Obviously neither one of us can answer that," Joey says. "But try this: What's the worst possible reason for him to keep that from you?"

I answer immediately. "He wants to get back with her."

She nods. "Okay. You saw them together. Does he want to get back together with Janie?"

I only have to remember his stiffness when she held on to his arm and gazed up at him. "No. He's not interested. She scares him."

"Okay," Joey says again. "Next-to-worst reason?"

I rub my eyes. "He wants to humiliate me."

Joey's voice is soft. "Does he?"

I shake my head. "He felt awful. If anything, he looked more embarrassed than I was."

She nods again. "Okay. What was his excuse? What did he tell you?"

I sigh. "That he can explain."

"Do you think he can?"

I nod. "Yeah, I think he's probably got a reasonable explanation for the whole thing. In fact, he didn't even know I was planning to go to the Portia Bancroft signing until this morning. Yesterday morning. Whatever. I didn't exactly give him a lot of time to clear things up. But he didn't stop me. He didn't say anything."

She nods again. "That's bad. Really bad. Do you want to give him a chance to clear things up?"

I didn't, not a few hours ago when I was in the middle of it all and feeling like a dummy. But now I follow Joey's lead and ask myself, really letting the answer settle in my heart.

"I do."

She claps her hands together once and nods. "Where is he now?" Joey asks.

Shrugging, I say, "Sleeping in his dorm room, I imagine."

She shoves my legs off her lap. "Then you know what you need to do. Put your coat on. You're knocking on a window."

I convince Joey to walk across campus with me, to come to the window. I realize the irony of me, a grown woman, going to a dorm room window and having a conversation with a boy who had to be inside by curfew. I'm not a bit confident that I know what to say.

"Do you know which room is his?" Joey asks as we stand there in the icy darkness. I realize that I don't. I have no idea. I stare at her. She whisper-laughs. "What do you want me to do? I can barely see over the ledge."

I shake my head and point at the side of the dorm building. "I am definitely not staring into every room to see if the dude sleeping inside it happens to be one of Us Weekly's hottest Hollywood stars under thirty."

"Okay," Joey says. "Maybe only the ones with lights on?"

I look around. "We're getting fired, aren't we?" I ask.

She shrugs. "Only if we get caught."

We hear the sound of a window opening above our heads. I back away from the building to look up.

A kid in a hoodie with messy hair leans out a second-floor window. The window beside him slides open.

The first kid leans way out, and hands something across to his neighbor then starts to duck back inside his room.

I make a "*psst*" sound. The boys both look down and see us standing in the snow. I point at them. "Creeping Death," I say.

As though it's a magic code word that unlocks a secret door, the first boy releases his hold on his window sill. "Oh, hey, Ms. Rogers."

I look at him again and recognize his face, although he's way more rumpled than he ever was in my AP chem class last year. "Dixon," I say.

The kid in the other window, now with his arms full of cat, asks, "How do you know about Creeping Death?"

I point to myself. "Huge Metallica fan," I say.

Beside me, Joey whispers, "What is happening right now?"

"Negotiations," I whisper back.

"Metallica? And what is he holding?"

I don't answer her. Addressing the boys on the second floor, I say, "Which window is Dr. Miller's?"

Both boys shake their heads. "We promised we wouldn't tell anyone," Dixon says.

"I'm not anyone," I say. "Just point."

The other kid says, "First floor. Last one on the right. But you didn't hear it from me." The window on his other side slides open and he hands the cat across the ledge to his neighbor. I turn to Joey.

"I've got this," I tell her.

"Oh, no," she says, shaking her head. "I've paid the price of admission, and I'm not leaving before the show's over."

She's grinning, and I'm pretty sure she's joking.

I say, "Thank you for being here with me, but it's time for you to go home."

She gives me a squeeze. "And you'll tell me all the relevant plot points later? Over coffee and a muffin?"

I nod. "Definitely. I won't leave out any of the important parts."

As she turns and walks away, she says over her shoulder, "I think you're going to have to explain some of it to me."

I imagine she's right.

Walking close to the building, I head for the last window on the right.

26

TY

I hear the taps, but I don't recognize that they're at my window until the second set. Tap-tap-tap.

I slip my fingers between two slats of my blinds and peek out. When I see Ginger standing there, in the dark, in the wind, in the middle of the night, outside my dorm room, I pull the cord and raise the blinds. I open my window and lean out.

My words come out as a sigh of relief. "You made it home," I say. Obviously.

She nods.

"I waited. For a while. On your front step."

It's true. I waited. But the words don't explain that from the second I returned to campus until the last moment I could walk away, okay *sprint* away, and be inside Rowan Hall before curfew, I sat on her concrete step, my back to her door, waiting and hoping and worrying about why it took so long for her to come back. I was so cold. I'd do it again if there was any chance of fixing what I broke.

"Are you okay?" I ask her.

She nods again.

"Can I explain?" I ask, my head and shoulders leaning out the window. I want her to step closer, but she doesn't.

She shifts her feet in the snow. "I think you can," she says. "And maybe you should, but I don't need you to do it right now."

This gives me a combination of relief and confidence. She trusts me. And I don't have to talk about Janie while I'm leaning out of a window. I don't want to talk about Janie. I want to talk about Ginger.

"What do you need me to do right now?" I ask.

She doesn't say anything. I don't know if she's thinking about how to answer me, or picking her way through a possible list of responses, or something else entirely.

I wait.

"I changed my mind," she says. The words come out in a cloud of frost.

I feel like I've been punched in the stomach. By a bear.

Oh, no. She could mean anything, but I'm afraid I know. She's changed her mind about us. About being together.

When I can breathe again, I say, "Okay," even though nothing about this feels okay. But what else am I supposed to say?

She nods. "I know what I said." Then she stops again, hugging her arms around herself.

I need her to keep talking. I need to know which of the things she said. What is she talking about? I lean a little farther out the window, trying to get closer to her. Trying to close some of this distance between us. Maybe then I'll know what she wants from me. What I can do to make up for this terrible night.

Finally, she shuffles her feet again and clears her throat.

"I know I told you we had to take it slow, but I don't want that anymore."

My body is a little ahead of my brain, because by the time I register what she's saying, I'm exhaling a huge, relieved breath. That could not have gone better. I grin.

"Don't move," I say. "Wait right there." I pull my head back into my room and then lean out again. "I mean, please wait for me. I'm coming out."

I tug on a hoodie and stuff my feet into the first pair of shoes I come across. I'm not even subtle as I throw my door open and run through the corridor and out of Rowan Hall.

She didn't move. She's here, standing in the little puddle of light from my bedroom window, her posture still and expectant, her face wiped free of makeup, a few strands of hair, loose from her braids, fluttering around her head in the breeze.

It is so cold.

I slow my steps enough that I'm not running at her. I don't want to look like I'm on the attack.

Walking a few feet closer to her, I hold out my hand. An appeal. On offering. A wish.

She looks from my hand to my face and back to my hand before she reaches toward me and takes my fingers in hers.

"I know mixed messages are the worst," she says in a whisper. "I don't want to be confusing. But I've regretted that stupid thing about taking it slow since about ten seconds after I said it."

Holding both her hands, I step closer. She does the same, and our foreheads touch. "You have no idea how happy I am to hear that," I say.

A little laugh escapes her, but I can hear fragility in it.

Our heads still together, I say, "I never want to make you cry again."

Her inhale shudders a bit, that shaky breath left over after tears. I pull both of her hands against my chest. "Ginger, I love you."

I didn't plan to say it. I've never said those words to her before. Not any of the times I've thought them.

It was unplanned, but I love the taste of the words in my mouth. "I love you," I say again, and I pull back a little. I want to see her face. I want her to see I'm serious.

"I'm not sure what you mean," she tells me. "I don't know how to believe you."

I lean closer, shifting my hands to cover hers. I whisper to her, and my words come out covered in clouds.

"You know the nights when sleep just won't come? You know that feeling of forcing yourself to stay in bed, just in case you might fall asleep? For hour after awful hour? And then the sky begins to lighten? First it turns from purple to blue, then it gets a little brighter and brighter until you know it's going to happen, that the sun's going to come up? And the day is a new one and it won't be so bad? Ginger, I love you like the sunrise."

I can't tell if I hear a laugh or a sob, but when I look at her face, I see it's both. She lets her tears fall as she smiles at me. When she wiggles her hands out of mine, she wraps her arms around me and says, "I love you, too. Like the sunrise."

I hold her face in my hands and kiss the trail of tears on either side of her mouth. She closes her eyes and lets her head tilt back, relaxing into my touch. I kiss the side of her mouth again, feeling her smile unspooling beneath my lips. One hand moves to the base of her neck, the other to her back as I press kiss after kiss into her mouth. She slides her hands into my hair and pulls me closer, like she can't get enough of me. Just like I can't get enough of her.

We only pull away when we hear cheering and clapping coming from Rowan Hall. Every room on this side of the building has lights on and blinds open, several boys pressing their faces against each window, watching the show Ginger and I unwittingly put on for them.

I hear Nam say, "Guys. Leave them alone. Give them some privacy."

Joel shoves him. "No way. Look how much we're learning about chemistry." The boys cheer some more.

Ginger ducks her head and laughs. I take a bow. "Go to bed," I say, not caring at all that they're not going to listen to me, much less obey my arbitrary commands.

When I feel a gentle pressure against my calf, I look down to see a mangy white cat circling my ankles. I reach down and pick it up, shuddering at the contact. Attached to a shoelace tied around its neck is a bottle cap with "CD" written on it in marker.

York leans out his window and says, "Creeping Death approves of you two." This is met with another round of applause and cheering. I set the matted cat back on the ground and it slinks toward a rowan tree in the corner of the building. We watch it climb the trunk and then leap onto the window ledge, where it slips into my still-open window.

Oh, gross.

I shudder, imagining fleas. Lice. Vermin of all kinds.

Ginger thinks the shiver is because I'm cold, so she wraps her arms around me to warm me up. I'm not going to tell her she's mistaken. I mean, it's frigid out here, and it feels amazing to be in her arms. And thoughts of Ginger are so much more pleasant than thoughts of whatever that cat has just carried into my room.

"I'm out past curfew," I whisper into her hair. "Walk me home?"

She nods. "Got to keep up appearances, Mr. Miller."

Arms wrapped around each other, we walk to the door, which of course is locked tight. And my key is in my room, probably being batted under the bed by the filthy, illegal dorm cat.

I whisper-shout, "Someone come let me in," before I take Ginger into my arms again and carry on where we left off.

I love Chamberlain Academy.

27

GINGER

I knew I liked teaching. I had no idea how much I'd love it when it means working in the same building as Ty. He comes to my classroom on breaks, or I go up to his. Sometimes we meet in the stairway like teenagers. I have come to love the stairway.

It is a far more romantic stairway than I would have supposed.

Over the years when I was without him, watching episodes of his new show over and over just to catch that look in his eyes, reading every tabloid news item that mentioned him, stalking his social media profiles, I could never get enough of looking at his face.

I can still never get enough of looking at his face. But now I get to watch him looking at me, too. I get to see him smile, just for me. I watch him reach for me. I feel his hands on me.

One day in late March, we get one of those weirdly warm, magical days the locals refer to as "false spring." I hold my afternoon classes outside, and I'm not alone. I see that lots of teachers have ditched the inside lesson plans and are winging it, just like me.

When I release the last class, I sit on a stone bench and turn my face up toward the sun. Eyes closed, I soak in every bit of warmth, knowing it can't last.

Loving it anyway.

I give a start as a hand touches my shoulder. "I was just going to kiss you," Ty whispers, "but I didn't want to risk getting punched."

"Have I ever punched you?" I ask, taking his hand and pulling him down to sit beside me.

"You probably wanted to once or twice," he says.

I shake my head, eyes closed and face tipped to the sun. "I will never admit to such a thing."

I feel his arm go behind me, and I make a humming sound of happiness. "This is a pretty good day."

Ty leans close to my ear and whispers, "Can I try to make it even better?"

I open my eyes and sit up straighter. "Right here?" I ask, trying to look appropriately shocked.

"At Lola's," he clarifies.

"This isn't about kissing," I say.

He shakes his head. "Not entirely. I want to tell you something."

"Just tell me now," I say.

"Call it my dramatic tendencies, but I want to keep it a surprise a little longer."

That's cute, I have to admit it. "How about a hint?"

"I'm sticking around a few more months after the semester is over. Want to spend the summer with me?"

I laugh. "Are you kidding? Of course I do. Especially if you keep taking me to dinner at Lola's."

"Consider it part of the deal."

He takes one of my braids in his hand and kisses my cheek.

I tuck my head into my favorite space between his neck and shoulder. "I suppose I accept this much of the story," I say, smiling and sighing. "But I hate to wait for the rest until dinner. And it's a shame to go inside on a perfect day like this."

"We can wait until the sun goes down, for dinner and for the rest of the news," he says, dropping another kiss on my cheek.

But it gets cold long before the sun goes down. We grab jackets and head down to Lola's, running into Hank and Dexter and Joey on the way. Turns out Ty had invited them, too.

Lola feeds us falafel and yellow rice, baba ghanoush, the most perfectly pillowy pita, and a salad that whispers hints of a summer to come. She really must be bribing someone for these tomatoes.

When we're fully satisfied from the amazing meal, Ty says, "I have some pretty great news to tell you."

Joey glances at me, her eyebrows raised, a look of "why did I not get a warning?" on her face. I give her a little shrug to tell her I don't know what the good news is. At least not all of it.

"Fleming Brothers productions will be filming a new show this summer, right here at Chamberlain. They're coming in a month to hold auditions, if any of you want to be in it. It's going to be amazing. And by that, I mean audacious and over the top, full of beautiful people and meme-ready one-liners. They're paying the school handsomely for the privilege of filming here, and it means I get to stay a little longer."

He squeezes my hand under the table.

Everyone says their own versions of congratulations, and the guys ask their questions. I smile and listen, but I don't say anything.

After a couple of minutes, Joey does a nod toward the restroom. I stand and follow her down the hall.

"You okay?" she says.

I force a smile. "Of course. How fun is this? Campus crawling with TV stars and film crews all summer? The best."

"And after?" she asks.

That's the question, isn't it?

After summer, what's going to happen between us?

She sees my eyes fill up and reaches over to hold my arm. "You haven't talked about it." It's not a question.

She nods as her answer to her own comment. "Okay. Dinner's over. You and Ty need to have some conversations."

I shake my head. "There's no hurry."

She squints at me. "I disagree. You don't need to have one more day of wondering or worry or sadness over this guy. He's crazy about you, and he doesn't want you to feel—" she pauses and gestures to my face, "this. Tell him you want to know his long-range plan."

Joey takes my hand and we walk back to the table, where she pulls on her coat and says, "Okay, boys. Time to go."

I sit beside Ty. My hand goes to his arm. "Wait," I say quietly, and we say goodbye to the others.

When they're gone and I'm sure I have myself all pulled together, I take a breath and speak. "Ty, I don't want to be demanding," I say, and the tears start to flow.

He doesn't respond. Probably because he's in shock. We have just gone from a celebration dinner to me in tears beside him.

"I'm not saying you have to make any long-term decisions right now," I say, sniffling and trying hard to pull myself together.

"I know you have basically unlimited career opportunities on the other side of the country, and I'm willing to do a long-distance relationship if you are. But I hate to think about you leaving."

"I'm not leaving," he says, his voice quiet. I'm sure he's trying to calm me so I don't make a scene in this public place.

I nod. "I know. It's only March. We have months left before you go. More months than I thought. I guess I'm just feeling how soon that end is coming, and I don't want to lose you."

He laughs.

He laughs?

"Did I say something funny?" I can feel a little spark of annoyance. "I'm bearing my soul here, mister."

"And I am very, very happy to hear it." He shifts a little, moving in his seat. He's reaching for something in his pocket. "But I meant what I said. I'm not leaving."

He pulls his hand from his jacket and there's something in his fist. He puts a tiny box on the table in front of me.

"Ginger," he says, and the way he's looking at me gives me the shivers all the way from my toes to the ends of my hair. "I have asked Dr. Moreau for a permanent place on the staff, and she took my request to the board. You are looking at the newest member of Chamberlain faculty."

I gasp. "No way."

He laughs and nods. "Way."

"That's amazing."

"It will be if I don't have to live in the dorm anymore," he says.

Now it's my turn to laugh. "I bet she'll offer you a faculty apartment."

He shakes his head. "I don't want one. I'm getting something better."

"A place in town?"

He nods.

"You've been looking at houses? To live in?" I can't keep the annoyance out of my voice at this. How is all of this a secret? And for how long?

He nods again.

"You want to stay off campus?" I can hear the surprise in my own voice.

"I do if you do," he says, sliding the little box closer to me.

Oh.

My mouth is definitely open. I look at the box. I look back at him. I point at it. "What is that?" I ask, but my voice comes out barely as a whisper.

"It's a box," he says.

I try to scowl, but I really can't make my mouth close, so I imagine the effect is not all that frightening.

He puts an elbow on the table and leans on his fist. "Aren't you at all interested in seeing what's in it?" he asks.

I shake my head.

He looks surprised now. "You're not?" A worried look settles on his face.

"See, if I don't look inside, I can imagine what might be in there," I say. "Once I open it, I will know for sure."

"Schrodinger's box," he says with a nod. "I promise there's not a cat inside. I've had more than enough of cats." He smiles that amazing smile at me. "I kind of think you'll like it," he says, and there's a hint of shyness there.

I slide the box off the table and open it up. Inside is a wide, silver band, filigreed with leaves. It's the most beautiful ring I've ever seen.

He reaches over and puts his hand around mine. "Can I put it on you?"

I nod, dumbstruck. He slides the ring onto a very important finger. It fits perfectly. And it looks magical. If a plant grew on my hand, it would look exactly like this.

"I love it," I say.

"I love you," he says back. "Ginger, I never want to go another day in my life without looking at your face and telling you I love you. I want you with me every day, and if you want that, too, I think we should get married."

I can feel another prickle of tears in my eyes, but this time, they're tears of happiness. "That's not actually a question," I say, my smile spreading wider by the second.

"And that's not an answer, but I'm getting the feeling we're reaching an agreement."

He shifts in his chair so he's facing me, looking right into my eyes. "Want to get married?" Ty asks, his fingers pushing a runaway hair behind my ear.

I nod my head. "Yeah. Do you?" I ask. He nods.

Then he's taking my face in his hands, drawing me close. As our lips meet, I feel certain that this is how I want to begin and end every day for the rest of our lives.

EPILOGUE

"Have you ever loved anything more in your life than this house?" Ginger asks me, her eyes shining. She has her hands clasped in front of her like they're holding her heart inside her body. Like if she let go, her excitement would burst a hole in her, making an escape.

"Yes."

She looks at me, shocked. "What do you mean, yes? How dare you?" she asks.

I hide my smile and give a little shrug. As if I don't care. I doubt she'll buy my act for long. "I've loved so many things more than this house. The stairway is narrow. The cellar smells like mud. The bricks on the fireplace—"

She interrupts me, a hand out as if to prevent my words from reaching her. "Stop right now," she says, "before you say something you're going to regret. Those bricks are everything to me."

I can't hide the smile now. "Everything?" I ask, and I know she can hear the teasing in my voice. "I thought the garden was everything. It can't all be everything, Ms. Rogers."

"See, now, that's where you're wrong. Again. It *can* all be everything. Including but not limited to the perfect tree-lined street, which, if I'm not mistaken, is called Green Leaf Lane. Who wouldn't want to live on Green Leaf Lane? Come on, man. Have you no soul at all?"

I wrap her in my arms. "I believe I have a bit of a soul, and it's all dedicated to answering your every wish. If you demand it, I will love this house almost as much," I drop my voice to a whisper and plant a kiss on her lips between each of the following words, "as I love you."

She pulls back and looks into my eyes. "I don't want you to settle. If you really don't love the cottage, we can keep looking."

Pretending to search her face, I say, "Can you say that again?"

"We can keep looking?" she says, as if she's unsure that's what I was asking for.

I shake my head. "Just 'cottage,' I mean."

She's grinning again. "Cottage," she says. Then in a whisper, her eyelashes fluttering. "Cottage."

"I'll admit it," I say, feigning resignation. "When it was only a house, I could take it or leave it. But now that I know it's a cottage, I'm not sure I'll ever be happy anywhere else."

She wraps her arms around my neck and pulls my face to hers. After a monumental kiss, she puts her hands on either side of my face and looks into my eyes again. "I promise, I'll do my best to make you happy everywhere. Anywhere."

I can't get enough of staring at her. Knowing that she's mine. I'm hers. We are ours.

But she's not finished. "And I really, really want to live here in this house—" she says, then stops, shakes her head, and revises, "—I mean, *cottage* with you forever." She tilts her head to the side, thinking. "Except when it's completely necessary to visit your fancy mansion in southern California. Then, I guess we can be happy there."

I clear my throat, nerves taking hold and making it hard to breathe. "What if I didn't have that fancy place anymore?" I ask.

She looks surprised. "You're selling your Burbank house?"

With a sigh, I say, "I'm thinking. Would you be totally disappointed if I did?"

She appears to be considering her answer, which I appreciate. I want to know the truth. Finally, she says, "I really can't imagine trying to fit into a life of palm trees and infinity pools. I wouldn't be sorry to stay here in Vermont forever." She takes my hand and I feel the truth of her words.

"I need to make things right," I say. Ginger knows what happened with Brady and Ellison. She knows they both disappeared and the money did, too. And she knows that although the Fleming brothers don't hold me responsible, I still feel like I am. That I should be.

"I want to pay back whatever I can, however long it takes."

She nods. "I get it. I would do the same."

I love that she feels this way. That she doesn't resent my errors in judgment.

And I'm so grateful that not all my decisions have proven to be bad ones. The show we've been filming here on campus this summer has been so much fun, and the initial episodes have gotten tremendous reviews. It seems like everyone loves it.

I love it.

I love doing the show, I love doing it here, on this campus that feels like home. I love that Ginger helps stage a few of the locations (with plants everywhere—and I mean *everywhere*). I love having friends who stayed on campus over the summer to play roles. I love the kids we work with in the show, and I love that, come fall, they'll all leave and I won't teach any of them. That would be way too weird.

Just then, my phone buzzes. I pull it out and see a message from Tanya, my agent.

'Great news. Post-production is way ahead of schedule. A major network has started a bidding auction to purchase rights to the series, and there are rumors of film adaptations. This is unbelievable, Tyson. Unprecedented. You've got a giant on your hands. Flemings are thrilled. You're making them rich. I promise to love fifteen percent of this show (and all your best ideas) forever.'

I show Ginger the text, and she grins and squeezes my arm.

"You think we'll ever see him?" she asks. I don't have to ask who she means. She gives me a soft look, and I know she's thinking about

Brady. She understands that his desertion is the one sore spot in this summer of so many great things.

I shake my head. "I think he's gone for good." It surprises me how comfortable I feel with that thought. I have admired—adored—him my whole life. But he's no longer the one whose opinion matters most. "And I'm okay with that."

"You're so much more than okay," she says, laying her head on my shoulder as we stand on Green Leaf Lane, staring at the front of the cottage. This place that will be our home. "You're divine. You're celestial. You're—"

"Are you forming a star metaphor?" I ask, teasing her.

She laughs. "You know it. I'm always brewing something brilliant in here," she says, tapping the side of her head. "Okay, but seriously? We have to hand it to Janie. Even though she wrote an entire book that basically said nothing, she's made a lot of people happy. And confident." She turns and our eyes meet. "She was part of our story."

"The conflict part," I say.

Ginger nods and laughs. "And everyone knows there's no story without conflict."

I take both her hands in mine. "I promise to offer you at least a little bit of struggle each day."

"Hey, same," she says, leaning in. I think she's planning to kiss me, but then she backs away. "See how well I can do it?" she asks, her eyes shining.

"You are very good at this," I say, pulling her close. "And I'm up for the challenge."

I kiss her, and in her return kiss, I feel every promise we've made to each other. Every agreement and disagreement. Every hope and dream we have for the future.

"Now," I say, when we've finished the kissing for the moment, "will you show me what you have in mind for the back garden?"

"I thought you'd never ask," she sings out, tugging me with her as she jogs around the side of the house. "I'm definitely going to need a freestanding office shed out here." She points to a clearing between two stands of huge trees. "I'll need a creative workspace to write my book reviews. And there's a poetry website that's recently come to my attention that deserves a shout-out."

"Poetry?" I ask.

"Trust me. It's brilliant."

"But what about chemistry?" I ask.

She wraps her arms around my waist. "Don't worry. I'll love chemistry forever. It's what brought us together. Both times."

"And," I say, nuzzling the space below her left ear, "it's what keeps us coming back for more."

"Forever," she says, and I feel her smiling as I kiss her again. And again. Forever.

ACKNOWLEDGMENTS

I taught high school for some delightful years. It was great. I didn't write much when I was teaching. But I got some ideas. And I made so many dear friends. So, thanks for that.

I feel like I should add that none of the fictional high school teachers at Chamberlain Academy are based on any of the actual human teachers I worked with. Sure. I'll say that.

And special thanks for friends who help make the writing better: Josi S. Kilpack, Nancy Campbell Allen, Brittany Larsen, Jennifer Moore, and Jenny Proctor. The mistakes are mine alone, but the process is so much less solitary when friends are along for the ride.

I love writing books. Thank you for reading them.

Join my newsletter for updates and special deals!

ABOUT THE AUTHOR

Becca Wilhite loves hiking, Broadway shows, rainstorms, food, books, and movies. She lives in the mountains and adores the ocean, and dreams of travel but loves staying home. Happiness is dabbling in lots of creative activities, afternoon naps, and cheese. All the cheese. You can find her at beccawilhite.com.

ALSO BY BECCA WILHITE

Made in United States
North Haven, CT
26 May 2023

37008555R00133